FINDING HEART

Colorado Veterans Book 2

TIFFANI LYNN

*Shanon,
I hope you enjoy this!
Happy Reading!*

COPYRIGHT

Finding Heart

Copyright 2017 by Tiffani Lynn

This book is a work of fiction. The names, characters, places, and incidents are products of the writer's imagination or have been used fictitiously and are not to be construed as real. Any resemblance to persons, living or dead, actual events, locales, or organizations is entirely coincidental.

ALL RIGHTS RESERVED. No part of this book may be used or reproduced in any manner whatsoever without written permission from the author.

For information contact Tiffani Lynn at www.tiffanilynn.com

Cover Design by Dar Albert, Wicked Smart Designs

Cover Photographer: Kruse Images and Photography

Cover Models: Amanda Joan & Jonny James

Editor: Twin Tweaks Editing

❃ Created with Vellum

DEDICATION

For my uncle, retired Master Sergeant Charles R. Moore USAF. Thank you for the years of dedication you gave to our country, first in active duty and then with civil service. If it wasn't for your time serving, I'd never have known you. You and my dad taught me that friendships forged during military service can be some of the most important in life. Your presence and active participation in our lives has been a game changer. We wouldn't be the same without you. I love you and am so thankful for you.

ACKNOWLEDGMENTS

As always my gratitude goes out to my amazing husband and three fantastic daughters. Your pride and encouragement have helped me to continue writing and sharing my words with the reading world. Teddy, thank you for giving me 20 years of happily ever after. I'm crossing my fingers you're ready for at least 20 more.

To the U.S. Marine and long time friend—who wishes to remain unnamed—thank you for giving up a chunk of your time to answer questions and share your story with me. When I left our meeting I was inspired to write and that's half the battle.

To Officer Alex Koszo of the Union Township Police Department, thank you for answering random questions about police procedure and lingo. I'm sure I didn't get it all correct but I got closer than I would've without your help. You're a great friend, an honorable man and I appreciate you more than you know.

Thank you former Army Staff Sergeant Matthew Musto for taking the time via text and phone to help me with ideas, information and inspiration. Your courage, strength and honor put you in a separate class from the rest of us. I'm so happy that you've finally found the other half of your heart. You earned the beauty and joy you are surrounded by. I wish you and Bailey many years of good health and happiness together.

Special gratitude to Andrea Musto for helping me get in contact with Matthew. You're an exceptional mother and friend and I admire you.

Tara Connor and Jessica Spriggs, thank you for answering my medical questions. Your responses to my crazy texts made me laugh and helped me so much. I love you ladies!

Finding the perfect image for this cover took forever and ended up being a team effort with the beautiful Amanda Joan. Once I saw Amanda's laughing smile in reaction to the tender kiss from the sexy Jonny James I knew I'd found exactly what I was looking for in this image by Shauna Kruse. Thank you Amanda Joan for taking the time to help me and for the friendship we're building. I adore you.

Mia Sparks, you rock and I appreciate you for a multitude of reasons.

The support and love from my TLC family is irreplaceable. Much love and gratitude to all of you. As always, what you find is what you find!

Judy Swinson, Kat Mizera, Katharina LeBoeuf and Lexi Post y'all have each helped me in one way or another and I appreciate your support, encouragement and assistance. Kat Mizera thanks for pushing me harder and making me dig deeper while writing this one, it's a much better story because of your input.

Ruth Schlabach thanks for helping me conquer Romantic Times in a variety of ways. Having you there meant so much. I also appreciate you wrestling my new banner into submission. I know I couldn't have done it without you.

Finally, I'll never tire of thanking my Beta Babes. April Klusman, Barbie Stokes Timpson, Gemma Blomquist, Jackie Ziegler, Judy Swinson, Kat Mizera, Lisa Qualls, Maria Robinette, Mia

Sparks, Rachel Garcia, Rachel Javier and Terri Kuebbeler if I had a million dollars for each of you it still wouldn't come close to your worth.

PROLOGUE

Dex

The harsh scent of smoke, sweat and dirt swirl everywhere, choking me. The constant pop of small arms fire seems to be coming from all sides. I realize it's partially an echo from the damn mountain we're stuck on, since the truth is we only have shots coming from two directions, but I can't figure out how many of those fuckers there are.

"Anybody hit?" I hear someone yell from my left side a little further down the line. Larkin was running point and Davis was between us. I glance to my right and see Davis hunkered down returning fire in a little trench area, but I don't see Larkin. "Larkin?" I yell. No answer. More shots come zinging past and I drop my head down so I don't end up with one between the eyes. "Stu?" I try again, louder. Still nothing. *Fuck!*

I pull the grenade from my vest, yank the pin and toss it toward the brush where the shots are coming from. "Cover me!" I yell at Davis and run for the last place I saw Stu. Stuart Larkin and I have been best friends for years now. We were lucky enough to meet in boot camp, go through sniper school together and then we were assigned to the same platoon. I've never had a friend or anyone else in my life like him. The fact that he's not responding has my blood pumping harder than it was even seconds ago when we were ambushed by the dirty bastards waiting about 30 meters out.

Larkin's boot is sticking out at an odd angle from behind a huge boulder so I dive toward him, avoiding the fire now aimed straight at me. His eyes are closed but I can barely see them because his helmet is skewed to cover his forehead and most of his eyes. He's eerily still but I don't have time to assess the situation because I can hear rustling in the bushes not far from me and the sounds are shifting more to my right, which means that they'll be on us in the next few seconds. I heft Larkin over my shoulders and run back down the path. With bullets zipping past my head in alarming numbers, one of the new guys runs up to help me with Larkin and must trigger an IED because one minute I'm yelling at him to get down and the next I'm being thrown off my feet and hurled through the air like I weigh nothing.

Heat more intense than I've ever felt in my life rushes up my back and consumes me, making me scream like I never have before. I roll around in the dirt until the fire is out. My whole fucking body hurts so bad I want to die but I have to get back to Stu; I'm praying he didn't get burnt too.

The smoke is thicker, the smell now more intense mingled with burnt flesh, and when I finally reach Larkin I realize he's long gone. With a bullet perfectly placed in the middle of his forehead there is no other possibility.

"NOOOOOOOOO! NO! NO!" I can't stop screaming. Between the pain in my back and the pain that my best and only real friend is gone, I don't care if I ever make it off this fucking mountain. I drop my head to Stu's chest and pray to a God that's never listened to a single plea I've made, to take me too. The last thing I hear is someone yell, "Dexter! Dexter!" and my world goes black.

Two Years Later...

I shoot up in bed, covered in sweat, panting like I'm still in the middle of a fire fight that happened two years ago. It's the same dream every single time and as real as the day it happened. I'll never be free of the memory and sometimes I feel like it's penance to pay for letting Stu get killed. I should have been running point that day, but we were in a hurry so he jumped in.

The light to my room flicks on and I'm momentarily blinded. "The fuck, Les?" I snap, and she flicks the light back off.

Stu's wife stands in the doorway with the hallway light to frame her silhouette, leaning against the doorjamb. She's breathing heavy and obviously freaked out. "Another one?" she asks.

I wipe the sweat dripping down my brow and answer. "Yeah. I'll be okay. Go back to bed. We have to be up in a few hours."

"Maybe you shouldn't go yet. The dreams are more frequent when you have too much going on in your head. You know you can stay here. None of us want you to leave."

I rub my eyes and lie back against the damp sheets and pat the empty area next to me. "Come here, Les." I can hear the patter of her small feet as she follows my directions and climbs up next to me, snuggling in close. Leslie Larkin and I have a strange relationship with Stu gone.

One drunken night about five years ago I promised Stu that if anything ever happened to him I would take care of his wife, Leslie, and their two kids, Rushton and Skylar. I never thought I'd really have to do it. He had too many things to live for; I was certain if something was going to happen it'd be to me since I had nothing to lose.

After Stu died and I recovered from the burns from the explosion, I tried to go back to Afghanistan. I didn't think I wanted to go back to civilian life, but without Stu, Army life sucked and I could never get past losing him. So when my enlistment was up I opted to get out and move to Tampa, Florida, to help Leslie and the kids. The plan was to stay with them until I found somewhere else to live nearby so I could make sure they were taken care of. That was a great idea in theory, but it didn't take into account that both Leslie and I were hurting and lonely. Over the six months that I've lived here, we've found comfort in each other in a way that now makes me sick. The sexual attraction was building for months before we finally got drunk enough to do something about it and the result was sloppy sex due to the amount of alcohol involved.

When it was all said and done we both cried, and I don't cry, not in front of anyone, ever. The level of guilt I felt was crushing. Stu was the best friend I'd ever had, closer than a brother and the only person that I've ever trusted. It didn't matter that he was gone when I took his wife to bed. That was *his* wife and always will be as far as I'm concerned. Because of that one drunken night, I knew I had to leave. Neither of us would ever move on if I stayed in Tampa; we had become a crutch for one another.

"Do you have to leave, Dex?" she whispers, her arm holding tight across my stomach.

"Les, you know I do. This isn't good for either of us. It was too easy to slip into being Stu's replacement and there is no way anyone can replace him. If I stay I'll always be the guy who tried to slide into his life and that's not me. I want you to move on and find someone that you can love separate from Stu. I want you to have a life again and not be so tied to his memories that you can't breathe. If it's me, you'll never be free.

"I'll keep in touch. I still plan to be here for the memorial every year and we'll work something out for me to see the kids in between. Don't think I'm dumping and running. I'm just giving us some breathing room. I love you, Leslie, but not the way you deserve and I think you feel the same about me. We've held each other up for a long time now. Besides, you know if you ever need me I'll be on the first flight back here."

"Colorado is a long way from here, Dex. You don't have to go that far to give us a little space. I know it's your hometown, but from what Stu said, you don't hold much love for the place considering what your childhood was like."

She's right. When I was eight and my grandmother died, I was thrust into foster care and shuffled around until I aged out of the system at 18 and joined the Army. Those are some horrible memories. However, when the headhunter called me to tell me he had two interviews lined up, one for the railroad in Kansas City, Missouri, and one for the police department in Colorado Springs, Colorado, I jumped at the latter option. My interview was easy and I was offered the job on the spot. I came back here to pack up what little I had and say my goodbyes. I love Rushton, Skylar and Leslie and hate to leave them, but I know it's the right thing.

I kiss the top of Leslie's head. "Les, Stuart Larkin was the best man I've ever known and I made a promise to him that I won't break. If you need me, call me. I love you guys, but I won't ever be Stu so I can't be plugged into his life like I'm an exchangeable part. Please understand I'm doing what's best for all of us."

Her sniffle tickles my ribs where her face is. "I know. I just don't want to go back to being alone. Besides, you remind me of him and when you're here I don't feel like he's so far away."

"I know, sweetie. I swear it'll be okay. Please trust me."

"If we're talking about moving on, are you going to get the skin grafts for the scar tissue on your back?"

"I already told you I can't."

"But that's not true, you can. The VA will even pay for it."

"Les, it's not that they won't do it, it's that I can't let them. That's my reminder that I lived and he died. I need that."

"Dex—"

"Shhh." I interrupt her. "I'm fine, just let it go."

"But you aren't if you still wake up soaked in the middle of the night, yelling for Stu. That's not normal. I'm not going to argue with you about it, but if it's really time to move on, I think you should have the surgery."

The next morning, I hug and kiss everyone and say my goodbyes. All three of them are crying so hard I feel sick to my stomach when the cab arrives to take me to the airport.

It's time to face life without Stuart Larkin again, for all of us, and I hate it. The pain I've felt after losing him is something I never want to experience again and I plan to keep everyone far enough away that I won't feel the absence if anyone else in my life leaves.

Chapter One

MARINA

Shivering half-naked against a cement wall is not how I planned to spend my night. I wish I could say this is the first time I've been in this position, but it's not. The question is, how will I get myself out of it tonight?

As the cop gives me a quick pat down over the scantily clothed areas of my body, I cringe, hating this. There have been too many times in my life that unwelcomed hands have been on my body and I'll never get used to it. My problem right now is I have no one to bail me out of jail if they arrest me. My best friend and roommate doesn't have the money and no one else I know does either.

The asshole cop takes things a little further, pausing his pat down for half a second before he flattens his palm on my hip and leans into my ear. "Chiquita, are you ready to make this an interesting night?"

Ugh, his breath stinks like the chili dog I'm sure he consumed at some point during his shift and his hands are clammy against my bare skin. I press my face harder to the cold cement wall in front of me, trying to escape this scenario. It's like a bad scene in a weekly television drama.

"What do you mean by more interesting?" I know what he means but I'm stalling, hoping for a miracle. My friend Fern is quiet next to me and I hope she stays that way. There's no reason for both of us to get what this guy is giving. Instead of telling me, he decides to show me by pressing his slight beer belly and hard crotch against my back. *Gross.*

He must be reading my thoughts because he tells me, "I think something can be worked out for you since you weren't holding the blow, but your friend over there won't have it so easy."

His left hand runs up the bare skin of my torso and over my breast while he continues to breathe all over the side of my face with his rancid chili-dog breath. *How do I manage to get myself into this shit?*

"If you're implying what I think you are, then my friend walks too," I say, doing my best to sound brave. If I have to do this with him, he better let us both go. *How am I going to get through this? Is this really happening?* Rougher than he's been thus far, he smashes me harder against the wall.

"Chiquita, you've got a choice and it's the only one you're getting. Your friend is gonna sit in a cell tonight. What you do from here decides if you do too."

My throat is dry suddenly, so I swallow hard, hoping to draw some moisture. I should've chosen to fight, knowing my psyche can't handle any more than it's had to over the years. I'm terrified of what's about to happen. I may have to go to jail tonight because the more seconds that tick by the less likely I am to do what he wants.

"What's it gonna be, chiquita?"

Why does he have to take such a sweet term of endearment and use it while he's being a douchebag? Fern moans and her knees give way. She slides to the ground next to us in a heap, but horny cop doesn't flinch.

"Fern!" I call to her and wiggle, trying to get to her, worried something's wrong. He continues to hold me where he wants me.

God, Fern! Why did you go back down this path? She was clean for a long time but from the story I got in the bathroom before we were thrown out of the club she started hanging with some ladies from her new job who pulled her back in. I can't believe she did this with me here tonight knowing how I feel about drugs. Drugs are the thieves of my childhood and they changed the path my life was on to a much darker and more painful one. Earlier, when she was gone to the bathroom a little too long, I went to check on her and found her doing lines of coke. We were in the middle of an argument about it when security busted through the door and hauled us out. Apparently, someone turned Fern in and since they saw me with her all night I was being tossed out too.

Now I'm wondering how much she did and if that was all she got into tonight. I call out to her again, "Fern! Answer me!"

There is still no reply and instead of the cop checking on her, he groans in my ear and dips his hand into my bra to grip my bare breast while I fight the urge to puke and lose my mind on him. I've heard other women talk about sleazy cops that take advantage of situations like the one I'm in, but this is the first time I've encountered it to this degree. Right now I can't be worried about Officer Sleazebag. I've got to get him off me and check on Fern; I know something isn't right.

"Chiquita, let's move this along and I'll check on your friend." *What a creep!*

"I don't think she's breathing. You need to check her now! I promise I'll do whatever you want if you check on her. Please!" My voice jumps up an octave as the panic weaves its way through my body. I'm saying a little prayer in my head as I try to twist my upper body, hoping to dislodge his hands. He smashes me tighter to the wall.

"Nah, I think you do this first and then I check on your friend."

Try a different tactic, I tell myself. I twist my upper body again and bend my knees a little. He pushes on me harder and I explain,

"I'm just trying to get on my knees. It's what you want, right?" My voice shakes like crazy but he backs off a little and I move into the position he wants. *What if I can't do this? What if Fern isn't okay over there?*

"No funny shit, chiquita. All the way to your knees and get busy or you're going downtown for possession and resisting arrest. I may even throw in an assault charge if you really piss me off."

Again, I glance over at Fern and still can't tell if she's breathing, but the extreme stillness of her body is freaking me out even more than the disgusting cop. The tremors in my hands are so bad I can't get his belt open and his hands bat me away as he loses patience. He almost has it open when a loud, deep voice booms through the night, startling us both. "What the fuck, Gino? You lost your damn mind? Get up, lady!"

I struggle to my feet as Gino hurries to re-buckle his belt. The loud voice belongs to a cop way bigger than the one I've been dealing with. He rushes over to Fern and bends down, putting fingers to her pulse point. Swearing loudly, he pulls out his radio and calls for an ambulance. I don't know if I should run or stand here or what. I need to make sure Fern's okay but if I stick around I'll probably get arrested. My wristlet with my ID, apartment key and money is on the ground a few feet away and I'm in platform wedges so I doubt I'll be able to get very far if I make a run for it. Besides, the cop whose face I haven't seen because he's been bent over Fern, looks way more fit than I am and I'm guessing he could catch me in a foot race even if I had on sneakers.

The cop by Fern is now kneeling on the ground by her lifeless form, starting chest compressions while Gino the asshole stands dumbfounded, staring at him.

"I need help over here, man!" the cop yells.

Gino continues to stand there and I want to slap the dickhead for delaying this long. That's my friend dying on the ground and he wanted to exploit the situation? I glance between them and realize Gino has no intention of moving so I hurry over to them and drop to my knees hard, scraping them on the gravel next to Fern.

"Come on, Fern! You can't go out like this! Not in a nasty parking lot, not right now!" I scream.

"Lady! Settle down, focus, and give her mouth-to-mouth when I tell you, but open her mouth and check her airway first."

I do as I'm told and see nothing.

"Swipe in there with your finger. If you find nothing, then hold her nose closed and seal your mouth over hers, and breath into her mouth when I tell you to. You'll give her two big breaths."

I swipe and find nothing so I do as he's instructed.

"Go, give her as much air as you can!" He barks the order and I comply, pulling away when I'm done.

"Again!"

He goes back to pumping on her chest, counting as he goes. Her lips are blue and I don't think she's going to make it. My whole body shakes as we repeat the process twice more. As we're finishing round three, the ambulance comes screaming into the parking lot and the paramedics take over. I stand up, my bloody knees knocking, my body suddenly cold in the warm summer evening. I'm unsure of what to do. *Am I getting arrested? Do I go to the hospital? Do I run?*

The CPR cop stands to his full height and I realize again that he's a beast, enormous in a way most men aren't. Even in my wedges the giant makes me look tiny. This guy is way taller than Gino the sleazy cop. Before I register much more than the size of this guy, he turns to Gino and says, "Get her wallet, man," pointing to my wristlet on the ground. Gino is pacing off to the side near my wallet as he runs his fingers through his hair, making it stand on end. I bet he's shitting Twinkies. He got busted ignoring a woman dying right next to him because he was going to force me to give him a blow job. *Jerk!*

My body shakes harder as the adrenaline wears off and I wrap my arms around my bare midriff, attempting to calm myself. I need to call Dee. She'll come get me and she'll know what to do. Oh, my God! What if Fern is dead?

"Miss." The humungous cop calls to me but I can't answer.

My body continues with the uncontrollable shakes. He moves in closer and leans down, trying to get to eye level with me. "Miss, you need to clean up those knees so they don't get infected."

I glance up and when we make eye contact, I'm tossed back in time 12 years, to my last foster home. *Oh, my God!* I'd know those eyes anywhere. I mean *anywhere*. No one has eyes that color of aquamarine-ocean perfection except Jasen Dexter. But the Jasen Dexter I knew was a skinny, gangly, short, teenage boy with zero body fat and even less muscle mass. I open my mouth to speak, but before I can say a word his head jerks and he steps back, shifting his eyes from my head to my toes. He shakes his head a little as his brows pull together.

Just when I think he's going to say something about recognizing me, Gino pipes up from behind him. "What are we gonna do, man? We takin' her in?"

Jase turns and glares at him with an expression that could melt metal. "You really think that's your best course of action right now? You really want a girl you were about to get a blow job from sitting in the same room with the sarge?" He throws his hands up in front of him. "Hey, man, if it's that important to you to take her in, by all means grab the cuffs."

Sleazy cop shakes his head vigorously. "Nah, dude. I don't want that shit, but what do I do with her?" *What the heck does he mean by that?*

"You let her go home or see her friend at the hospital or go back inside if she really wants, and then you go back to the precinct and fill out a report on the girl that we sent to the hospital."

I shift on my now ridiculously uncomfortable wedges as the tremors continue, and for the first time in a long time I try to stay unnoticed. Under normal circumstances I'm trying to be noticed by anyone and everyone. I want to be entertaining enough to not be forgotten and to keep people hanging around. Being alone is not something I handle well.

Finally, Jase turns back around to face me and I glance at his name tag to make sure I'm not dreaming this. I haven't seen him since I was 16 years old. Sure as the sun rises, the name DEXTER is printed over his left breast.

"Jase," I whisper, absolutely floored that he's standing in front of me larger than life.

His expression softens briefly as his eyes search my face and I can tell the moment that recognition sets in fully. He knows who I am.

"Marina, what the hell are you doing? Are you all coked up too?" he blurts out in a harsh tone that's not at all what I was expecting. Not hello or hi, so good to see you. Two words. Complete. Asshole. Just like his partner.

"No, I'm not coked up!" I tell him indignantly as I cross my arms over my chest.

Leaning down into me with his eyes blazing fury, he growls, "Well, I almost think that would better explain why your friend was dying in the dirt next to you and you're on your knees in front of Gino with his cock in your hands!"

I gasp at what he's implying. How does he not know his partner is a douchebag? *Asshole, asshole, asshole!* We're only inches apart when he finishes and although I'm pissed, I'm reminded of the power of his eyes. They say eyes are the windows to the soul and it's never been truer than with Jase, but I'm not so overwhelmed with his eyes that I won't fight back. He may be big, but I guarantee I'm tougher. I'd never leave a friend in need, especially for a parking lot blow job. I'm nothing if not loyal.

"His pants weren't even unzipped. I didn't have his cock in my hand yet. He hadn't gotten that far!"

"Looked like it to me."

"Maybe you should get some glasses, Jase, and while you're at it, get a conscience for Gino over there." I flap my hand toward his partner. "I wasn't about to do that because I wanted to. I tried to get him to check on Fern, but he was more worried about forcing his dick down my throat, so maybe you should stop judging me and worry about your partner!" My chest heaves as I finish. I'm so pissed at him! I don't see him for 12 years and the first thing he says once he realizes it's me is completely offensive? This is not the Jasen Dexter I remember.

Chapter Two
DEX

The crazy girl in front of me who was just kneeling in front of Gino, ready to suck him off, is Marina Rossi. Sweet, gentle, Marina. What the hell happened? After all she went through when she was young I find her now in a public place, barely dressed, covered in tattoos and piercings, and out with a chick who just overdosed on coke. Why would she be around people like that after the damage drugs did to her family?

"Well, we aren't talking about Gino. We're talking about you. What the hell are you doing out here dressed like that, acting like that?" I gesture at Gino. "And what are you doing hanging with a girl who's all coked up?"

Her sigh is deep before she responds in a quieter voice. "Fern is my friend, has been for several years. I didn't know she had the coke until right before she got busted with it in the club. Fern was clean for a long time. This time came as a shock to me. I wasn't acting like anything. Your partner was trying to force me to go down on him. You tell me how I get out of that situation without going to jail for assaulting a police officer, which he threatened me with, by the way. I'm not proud of being in this situation in the first place, but not all of us grew up as well as you did. Don't act like you have a clue what I've been through over the last 12 years, especially when I did nothing wrong. Now, I really want to get to the hospital to check on Fern. Are you going to arrest me or not?"

Layers of sadness and a touch of defiance thread her voice. There's no way I could arrest her after the way the rest of the night has gone. It's likely her friend is dead and although I detest drugs, I know how it is to lose a friend. Besides, what did she actually do? There have been whispers about stuff like this with Gino since I started the force two years ago, but I've never gotten confirmation on any of it until now.

"Why were you about to be arrested?"

Gino tries to answer from his place behind me and I hold up a hand to silence him. He's an asshole. I'll be glad when my real partner is back from vacation. Quinn would never pull any of the shit Gino does. Now I see why he has problems keeping partners.

"I was with Fern when club security busted her. As they were dragging her outside, they saw your buddy walking past and passed her off to him. Because I was with her I got lumped in with her drug mess. You can do a drug test on me. You'll find nothing. Gino decided that I needed to work my way out of a visit to the jail tonight. I don't have the money for bail so I was about to have to do something I didn't want to do."

God, this girl is a hot mess, but she didn't do anything wrong and she needs to get to the hospital because I have a feeling she needs to say her goodbyes.

"Alright, go check on your friend, but you need to stay away from that stuff and those kinds of people. If I hadn't walked up it could have been so much worse for you. You know better than anyone what drugs can do to your life. I'll handle Gino. I'm sorry about how he treated you; that would never happen if I was with him." I turn and walk away because if I stand here and talk to her, I might discover I give a shit about her and that's not an option. It's bad enough I have the Rivers and Larkin families to care about. I don't need anyone else to add to the list.

"Jase." She calls to me using the name I haven't heard in many years so I turn back. Her mouth twists a little before she says rather softly, "Thank you."

I nod and continue to the cruiser parked in the back of the lot. Gino falls into step beside me and I shush him as soon as he opens his mouth. I don't want to hear what he has to say. When I get in the car, I wait and watch as Marina tries to hail a cab. I won't leave until she gets a ride out of here. She might be a grown woman but she obviously has no sense of self-protection; she has no idea how unsafe it is for her to be standing in that poor excuse for clothing on the street at night alone.

WONDERING IF FERN PULLED THROUGH IS EATING ME ALIVE. I see this kind of stuff often, but knowing she's Marina's friend has bothered me. She's known so much loss in her life, and that's just what I know about, so I give in to the curiosity and take a trip to the hospital to see if Fern made it.

Why would Marina friend someone like that, especially with her history? I'll never forget her story as long as I live. Although it's not much different than a lot of kids in foster care, something about hers got to me. It changed me.

Her dad died in some freak accident when Mari was four or five. Her mom was apparently weak because she fell into a drug habit not long after the dad died, and she found a new husband with his own drug issues. When her mom was too strung out to whore herself out for their drugs, the stepdad started pimping Mari and her sister, who is only two years older than her. She was barely old enough to wear a bra when it started. There's more to it but that's the basic story. If I were her, I'd stay light years away from that shit.

As I reach the front desk the middle-aged receptionist smiles up at me like I hung the moon. Hopefully this will make getting information easier. I smile back.

"Hi, I sent a young woman in last night in an ambulance. Overdose. I didn't get a last name, just a first. Can you tell me if she is still a patient here?"

She runs her pointer finger across her lips and her eyes roam my body. Damn, not this again. When women notice I'm not wearing a wedding ring, especially while I'm in uniform, they pull out all the stops. I'm not interested. I just want to be left alone.

"Well, officer, I suppose I could check for you." Her attempt at a sexy voice fails in a big way. I stare at her, giving her no reaction. Sighing, she moves her focus to my requested task and types her password into her computer. After five minutes of her searching and her unsubtle attempt at flirting, I finally get my answer. Fern's alive, but barely. She's on life support in the ICU. I'm not sure why but I make my way to the seventh floor and through the security doors. When I approach the nurses' desk I turn on the charm, hoping to avoid a bunch of questions about why I'm here. An older nurse shows me to Fern's room where I find her alone and seemingly hooked up to every machine the hospital has to offer. She looks like a broken teenager, not a grown woman, but drugs will do that. I stand there for a few minutes before I finally tire of studying the poor young woman in front of me and return to the station.

I'm pissed as hell that Gino didn't do anything to help her when she hit the ground. She might not be as bad as she is if he'd done something sooner. It's not his fault that she's a junkie but it's his fault that she went unresponsive so long without help.

I'M BACK AT MY DESK WORKING ON PAPERWORK LATER IN THE day, the worst part of my job, which I usually avoid at all costs. But after Gino screwed up so bad last night I told the captain that

I wouldn't work with him anymore. My partner, Quincy Rivers, will be back soon enough so for now I'll tie up all the loose ends at the office and fill in where I'm needed—anywhere but with Gino.

As I'm clicking save on the third form of the day, I hear a very girlish giggle and look up to see who it is. We have four women in this department. One is my partner and she's not here, one is old enough she'll likely retire in the next year, so girlish is not what I would use to describe her laughter, one is sitting across from me and has been quiet since she arrived, and the last one smokes a pack a day and sounds like it. The high-pitched laughter is not normal for this room. I hear it again, followed by the deep timbre of Denatto's voice. "Yeah, Dex is right over there but if you get tired of his grumpy ass, you know where to find me." Denatto's Mr. Charming today. Great. When my eyes make contact with Marina's, her giggle dies in her throat and the smile slides away. My eyes—drawn in by the exposed skin—roam the length of her body before they return to her face.

Oh, hell! What is she wearing today? Does the girl own any clothes that cover her body? If I were her man, we'd be having words. A red tank top that barely covers her breasts leaves her whole stomach bare. The short jean shorts she's wearing leave her legs exposed almost indecently. I pause at the scabs on her knees from the parking gravel before my eyes move down to note the sparkly flip flips that adorn her little feet. The tattoos on her belly disappear up into the tank top and in the light of day I can see a bunch more on her arms that I didn't see last night. When my gaze returns to her face I notice a good amount of makeup coating her face. *What is she doing here?* I wonder if she's here to report Gino. I wouldn't blame her, but I don't think it's a great move considering she was trying to bribe a cop with a blow job and hanging out with a girl who overdosed.

"Marina," I greet her cautiously.

"Jase."

A sliver of warmth weaves its way into my gut. No one calls me Jase anymore. I've been Dex, short for my last name, Dexter, since I went into the Army 12 years ago. I don't respond; I wait her out to see what she says.

"I thought I should come down here and thank you in person for letting me off last night." She steps in closer to me than is normal and I can smell the bubblegum-scented lip gloss keeping her lips shiny. Her eyes steal my attention the same as when we were young and I can't look anywhere else for the moment. They're the most intriguing shade of mossy green with little brown flecks that look like they slipped in accidentally when God was creating them.

The hardware and plethora of makeup detract from her beauty and I'd like to tell her to remove it all so I can see the woman underneath, but that would be pointless since I don't plan to see her again after this. Why do some females think they need to be coated in layers of makeup? Natural is so much more appealing to me. Not that I want her to appeal to me.

"You don't need to thank me. You didn't do anything that warranted an arrest as far as I was concerned." I continue to stare at her. If I don't say a lot, I think she'll be on her way.

She twirls a lock of dyed reddish-purple hair around her pointer finger and glances at the ground. She used to do the same thing when we were teenagers and she was nervous or uncertain. I'd spend hours of our days studying everything about her. I had every mannerism, every expression, every outfit, every kind of smile and every variety of frown memorized. It's funny that some of those things haven't changed, or my gut response to them. I want to reach out and soothe her.

"So whatcha been up to? I haven't seen you in years. In fact, the last time I saw you I was taller and weighed more than you." She giggles and bites her bottom lip. Her giggle is cute but annoying at the same time. I don't want to find anything about her cute. Adding someone to my social circle is not on my agenda so small talk makes no sense to me and this qualifies as such. I avoid any kind of emotional connection whenever possible. The Larkin and Rivers families sort of scooted in there under the radar and added themselves to my life without me noticing until it was too late. Surely she doesn't want to be friends after all this time. Doesn't she have anything better to do?

"I grew up, that's all. A lot of time has passed." If I don't elaborate she'll realize I have nothing to say and be on her way.

"I heard you went into the military."

I wonder who told her. I was removed from the foster home we both lived in six months before I enlisted. I'm not sure how she would've found that information out.

"I did, I went into the Army." I refuse to stand here and make small talk so I'm going to keep my answers short and sweet. A trip down memory lane isn't where I want to go tonight. "Listen, Marina, I have a bunch of paperwork to do so I'd better get back to it."

Her gaze shifts to my lips, pauses briefly and then moves to my feet as her finger continues to twirl her hair even tighter. Her voice is a little quieter when she says, "Oh." She swallows hard. Shit, I hurt her feelings. My gut sours a little. This is what I'm trying to avoid. I don't want to care that I hurt her feelings. It's obvious I don't know her anymore and I need to keep it that way.

"I'll let you get back to it then. Um..." She pauses and glances back up to me and I fight with myself not to try and comfort her. I stay quiet. "So, thanks again. And um...in case you were wondering, Fern is alive, but barely. They told me not to get my hopes up."

Without thinking first, I answer, "Yeah, I know." Shit. I didn't want her to know I checked on her friend.

Her gaze shoots back to mine and surprise is written all over her face. "You do?"

I make up a lie because I don't want her to think I have a soul left—one she can cling to. "It's part of my report. I called. Sorry about your friend." I take a step back to reiterate that I have to go and she turns like she's going to walk away, but looks back at me over her shoulder and says, "I'm sorry I took up your time, Jase, but I'm glad I got to see you, to know you're okay. You're the only one I ever really cared about in the system and well, I'm glad you're okay." That was a direct hit to my heart.

Before I can reply she strides across the room and pushes through the door to the lobby. When the door closes, I turn back to my desk and of course Gino the asshole is propped against it. *What the hell does he want?*

"So, I see how it is. You pull her off my dick so she can jump on yours. Maybe that's what's behind the super-partnership with you and Quinn. Now that she's out of town you've got to get it from somewhere else."

This guy is such a dick. "Fuck off, Gino. I didn't say anything about that shit from last night to the captain, but that can be remedied. I'm not in the mood for you."

"Yeah, I heard you asked not to work with me. You trying to fuck up my promotion?"

"If your promotion gets fucked up it won't be from anything that has to do with me. You'll do that to yourself. Now step the fuck away from my desk and go find something else to do."

He shakes his head and struts away like he owns the place. What an asshole.

Chapter Three
MARINA

My last memory of Jase Dexter is a sweet one. One of the boys in the house we lived in, Freddy Vines, had gotten wind of what my stepfather used to use me for and decided that he needed sexual favors too. Freddy was the biggest guy in the house, even towering over the foster father, and everyone feared him.

Jase had been my confidant for the whole nine months we lived together. He was lanky and scrawny and awkward. So, to a girl like me who'd been overpowered by larger men most of her life, a boy like him was safe to be around. I told Jase what Freddy said and he told me he'd handle it. Of course, I continued to be terrified because there was no way a little guy like Jase could handle it, but I never told him that.

So late that night when the door clicked open to the room I shared with two other girls, I knew Freddy had come for me. My heart pounded and tears welled up in my eyes. I didn't want to do whatever he had in mind.

He leaned into my ear and whispered, "Don't make a noise. Don't say a word. Go to the bathroom."

Too afraid not to do what he said, I got up and shuffled slowly toward the bathroom. I was going too slowly for his taste so he shoved me from behind and I smacked into the wall with a loud thud. Freddy leaned into me from behind and growled, "Get in the fucking bathroom, Marina, and take care of business. No one's gonna hear you so stop trying to wake the house. It's dick-sucking time." The tears sitting at the edge of my eyelids splashed down my face as I realized I was going to have to go through with this.

The hallway was dark but the nightlight in the bathroom was on, giving the space an eerie glow when I entered with shaky legs. Freddy was still two steps behind me in the hallway when I heard a thump, thump, thump, an oooffff and an, "Oh shit." That was followed by a louder thump and a thud loud enough that the door to the foster parents' room flung open and the father came out with a baseball bat in his hand that was barely visible in the darkness. He flipped the light switch and I squinted.

Freddy wasn't anywhere in sight, but Jase stood about three feet from me at the top of the stairs, looking down. His fists were balled up and his chest was heaving. The foster mom rushed out of the room tugging her robe closed, maneuvered in front of the father and ran to me, asking, "Marina? What's going on?"

I had no idea what to say. I wasn't sure if I should tell her that Freddy wanted a blow job and was going to force me. I didn't think she wanted the truth so I shrugged my shoulders as she hurried past me and looked down the stairs. She shrieked and took off to the bottom, screaming the whole way.

Later I found out that Jase knew when he heard the thump against the wall what was going on and knew surprise would work in his favor, so he ran at Freddy and put all his weight into knocking the kid down the stairs. The cops showed up, the social worker showed up, the ambulance showed up and took Freddy to the hospital, and then we were questioned for hours by the police and the social worker.

When the other boys who shared a room with Freddy confirmed our story, the Foster parents sent us to bed. I was still scared even with Freddy gone so once the house was quiet again I snuck into Jase's room, crawled under his covers and snuggled up to his bony chest and begged him to wrap his lanky arms around me. He held me the rest of the night and right before dawn he sent me back to my bed so we wouldn't get in trouble.

The next day a psychologist came to the house and spoke with both of us privately. Turns out that wasn't the first time Freddy had been accused of this stuff and they wanted to find out if he'd done anything before that. I kind of hoped the jerk was dead, but he only had a broken collarbone, a dislocated shoulder and a concussion. They decided to put him in a state facility because of the liability.

That night Jase slipped into my bed this time and held me again. I'll never forget the feel of his bony arms wrapped around me. You'd think it was uncomfortable, but it wasn't. His arms provided a safety I couldn't remember feeling before then and haven't since.

Jase whispered into my ear, "Tomorrow they're gonna separate us, Mari." He wasn't Spanish but his Spanish accent was strong when he called me that. It sounded like he was saying Ma-dee. "I heard them talking downstairs. They don't want us to get too close." He moved his hand down between us, placing something cold in my hand and said, "I want you to have this. It was my grandma's. The picture fell out a long time ago but it's real silver and it's pretty. You deserve pretty things, Mari. You deserve more than what you've been given."

"I can't take your grandma's locket."

"Yeah, you can. You deserve it. Someday when you find someone you love you can put their picture inside and wear it close to your heart."

"Jase," I whispered as emotion clogged my throat.

"Don't let anyone hurt you anymore. If there's another boy

like Freddy, tell on him. I won't be there to help you." He moved his arm around me and pulled me tight to his chest while I clung to the silver locket in my hand.

"Jase—"

"Mari, shhh."

I didn't want to upset him so I nuzzled in close to him and fell asleep. When I woke the next morning, I was alone. I jumped up, threw my clothes on and ran downstairs, afraid that he was gone and I wouldn't get to say goodbye. The social worker was passing through the doorway and I caught sight of Jase's royal blue T-shirt he wore often already in front of her.

I thumped my way down the stairs at warp speed and screamed his name as I rushed out through the screen door and flung myself at him. I knew he couldn't stay, but my heart was breaking and I couldn't help but beg him. I needed someone with me who didn't try to use me for sexual favors, who protected me, who cared about me.

"Please, please, please don't go!" I begged as if he had control of what was happening.

He held me close while I wrapped myself around his scrawny body and held tight, all the while crying. The social worker said something I couldn't hear clearly above my sobs and I felt his body jerk and heard him say, "Give me a minute, will ya? Hasn't she been through enough? Let us say goodbye."

"Mari. Mari, stop. Listen to me. I can't stay. They won't let me. But remember what I said. Take care of you. Protect yourself at all costs and tell if you have to. Don't let anyone take advantage of you ever again. Mari, you're beautiful and sweet and amazing, so much better than the rest of us. Keep the locket close to you and know I'll always think of you." Then he kissed the side of my head because he wasn't tall enough to reach the top. As he stepped away and climbed in the backseat of the car he said, "You're gonna be okay."

The last glimpse I had of Jasen Dexter was of his gorgeous aquamarine eyes luminous with tears that sat on the edges of his eyelids but never fell. He was tough as nails even back then.

Shame courses through my veins as I think about him catching me about to give a blow job to get out of that situation with Fern. You'd think with everything I went through as a kid I'd avoid it at all costs, but I'm broker than broke and knew I'd rather do that than end up in jail and not have a way to get out.

I wish I were intuitive enough to never end up in a place where that's even an option, but on occasion it's the people I'm friends with who get me into situations I'd never otherwise be in. I shove the thought aside and catch the bus back to my apartment. *God, this place is a shithole.* Dee, my roommate and best friend, will be home in an hour and I can tell her about Jase.

She's been hearing about him now for years. She knows everything about him, including my encounter the other night. She warned me to stay away from him, said he obviously wasn't the warm and fuzzy guy I remember, but I couldn't help myself. Just like when we were kids, there was something about him I found comforting, even if he scowls at me now.

As if to remind myself that the Jase Dexter I knew still exists, I go to the back of my closet and pull down the shoebox that holds the few things I've kept from my childhood. In the bottom of the box, under a couple of pictures, is the silver heart locket that Jase gave me. As my most cherished possession, I used to wear the locket everywhere, but it was almost taken from me once and I freaked. Now to keep it safe it stays hidden. Threading my fingers through the silver chain, I lift and pull out the silver heart. It's tarnished and needs to be cleaned, but it's still the most beautiful thing that I own besides the ruby belly button ring that Dee gave me for Christmas one year.

Jase told me when I found someone I love to put their picture inside and keep it close to my heart. I did the best I could to follow his instructions. I open the locket and find the contents intact. I smile a little, close it and put it all away. Maybe someday my life will be stable enough to wear it every day like I want to.

Chapter Four

DEX

Damn it! Why am I still thinking about Marina? She's a whole ball of trouble that keeps rolling my way. I've been alone for too many days in a row and usually I like that, but with Marina resurfacing in my life it's turned my normally quiet thoughts to a chaotic chatterbox of noise. Memories of watching her across the room at our foster home, thinking she's the most beautiful thing I've ever seen and later at night waking up from a wet dream because she had my teenage boy, hormone-riddled body all jacked up, have taken up residence in my mind and won't stop. She's tempting, but she's a disaster in every sense of the word and I need her to stay away from me. I'm certain with how rude I was today at the station that she got the picture, which should make me happy, but to make things more confusing, it makes me angry. *What the hell is wrong with me?*

Thank God Quinn and Judson are back home. Quinn and I started out as partners a couple of years ago and hit it off instantly. She wasn't pushy like most of the women I've encountered in my life but she knew exactly the questions to ask to find the answers she wanted. Instead of my quiet demeanor driving her nuts, it seemed to settle her. When I met her boyfriend—at the time—Judson, it didn't take long to figure out why she handled me so well. He and I are similar people and we rolled right into a good friendship. They were my first real friends since Stu and his family and I cherish every moment with them. I'd never admit that out loud because that would make me a serious pussy, but it's the truth.

Today, I felt it necessary to be around people who don't annoy the hell out of me and also don't stir up the hornets' nest of emotion buried within. Running into Marina, especially under the circumstances, has left me feeling off-kilter. I need to be with people who stabilize me and that's something the Rivers family does with ease.

I finally pull into the driveway of Daisy Rivers Ranch, Quinn and Judson's home, and watch as Carlo races out the front door and toward my car. This kind of excitement doesn't seem normal for a 12-year-old boy, but he's not normal by anyone's standards. Extraordinary is the only term I'd use for him. He's come a long way in a short time since the Rivers have made him part of their family and I've enjoyed watching it.

He and I have a special relationship considering we started life pretty much the same way, with messed up families and foster care, but his is headed in a better direction than mine was at that age, thanks to Quinn and Judson. They were his foster parents for a short while but after Judson saved Carlo and Carlo saved Judson, literally, there was no doubt they would adopt him. If they wouldn't have, I would've applied to do it. He's such a great kid with so much potential, there's no way I could've allowed it to be wasted in the foster system.

Quinn steps out on the porch with her six-month-old baby, Lila, in her arms about the time Carlo is crashing into me. I think it's cool he's turned into a hugger after living with them. I'm not that way with anyone else except him and Lila and Stu's kids, but I can't seem to help it with them and they don't give me a choice. Carlo used to try to play it cool but the Rivers squashed that quickly and if they hadn't handled it, Quinn's mom would have. That kid gets more hugs when she's visiting than he had in his whole life before that.

"Hey, dude! Did you have fun on vacation?"

"Yeah! They had this roller coaster made of wood and it jerked us all over the place. And Grandma and Grandpa Hannigan took me to this place with a huge swimming pool and rides and stuff. I love Ohio!"

"Never thought I'd hear anyone say that," I murmur as Quinn comes up behind him.

"Dex, one day you'll come to Mom and Dad's with me and see what all the fuss is about. They were disappointed you didn't come this time."

"I know, but my vacation time is in Florida. You know this."

"I know, but you could've come for a few days and shortened your trip to Florida."

"Maybe next year. This is a big year. I promised I'd be there."

"I know. I just missed you."

Carlo steps out of the way so Quinn can hug me and Lila turns in her arms and latches on to my shirt with a squeal. I hug them both and secure the baby in my arms as she smiles up at me, drool running down her chin.

Judson's voice booms behind me. "Dex! My competition! How are you man?" We shake hands and I give him the best stern face I can. "Competition?"

"Yeah, my family only wants to talk about Dex this and Uncle Dex that and Uncle Dex is the best. If it were anyone else, I'd have already kicked your ass for stealing my family. They're obsessed with you!" He chuckles and the smile he wears tells me that he's not really jealous. Judson is also a veteran. He was wounded in combat worse than I was and dragged himself through hell to get to this point in his life. He also lost guys when he lost the lower part of his leg and understands how that messes up your head. He probably understands me better than anyone.

"It's a ranger thing. Squids just aren't as cool."

"Screw you, man. I was a damn SEAL. There's nothing cooler than that!"

Quinn interjects, "Quit being childish, you two. Judd, finish with the horses and get inside for dinner. Carlo, finish your homework so you can hang with Uncle Dexter. For now," she points to me, "you can follow me to the kitchen so I can catch up on all the gossip at work. Besides, Lila wants some time to drool all over her uncle." She cackles as she turns and walks back into the house. The baby grabs my bottom lip, pulls and squawks a bunch of baby babble before I smile at her and follow Quinn inside.

"So what did I miss at work this week? How'd it go with Gino?"

"Fuck him! He's a dick."

Her head whips my way and she glares at me. "If Lila spits that out as some of her first words I'll shoot you in the butt. Now watch your language. Although I agree there's something super sleazy about him, you need to find a cleaner way to tell me about your week."

I feign fear and hold the baby in front of me as a shield.

"She can't protect you."

I laugh for a few seconds and then fill her in on everything that happened. She finishes stirring and places the spoon on the stove. Then she turns around and crosses her arms over her chest as she rests her hip against the counter. If looks could kill, Gino would be dead.

"What a dick!" she blurts.

I widen my eyes at her, over-exaggerating the gesture because she gave me hell earlier.

"Oh, shut up. You were right. Strong issues require strong responses. I can't wait to get back to work just so I can use a bunch of cuss words in a row. My brain is tired of behaving. So, tell me about this Marina Rossi chick."

"Nothing to tell. We lived in the same foster house for a little while. Then they moved me again."

Her eyes narrow on me. *Shit*.

"It's more than that. Tell me."

"It's not." I refuse to open that can of worms. Besides, what would I say? I was in love with her from afar when I was young? That I saved her from either getting raped or being forced to suck some dude's dick one night and then I got to hold her two nights in a row before they split us up? Do I say that I thought about her no less than a 1000 times while I was on deployment? Nope. Then Quinn will pester me about it. And I don't need the kind of crazy that follows Mari, not in my life. She could derail a train just by standing near the tracks, and it'll take a certain kind of man or friend to change that. I'm not that guy.

Quinn's eyes stay trained on me as she says, "You care about this girl; it's obvious even if you want to deny it. The look on your face tells me more than you think. We talk about everything so I don't understand why you won't tell me what the deal is."

"Just drop it. The story here is Gino. I refused to work with him the last couple of days after that incident. I don't trust him and I don't like him. Any man that could treat a woman that way is a di—um, jerk, and doesn't deserve to wear a badge."

"Well, I'll be back tomorrow. I was afraid you wouldn't miss me." Her grin tells me she's full of shit; she knows I missed her. I'm a little concerned that the captain will try to stick her with Gino when I'm in Florida, but Quinn has proven she can take care of herself. However, if he tries anything stupid I'll kill him when I get back.

After dinner, I spend an hour playing video games with Carlo and hanging with him while he reads out loud to me. Before Quinn and Judson, no one ever read with him. I never got that either as a kid and didn't realize what I was missing out on until I did it with Carlo one time. He's 12 years old now and when they asked if he wanted to read alone he said no. He liked it. He said most kids his age don't do that anymore but he has time to make up for. I like that about the kid. He doesn't care what anyone thinks of him. He does what feels right and oddly enough, his moral compass always points him in the right direction.

THREE DAYS LATER, QUINN AND I ARE IN THE BREAK ROOM chowing down on our lunch when Myrtle, our ancient white-haired receptionist, sticks her head in the door. "Dex, you've got a call. I tried to forward it to your phone but you weren't picking it up. One of the guys said you were here. Line two."

I pat my pocket and realize my phone must be sitting on my desk. Who the hell is calling the station to talk to me? I pick up and answer, "Dexter."

"Jase. Um...It's Marina. Don't be mad but I need your help." My body stills but my heart rate picks up. The logical side of my brain is pissed as hell that she's calling and the side I obviously have zero control over is ready to fly into action with whatever her request is. The dueling responses have me feeling off-balance and irritated.

"What's up?" I attempt to keep my tone businesslike.

"I'm in a little bit of trouble." *Shit.*

Impatience that's very unlike me flares in my gut. "What kind of trouble? Spit it out."

"Don't be mean. I'm at the hospital. If you won't come they'll have me arrested. I can't afford bail. Please help me." *Damn it!* This girl is killing me with her drama. Why is she calling me? I probably should ask why she'd be getting arrested at the hospital, but I don't think sitting on the phone hashing it out will help.

"Give me a few minutes to get over there." I hang up, not waiting to hear what else she has to say. I got her out of that situation with Gino a week ago and can't imagine what she could possibly have going on now? I snatch my trash off the table and toss it in the garbage can. Quinn follows me out the door. "What's going on, Dex?"

"Nothing. I'll take care of it."

"Tell me what's going on," she insists.

"No. I've got it."

She grabs my arm to stop me and I spin on her. She must see the anger in my eyes because she takes a step back. I never turn like that on her and hate that she had to back away from me.

"Dex?" Her eyes are pleading with me. She's worried. I did get spun up pretty fast. As soon as I heard Mari's voice my heart rate shot up, and then to find out she's in trouble again pissed me off.

"Look, the girl, Marina, I told you about? She's in trouble at the hospital. She didn't say what it was, but she wants me to come help her. I'll be back in a little while."

"No."

I flinch, what does she mean no? "What?"

"I said no. I'm going with you."

"Quinn."

"I'm going. You won't change my mind. Come on, you can drive." I say nothing in response since arguing with her is pointless:;I always lose.

When we finally find Marina, I can see her through the square glass window of the wooden door leading to the hospital security office where she's sitting. A short, stout, out-of-shape security guard with a horrible comb-over is glaring at her as she drums her fingers on the table. Quinn pushes in front of me and takes the lead despite our conversation in the car.

She turns her attention to the guard. "I'm Officer Rivers and this is my partner, Officer Dexter. What seems to be the problem?"

"She was raising hell in the ICU. You can't do that in this hospital. She's not even family. She shouldn't have been in there in the first place."

Quinn turns to face Marina who's staring at me. I refuse to look directly at Marina; it will only pull me in deeper.

Marina speaks before anything else can be said. "They're taking Fern off life support. They're gonna let her die. She doesn't have any family to fight for her. They can't let her go. She's not ready." I can't help but focus on her now as her horrified tone digs at my insides. Her eyes are wide and frightened, a look I remember well. My chest squeezes at the memory of her running down the steps of the foster home as I was loading up to leave that last time.

Quinn leads the conversation with the security guard. "We'll take care of her, but first I'd like to talk to the head nurse in the ICU. Can you take me up there? Officer Dexter will stay with Miss Rossi." The guard looks between us like he's unsure, but finally he gives in. The two exit the room and it's just me and Marina left. Suddenly the years melt away and the pressure on my chest increases. Marina's face is tear streaked and her eyes are bright and damp. I want to fix this for her so she won't look this way. She's making my stomach churn with emotion and I can't afford messy feelings from the past that mean nothing.

"Marina, why are you doing this? By law you have no say and can't fix this. She's a junkie. She almost got you arrested once before. She's better off out of this life anyway. You know how hard it is for addicts to get clean and stay that way."

"Jase, how can you be so cruel?" she whispers.

Why is this pressure in my chest getting worse? Am I having a heart attack?

She continues, "Please don't say that. Everyone deserves a second chance. She doesn't deserve to die because she made a mistake. If that were the case I wouldn't be here." I can't imagine the mistakes she's made over the years consider the situations I've encountered with her over the last week, but the thought of her gone makes me a little dizzy. What the hell is wrong with me? She's not someone who should concern me.

I take a deep breath and stare into her eyes; they're lethal they're so beautiful, but I need her to listen to me and understand I'm not trying to be a jerk, so I'll take the risk of staring into them. I care, even as much as I don't want to, I still do. I wipe my palms on my pants, and place one on the table. When I wiggle my fingers at her she glances down and then back up at me, confused by the gesture. Wiggling my fingers again, I say, "Marina." Finally, she places her hand in mine and I close my fingers around it. Warmth from her touch spreads up my arm in a way I've never felt before. *Focus!* "If they want to pull the plug it's because she's already gone. They don't stop life support on patients for the hell of it. There are laws about those kinds of things. You've got to let her go. Sometimes it's not what we want, but it's what's best." I squeeze her hand tighter for support but not hard enough to hurt.

The tears she was holding back are now falling as her head lowers and her shoulders sag. "I don't want her to die alone. She has no one else. No one cares. Please don't let her die alone." She pleads with me. About that time Quinn comes back in and her eyes quickly flick to our hands joined on the table and then to me. When I see the look on Quinn's face I know she needs to talk to me before she addresses Marina, so I give Marina a light squeeze and slip my hand out from under hers. Quinn and I move to the far side of the room and whisper.

"She's brain-dead. They're ending life support. There's nothing we can do and frankly nothing we should do. She's gone. What did you get out of her?"

"She doesn't want to let her go. Fern has no one else and she doesn't want her to die alone."

"That's an easy fix." She leans in closer and quietly says, "You can tell me all day long this woman means nothing to you, but the only hands I've ever seen you hold belong to members of my family. We *will* talk about this, Dex." Turning to the security guard who followed her back into the room, she says, "Miss Rossi has been cleared by the charge nurse to sit with the patient until she's gone." He opens his mouth to protest but Quinn holds up a hand. "I've agreed to stay with them to make sure protocol is followed and she doesn't disturb anyone else. It's already been cleared but they're ready now, so we need to go."

Marina stands abruptly and darts for the door. Out of instinct I wrap an arm around her chest and pull her back to me. I want to comfort her and calm her. Her whole body vibrates with tension and she needs to settle down or this will get bad. Quinn's eyes widen at my reaction.

I lean down and whisper in Marina's ear, "Calm down or they'll make us remove you and will likely press charges. I'll go with you."

She surprises me by saying, "No! You don't care about my friend. You think the junkie got what she deserves. I'd rather take your partner."

She wiggles out of my grasp and I blurt, "Mari! Wait." We both freeze because I haven't called her that since the day we said goodbye. As far as I know, no one called her that but me. Then I step closer, unable to let her face this without me. "Mari, I do care. I'm sorry you think I don't. Quinn can come, but I'm coming too." We stare at each other for a long, uncomfortable moment as security and Quinn stand awkwardly aside. Her wide sad eyes remind me of our history. So many memories are pouring between us as we stand there that the air grows thicker with more emotion.

The whole encounter is way too heavy for me to deal with, but for whatever reason, I won't let her face this without me. As the three of us head to Fern's room, I remind myself that I need to put some space between Marina and me. I can't allow her to drag emotion out of me like this. We have some history but that's it. I don't need to have a human cyclone blowing around in my life. I just need to lock it down and treat this situation like any other work related scenario.

The nurse is kind enough to pull in two extra chairs for Quinn and me, but we don't sit down. Mari drags the chair that was already in there close to the bed to sit in and holds Fern's lifeless hand while she waits quietly.

The nurse breaks the silence as she removes the IV and all the additional tubing and explains, "Marco, the respiratory therapist, will be here in a moment to turn off the machine. Fern can't feel anything so this won't hurt. It may happen right away or it may take several hours, I can't give you an exact answer because everyone is different. I know this is difficult and I'm sorry for your loss."

Quinn and I stand out of the way until Mari glances back at us and the look on her face brings the pressure back to my chest. The instinct to comfort her is overwhelming, so I step forward and place my hand on her shoulder and squeeze lightly. Quinn pulls her chair up on the other side and holds Mari's free hand. The respiratory therapist strides into the room, all businesslike. He must do this often to not even appear phased by what he's about to do. Right before he turns the power off, he looks up at us and asks, "Do you have any questions?"

"Are you sure she's not coming back?" Mari croaks.

"Three doctors reviewed the tests, the chart, and examined the patient, and all three agreed. I'm sorry. I wish I had a different answer."

Sniffling, she wipes her nose on her sleeve and all her muscles tense as the power to the machine is turned off and the tubing that leads to the ventilator is disconnected.

In less than 15 minutes Fern is gone and Marina is a mess. We allow her a few minutes alone with Fern's body and when it's time to go, she won't move. Afraid that she'll lose it, I scoop her up in my arms and stride out of the room before she has time to argue. Surprisingly she wraps her arms around my neck and cries into my scratchy uniform shirt.

There is no doubt in my mind that I need to take her home and put some space between us before she completely disarms me. Knowing she's hurting is almost more than I can handle.

Something deep within me fights against my conscious choice to distance myself from her. The urge to comfort her is difficult to deny.

Quinn opens the rear passenger door of the cruiser as I'm returning Marina to her feet. I hold her there, allowing her to get her balance and settle down a little. After a few seconds, she scoots in, sniffling, but quiet. Once I'm in the driver's seat I study her from the rearview mirror, wishing I could take that look off her face. Quinn climbs in the front seat and quietly says, "I'm glad we're taking her home. I didn't want her to ride the bus. It's been a rough day."

I don't say it out loud but there is no way in hell I would've allowed her to get on a bus alone after this. Instead of responding I ask, "Can you check in and make sure we didn't miss anything?" Quinn calls and all is well so I pull out of the parking lot.

As we drive to the address Marina gave us, I alternate between watching the road and watching her while my emotions volley all over the place. I need to get away from her. I'm known for how even-keeled and in control I am but she seems to stir the pot and flip my world upside down. I need to go back to my life before Mari reentered it.

Because I was so distracted by her sad eyes and thoughts of escaping her, I didn't pay attention to the neighborhood we were going to. Son of a bitch! This is one of the worst neighborhoods in Colorado Springs. She lives here?

The complex she lives in is one of the better ones but when I say *better* I mean better for this area. Not necessarily *decent* by anyone's standards. She's struggling in more ways than one. How has she made it this long?

When I pull into a parking spot, Quinn and I exchange a glance and I know she's thinking the same thing I am, we don't want to leave her here.

Chapter Five
MARINA

I can't decide if I want to slap him or kiss him. One minute he's a standoffish jerk and the next he's melting like warm chocolate right in front of my eyes. That's the Jase I remember, the melty one. There was nothing I needed more than him to carry me out of that hospital room. His sturdy chest, strong arms and comforting heartbeat were exactly what I was in desperate need of. Not the uptight, overly controlled dickhead that acts like he doesn't care about anything.

I turn to Officer Rivers. "Thank you for taking care of things and working it out for me to be there." Then I turn my attention to Jase. "I know that's not how you wanted to spend your day and I'd like to say I'm sorry I messed up your plans, but the truth is I'm not. I didn't know what else to do and calling you turned out to be the right thing. I appreciate you being there for me and for the ride. I know I've passed my quota on favors so I won't bug you anymore. Take care of yourself." Without another word, I slip out of the car and walk toward the building.

I stop and turn when Officer Rivers yells, "Marina!" She jots something down on a card, jogs to where I am and hands it to me. "Here's my number, both the station number and my cell. If you call late I may not hear it, so leave me a message. I turn off the ringer so it doesn't wake everyone in the house after hours. If you need something, call me. I'm sorry about your friend." She pats my shoulder and jogs back to the car.

Jase is still staring at me through the windshield but I can't let that get to me. Despite the sweet moments I've seen from him today, it's clear he doesn't care to see or deal with me again so I turn and continue inside to my subpar apartment and my less than stellar life. Although, I can't seem to allow myself to be too upset about my living situation when I at least have my life to live. Shitty or not, it beats the alternative. Today was another crappy reminder that I'd rather live a hard life than have no life at all.

It's obvious I'm not Irish since I have absolutely no luck. I haven't figured out how it is that I seem to be able to screw up an already major screw-up, but I always do. I can never have a regular problem, solve it and move on. Nope. Each incident has to be bigger than the last. Although I don't know how getting busted being forced to suck off a cop in order to avoid jail while my friend dies on the ground next to me can be beat, but hey, I can try.

After watching Fern die, sadness sort of set in and I walked around the rest of the day feeling numb and it never occurred to me to check my work schedule for updates. Of course, because it's my life and my luck, I was scheduled at the last minute to work yesterday and didn't show up. They were shorthanded and there was a birthday party on top of it. Apparently, the place was a zoo and everyone was flaming mad at me. The manager yelled at me for 10 minutes and then threatened my job when I showed up today. I think he would've fired me if he didn't need me on the floor so badly today.

One of the girls I work with, Cindy, tends to sleep with the customers—too many, too often. We look a little bit alike in that we both have tattoos, piercings and hair with colorful streaks but she's much shorter than I am with thin lips and a shrill voice. Of course, her boobs are *way* bigger than mine and I think that's the appeal for the men. Midway through my shift a woman with a fierce scowl storms through the front door, past the hostess, and around to the bar like her ass is on fire. The frizzy brown hair she should've stopped perming years ago gives her a weathered look. With eye makeup reminiscent of an '80s hairband groupie and clothes that are clearly a size too small, she's a frightening site. She's waving a phone in the air and screaming about wanting to see the chick with the tattoos. Cindy is off today so the two servers and bartender turn and point to me.

The woman rushes over to me and it's obvious she's crazy-mad, but I've never seen her before so I can't figure out why. I'm holding an empty tray ready to bus the table behind me, wondering what in the hell her problem is. Thinking maybe she's going to yell at me, I don't see it coming when she pulls her fist back and punches me in the face, sending me backwards several steps and over a nearby table. I crash to the ground, along with all the leftover dishes on the table, and when I stand she comes back for me again. I was unprepared once, but it won't happen like that again. I snatch the tray up off the floor and swing at her with the bottom side toward her face. She swipes at it and tackles me to the ground, knocking more tables and dishes over. Now she's straddling me and swinging like a maniac as I do my best to protect my face. *What the hell is going on? Who is this lady?*

Finally, she's pulled off me and I look up to see the daytime manager holding a squirming, screaming woman. Gingerly, I get up and face my boss.

"What the hell is going on, Marina?"

The woman shouts, "That bitch fucked my husband and got knocked up!"

What the hell is she talking about? "I'm not pregnant. And I doubt I screwed your husband!" I yell back at her.

"My friend saw the tattooed waitress from this place go into a motel with him last week. Now he's leaving me because she's pregnant and says it's his. That's you, bitch! When I asked for the tattooed one, they pointed at you! Now tell me why you fucked my husband!" she screams as her already red face morphs to a purplish color. Families and old people have all stopped eating to watch this spectacle.

"I didn't screw your husband!"

Still a little dizzy from the tumble I took and the head smack to the floor, I forget to tell her that I'm not the only tattooed waitress here.

"You goddamned husband-stealing whore!" she screeches at me. "You try to look all exotic with your piercings, tattoos and colorful hair but you're just a husband-stealing whore!"

Before I can say anything else two very familiar cops come through the door. Of course it's them, because why would anyone other than Jase and Officer Rivers be privy to the latest episode of my-life-is-a-shit-show? If there were a rock in this room, I'd crawl under it.

As soon as they get a look at me, Jase's face turns to stone and Officer Rivers's softens. She takes the lead. "What's the issue here?"

My boss tries to tell them I was attacked at the same time as the crazy woman starts yelling about me being a husband-stealing whore again. Jase stifles the woman with a low verbal warning I can't hear and then he stares daggers through me.

I yell loud enough to stop chatter in the entire restaurant. "I didn't touch her husband! I don't even know who he is!" You can hear a pin drop by the time I finish.

My boss comes over and says, "I don't care if you did or you didn't. This woman thinks you did and destroyed my restaurant trying to get to you. I don't need your chaos, Marina. You're fired.

Get your stuff and get out. If I could count on you to be here on time or at all and do your job, I might listen to what you have to say, but the truth is I don't care and I don't believe you anyway."

Unbelievable. Now he's poked the dragon and I'm ready to breathe fire. "Has anyone noticed that *Cindy* has tattoos, piercings and streaks in her hair too? Or that she sleeps with the customers? I don't! I've never slept with a customer." The woman finally stops struggling and stares at me for a minute and then at my chest. She swallows hard and flips her eyes back to mine before she says solemnly, "You don't have huge boobs."

"No, lady, I don't! That's Cindy. Thanks to you and her slutty leg spreading, though, I no longer have a job. I hope you feel good about that!" I wiggle out of my boss's grip and go to the back to get my stuff. Jase follows me.

When the door swings closed behind us, he asks, "Marina, why does drama always follow you?" *Is he for real?* My anger explodes like Mount St. Helens and I turn and yell, "Screw you, Jase! Not everyone got out of this fucking pit and made a life. I'm stuck here on the bottom rung and no matter how hard I try I can't climb any higher out of the depths of hell. If you're going to arrest me just do it. At least that way I'll have somewhere to sleep. If not, let me get my shit and get on my way so I can find another hellhole to work in so maybe I can pay my rent and avoid living on the streets again." His already tense muscles turn to stone.

"Mari! You say it's not your fault, but I've never met anyone who ends up in as many situations as you do. Seriously, this is the third one in a week. Some of this could be the choices you make."

Oh, my God! If I could slap him, I would. Then I'd really go to jail. Assaulting a police officer, that would make a lovely addition to my rap sheet.

"The first night I saw you I was with a friend who'd started using drugs again and I didn't know it. The second time was me trying to take care of a dying friend. Today? Today has absolutely nothing to do with me except that I happen to have tattoos like the waitress who *is* a husband-stealing whore. My boss fired me more because he was mad that I accidentally missed my shift yesterday after watching my friend die. How could I have changed any of that? Realistically I couldn't, not without changing who I am, which is a loyal friend. I'm sorry you don't like it."

I spin back around, grab my purse and pull off my apron. Today's tips get shoved in my pocket and then I toss my apron at my manager who is now blocking the doorway as he listens to our exchange. Without another word, I storm past both of those idiots and out the door. When I glance down at my dollar store watch and realize the bus doesn't run for another 45 minutes, I want to scream. Why can't even the littlest thing work in my favor? You know what? I can walk. It will be a haul but at this point who cares? It'll be better than sitting here stewing in my anger and self-loathing. As I turn to do just that, I see Officer Rivers striding up to me.

"Marina, wait. Are you okay? You're still bleeding."

"I am?" A quick survey of my limbs reveals nothing. She reaches out and swipes under my chin and comes away with blood on her fingers. I hate the sight of blood; it turns my stomach. My head swims and I wobble as I process the scarlet wet streak on her fingers. She reaches out to steady me.

"Come on. Let's get you cleaned up. You may need stitches." I let her support me a little, afraid that the wooziness will send me to the ground for more injuries.

"I don't have insurance. I can't afford to get stitched up. I'll clean it up at home and tape it together. It'll be fine, officer," I say, feeling the defeat of the last week and even the last few years all the way to my soul. Why do I fight so hard to keep going when it always turns out bad? Maybe not always this bad, but nothing is ever roses for me. It's just a fact of life.

"You aren't cleaning this up yourself. I'll handle the bill."

"No way. I don't take charity. I'll be fine."

She gently pulls me back to the restaurant and I begin to protest when the manager glares at me.

Quinn whispers in my ear, "Shhh, let me handle this."

"Did you notice the blood when she walked out of here?" The tone of her voice makes it clear she's not happy. My manager nods, glowering at me as he does.

"It's in your best interest to file a report and send her to get this taken care of on the company dime or she can sue you if anything happens since she was on company property and on the time clock." Glaring at me he mutters under his breath several words that sound a lot like cuss words, he finally gives in and says, "I'll get the paperwork started."

Two hours later, Quinn and Jase, who still hasn't spoken to me since our altercation in the staff locker room, drive me home. I ended up with five stitches in my chin. I have a few other bruises and some I'm certain will show later, but I don't care right now. I just want to go home and get some rest. I can figure out what tomorrow's survival tactics will include when I wake up.

It's dark and the neighborhood's sketchy population that's usually hidden during the day is roaming the streets while some are huddled on street corners, so Quinn insists on walking me to my door. I let her, because with my luck I'd get robbed of my last $80 on the way to my door.

Of course, because it wouldn't be *my* life if this weren't the case, my front door is open a little when I arrive. I would think it's weird if I couldn't hear Dee's voice coming from within. A quick peek inside allows me to see Dee standing with another uniformed officer. Tears stream down her face as she runs for me. When she reaches me, she throws her arms around me. I hold tight and close my eyes because I need the hug as bad as she obviously does, but I'm a little freaked out not knowing what's going on.

"What is it, Dee?" She leans back to gain eye contact and the bloodshot state of her eyes alerts me to the fact that she's probably been crying a lot longer than a few minutes. She turns and waves her hand toward the room like a game show hostess. It takes everything in me to remain upright as the scene of what I walked in on settles inside me. There's nothing here. No pink and white floral couch straight ahead, no ratty brown recliner to the left, no flat-screen TV to my right. No pictures of me, Dee and Reggie, or our other friends, or Dee's family on the walls. On the back wall, before you reach the hallway, there is no framed poster print of Gustav Klimt's *The Kiss* hanging up. Even our old scatter rugs are gone. Not even a dead leaf from the one houseplant we've managed to keep alive can be seen. Nothing that was in the room when I left earlier today remains.

A few dust bunnies gather near the corners and a few handprints I didn't notice before are visible on the walls.

"What the hell, Dee? Are you leaving?" I can't come up with a better explanation for why everything would be gone, even if that doesn't add up either.

"No, honey." Her lower lip trembles as she replies, "I'd never leave you. We've been robbed."

I glance over to the cop, who nods, reinforcing what Dee told me. My eyes widen as panic shoots through me and I dart toward my room. The only thing I care about is that damn shoebox. The only important things that I own are in there. *Please let it be in there. Please let it be in there.*

The closet door is standing open and everything is gone, including my sacred shoebox. There's not even lint on the floor. That's the end of it. The one finger grip I had on my control and sanity is finally gone and I lose it. My knees give way and I land hard on them. I only stay in that position long enough to transition to a little ball on the floor. The tears flow hard and heavy. Neither of us had anything expensive other than the TV. Why would anyone want my hand-me-down dresser or my ratty old tennis shoes? None of that meant a damn thing to me until losing it meant I have absolutely nothing. I only have what I'm wearing.

That shoebox held the few pictures I had of my grandparents, the only picture of my sister, my favorite shirt—which was my sister's, and the beautiful silver locket that Jase gave me when we were in foster care.

Now I have no job, no belongings, no car and hardly any money. Who takes someone's clothes? They weren't designer brands. They were cheap. I don't even have a pillow or blanket to sleep on the floor with, thanks to our burglar.

A warm body curls around mine and holds me close with an arm around my waist. I know it's Dee because she's done this before when I've fallen apart, which doesn't happen often, but it does on occasion when my shitty life proves it can get shittier. She holds tight and stays quiet until I settle down. I can hear voices in the living room, but they all leave us alone.

"Dee, why does God hate me? I try to be a good person. I don't understand why things keep piling up." My heart hurts for what I've lost. It doesn't feel like I can dig myself out of the hole I seem to be in. As a matter of fact, I feel like the more I dig, the more dirt someone else piles on me to keep me down.

"It's not your fault, honey. God doesn't hate you. This is just life for people like us. It happens. This sucks, but at least we weren't home so we weren't hurt. We have each other. No matter what stuff is gone, we still have each other. I'm not going anywhere." She squeezes tighter to make her point. I lace my fingers through hers over my belly and lie there in the middle of my floor, trying to be thankful that I still have Dee. Without her I'd have almost no one, well, no one of substance anyway. I hate to be alone, am absolutely terrified I'll end up completely alone in this world, so I cling to anyone who gets close enough to me. Fern dying yesterday didn't help that feeling. Dee's been with me the longest. I met her a couple of years after I got off the street.

After a few more minutes go by, a shadow crosses the door and Jase's deep voice echoes in the bare room, "Do you have anywhere to stay?"

I don't answer. He's seen enough of my humiliation this week and doesn't need to see more. The truth is, I don't have anywhere else to go. I could stay with my friend Callie but she lives almost an hour outside the city and I don't have a car to commute that far.

Dee answers for both of us as she climbs to her feet and helps me up. "We'll work it out. We always do." I wipe away the tears that collected on the side of my face and clear my throat. Dee leads the way past Jase into the living room where the cop who was standing with Dee when I came in is talking with Quinn. They both turn to us and the first cop says, "I need you to review this list your roommate gave us, add anything else you can think of and then sign it. I'll call you if we have any questions or anything turns up." He looks at me. "Did you have anything valuable stolen? Your roommate didn't think you did but I wanted to confirm."

"Yes, I did," I answer in a low voice. I don't want to share with the room that I kept that damn necklace that meant so much to me when it obviously never meant anything to him. If it did he wouldn't treat me, the person he gave it to, like I'm a huge inconvenience every time he sees me.

Dee's eyebrows draw down, the question obvious in her eyes. "A silver necklace. It had a silver heart-shaped locket attached," I tell the cop in a quiet voice.

Dee gasps and nods rapidly, "Oh God, the shoebox! Oh, honey, I'm so sorry." I choke back a sob and shake my head fast, trying to clear the urge to break down. If I start again I won't stop and I'm tired of appearing weak. She clamps her lips shut.

The cop looks at us and instructs, "I recommend you don't stay here until the landlord gets the locks fixed. Call me if you think of anything else." Then he exits, leaving us with Jase and Quinn. Quinn takes the moment to introduce herself and Jase. Dee's eyes widen for a second when she recognizes the name, but other than that she doesn't respond.

Quinn turns to me, "Do you have somewhere to stay?"

Again, Dee answers. "We'll work it out. Between her tips and mine we'll be fine."

Before she can say more I interrupt, dreading having to tell her the latest news. "Dee, I've got enough for tonight and maybe tomorrow night, but I lost my job today." She looks back to me and I lift my chin and point so she can see the stitches.

"Shit. What the hell! Is this why they came home with you?"

"Kinda. It's a long story, but the end is me losing my job."

"Damn it."

"Yeah, I'm sorry."

Dee shakes her head like she's disappointed in me. To be fair, she's put up with a lot of irresponsible shit from me over the years. Even if this isn't my fault, the 100 other things that came up over time are.

"It's okay. We'll work it out. We always do," she repeats after a deep sigh.

Quinn stares at a quiet Jase for several long seconds before she finally looks back at us and speaks up, "I've got somewhere you can stay for a few days. We've got an extra room. I mean, you'll have to share, but it's nice and clean. If my husband and two kids don't bother you, it should work for short term."

"No way. We aren't intruding on your family. You've been kind enough to me. We'll be fine. Besides, Dee can stay with her boyfriend. I'll work something out."

Jase never says a word. One minute tender, the next distant. Whatever. I wonder if the Army made him this way. He wasn't like this when I knew him before. He was quiet but not withdrawn.

Quinn doesn't take no for an answer. "Come on, you can follow us. The officer that was just here told me you have a car, Dee. I have clothes that you can fit into. They might fall off of Marina but they'll be clean. Come on. If you hate it, you can find somewhere else tomorrow."

We don't have any choice except the fleabag motel up the road. Well, Dee does. She could stay with Reggie, but I don't like or trust his roommate so I won't go near the place when he's not there. She's such a good friend though that she won't leave me to deal with this alone.

"Okay, but just for tonight." I'll take the help because I may need that last little bit of money from tips to go toward clothes and food for a bit, until I can get a paycheck.

An hour later we're having dinner with the second hottest guy I've ever seen, Quinn's husband Judson, a cute tween-age boy they adopted named Carlo, and their darling baby girl, Lila, in the Rivers' beautiful ranch house. It was too dark to see anything except the outline of the barn and horse pen when we pulled up, but her husband, Judson, says he'll take us out to see the horses in the morning.

After leading us here and introducing us to everyone, Quinn and Jase returned to work. I thought it might be weird to be left here with people we don't know, but Carlo has been very animated as he talks to us, like he's enjoying having an audience. Judson is quiet, but not uncomfortably so, almost like he's always this way. It's as if he's taking everything in.

While I sit at this table, in a real family home, my heart aches for everything I never had. A family is the only thing I've ever wanted; people to love me that I can love in return. The warmth and happiness that I see in this room is my dream, not the family that I grew up with.

Chapter Six
DEX

I'm angry at Quinn and it's time to find out why she took them in. "Quinn, what the hell were you thinking?" I flash her a look filled with all the attitude I can muster.

"What? I couldn't leave them there. They didn't have anywhere to go. I don't know how you could leave them considering you know Marina and obviously feel something for her. You can deny it all day long, Dex, but I know you and it's obvious that she matters to you."

"Marina is a footlocker of misfortune and you don't need that in your house. Your family has been through enough."

"Do *you* want to give them somewhere to stay?"

"No," I grumble. Marina at my place? That's asking for trouble. "But you need to think of Carlo. Who knows what those two women will bring to your house."

"Don't lecture me on Carlo. Either I take them in, or you do. For now, they're at my house with my family. If you feel strongly enough that they don't belong there, you can take them to your place; if you don't, then shut up. You know I can't leave them out there when they have no place to go."

"Marina said something about Dee's boyfriend."

"Did you get a look at Marina's face when she thought Dee might go there? She was terrified. After everything she's been through, I don't know how you can be ready to leave her on a street corner and be done with her. Especially since you have some kind of history with her you're not talking about."

I flinch, knowing she's right and feeling a little bit of guilt about it, but I didn't ask for any of this. I don't understand how these women became my responsibility. How did I end up with a do-good partner? I'll never be able to get rid of Marina now.

AS WE FINISH UP THE DAY, I FACE THE GUILT THAT'S BEEN weighing on me since Quinn called me out. I have the space to put the ladies up and it's safer for Quinn's family for them to stay with me in case there's a problem we aren't aware of.

On our way to the parking lot I finally cave. "I'll come get them; let me follow you home."

"Why? They aren't bothering me. Sounds like my family likes them, if the last five texts from Carlo and Judd are anything to go by."

"I don't want to take a chance that there will be problems. I'll get them set up and then stay out of their way. Besides I leave for Florida soon."

Quinn studies me for a long time before she finally says, "Fine, follow me then."

WHEN WE WALK THROUGH THE DOOR TO QUINN'S HOUSE, I'M stopped dead in my tracks by the sight of Marina with Lila on her hip. Mari's hair is pulled up in a messy knot on her head and the tip of a tattoo at her neck is peeking out along her shirt collar, but not enough to see what it is exactly. They're facing the window, away from us, and it only takes a second to figure out they're laughing at their reflections. Mari does something and Lila giggles uncontrollably. Then Mari laughs. When they both settle down it starts again.

I'd love to look away but I can't. It's beautiful and in that moment, I'm speechless and pulled back in time to the second week Mari was staying with the foster family. I'd been there longer and when she arrived I couldn't get enough of her. Everything about her, from the sound of her voice to her boisterous laughter, the scent of her shampoo, and the delicate curve of her neck, made me stupid with obsession. There were other girls her age at the house, but none of them affected me the way she did. Sometimes I'd sit outside of whatever room she was in and soak in the sweet cadence of her voice, even if the conversation was stupid.

There was one time when Mari was in a bedroom with one of the littler girls in the house and they were giggling about something. Within a couple of minutes the giggles turned into hardcore laughter, practically obnoxious in its volume, but I was certain I'd never heard anything more amazing. I don't know why it hit me like it did then or now, but I can only classify her laughter as magical. I'll never admit that to anyone else. I'd be labeled a pussy for the rest of my life. Especially since she irritates me so badly now with everything else she does.

I don't know how long I stand there and watch this little scene, but I don't snap out of it until I hear Judson call my name. Shit. I was hoping no one noticed, but of course that's not an option in this house. When I glance around I realize everyone else is staring at me. Quinn is doing her best to hide a smile and Judson is flat-out laughing at me. *Fucker*.

"What?" I ask, narrowing my eyes at them, but I don't wait for the answer to my question. "Marina and Dee, I'm taking you guys with me."

Marina's head whips around and the smile she had on her face slides off slowly. "Why?"

"Just because. They have enough going on without all of this. I have room at my place for you two and it won't disrupt the kids' schedules."

Judson opens his mouth to say something but Quinn clears her throat and gives him a quick shake of her head to shut him up.

Marina looks a little hurt as she passes Lila to Quinn. "I'm sorry if we invaded your family time. They're great kids. Let me slip on my shoes and I'll be ready." She's crushed and like every other emotion she experiences, she can't hide it. Damn. I feel like an ass, but I don't need her getting attached to the Rivers family when she'll be gone soon. Besides, I have no idea what kind of trouble is following her this time and I don't want it on their doorstep.

"Hold on. Let me grab some clothes for you guys. I'll be right back," Quinn calls over her shoulder as she rushes out of the room.

There's an uncomfortable silence as we wait, so Judson asks, "Can I talk to you out back?" I nod and turn for the door when I hear him tell Carlo, "Take your sister to her room and play with her for a little bit, please. Say goodnight to the ladies."

Once the door is closed, Judson asks, "Dex, what the hell is going on? You know having them stay at our place isn't an issue. I'm missing something here, but I don't know what it is. You gonna tell me?"

I lean over and prop my elbows on the railing of their wrap-around porch and release a deep breath, feeling like I've been holding it in for hours. "There's a lot you don't know. I'm sure Quinn will fill you in, but basically Marina is a mess. Although I don't think she means to, she keeps ending up in trouble. It's one issue after another with her and I don't want your kids exposed to that. You guys have been through enough."

"She's fine. I think I'm a pretty good judge of character and I'm telling you, any problems she has aren't totally her fault. She may have judgment issues, but she's got a good heart."

"Dude, you don't know her. I'll explain everything another time, but I can't go there now. I'm taking them with me. It'll be better that way. I'll also be gone to Florida in a couple of days, so they'll have the place to themselves."

He throws his hands up as he backs away. "Okay, your call, but if it doesn't work there they can come back here."

My apartment doesn't have the comfortable feel of home like Quinn's house does but it's clean and has enough room to accommodate us all. An interior decorator I'm not. Both guest rooms have a queen-sized bed with solid navy bedding and a matching dresser. I don't have anything hanging on the walls in those rooms so they're a little on the sparse side. I know it's weird that a single guy has a three-bedroom apartment, but after a lifetime of having no space, I felt I needed room to breathe.

The living room has the most comfortable couch I could find. It's big and firm but fluffy. The sales lady called the color chocolate, but let's call a spade a spade, it's brown. Next to that are a tan, leather recliner, also very comfortable, a coffee table and an end table. The only pictures I have on the walls are two collages Quinn made for me for Christmas, of me with the Rivers kids and me with the Larkin kids. They were the best present I've ever received so they're on a wall all by themselves, where I can see them every day. I'm definitely not the kind of guy who knows how to entertain but hopefully the fact that the ladies are in a safe, clean home will outweigh the less aesthetically pleasing aspects of my place. When everyone is settled, I go to bed. They stay up to watch TV. Their alternating laughter at whatever is on and whispered conversation can be heard through the thin walls, although

I have no idea what exactly they're saying. I fall asleep quickly, but another combat nightmare wakes me. Once again I'm covered in sweat, unable to catch my breath feeling like I just stepped off the battlefield and I want to puke. I lie there for a bit trying to calm myself and go back to sleep but I finally realize that when the dream is so real you can practically smell the burning flesh, rest suddenly becomes unnecessary.

Giving up on the idea of sleep, I tug on my jogging pants, sneakers and a hoodie. Then I shove a $20 bill in my pocket along with an apartment key and slip out for a run. This is nothing new. It's the only way I've found to burn through the remnants of war that stirs in my brain some nights. As I'm crossing the living room, I see Marina slip into Dee's room and wonder if she's okay, but I know I need to keep my distance so I continue on my mission.

A few minutes later and three blocks down, I see Marv curled up along a wall, with the blanket I got him last winter wrapped around his body. His head is propped on his duffel bag like it's a pillow, but he sits up when he sees me and gives me a half toothless smile.

Marv and I met several years ago when I was out for a jog one night. A mentally unstable homeless woman was attempting to steal his stuff and they were fighting over it. I intervened and something about the salty old homeless guy had me coming back to check on him. Turns out he's homeless by choice and not circumstance. As a veteran of the Marine Corps from the Vietnam era, he came home to a country that hated him and he didn't handle it well. Within five or six years he quit his last job, sold or gave away almost everything he had and moved out onto the street. I asked why he didn't go down to one of the states with a warm climate and he said he loved this town and wanted to stay. It's a shame that America couldn't get its act together to welcome a man like him home with open arms. Who knows what he would've become. Marv is a genius with equally impressive street smarts and is a funny son of a bitch to top it off. When I can't sleep I usually take a run and stop off to see him while I'm at it.

"Dex." He nods.

I sit down next to him. "Marv, how's it going?"

"Can't complain."

"You cold?" Tonight he probably isn't, but there are a lot of nights I know he has to be.

"Nah. I've got a good blanket." He winks at me. "You doin' okay?"

"Yeah. Got visitors at my place and I can't sleep. Thought I'd run to see if I could wear myself out."

"Family?" he asks and I realize we've never talked about my family or lack thereof before.

"Nah, don't have any family."

"Women?"

I smile a little as I answer because he always wants to know about my dates so it shouldn't surprise me that he's asking about the ladies. "Yeah."

"They good looking?"

I smirk at him. He's homeless and eating out of dumpsters most days, but he hasn't lost his sense of humor. I tried to get him to stay with me for a little while last winter, but he only took me up on it one night when the shelter was full. Women should be the last thing on his mind.

"Do I look like I'd have ugly women at my house?" I joke. There aren't many people I can talk to like I do him, so he gets a rare glimpse of me that no one else does.

"If I thought you were with either of them then I'd say no, but no man with a gorgeous woman in his bed is out running and hanging out with a guy like me in the middle of the night."

"Yeah, well, one of them I don't know and the other is a handful."

"Those are the best kind, my friend. They keep you on your

toes. I had a woman like that once. I just wasn't man enough to keep her. Maybe you need to go home and work on that."

Laughter, deep and hearty, spills out of me at his comment. Marina would keep me on my toes all right. I don't think I could deal with all the piercings and the makeup though. The tattoos don't bother me, but I feel like she's overdoing it with the other stuff. Besides, tornados don't even spin up stuff as fast as she does. It's all too much for me. I've never seen anyone get into the trouble she does. I'd cringe every time the phone rang, worried about what she's gotten herself into this time. Whatever. I can't have anyone in my space and business all the time anyway. I crave the silence and I've spent too many years doing my own thing; adding someone else to the mix would only complicate my life.

"Here man. Get a burger, you're getting too skinny." I place the $20 in his hand and stand.

"I don't need your money." He scowls at me as he tries to hand it back.

"No, but you need a burger. You're gonna waste away if you don't start woofing down some fast food." His laughter follows me as I jog away feeling a little bit better.

When I return to the apartment, it's quiet and the door to Mari's room is still open the way she left it when she went to Dee's room. I wonder what made her go in there. The mattress on her bed is new so it should be comfortable.

THE AROMA OF COFFEE FILLS THE AIR WHEN DEE TIPTOES OUT of her room the next morning. Mari's door is still open so I figure she stayed with Dee. Maybe they're lovers. That didn't cross my mind until now but it wouldn't surprise me. I'm finding that nothing with Marina surprises me.

"Morning," she mutters.

"Morning. You sleep okay?"

"It would have been better if Marina wasn't wrapped around me like a koala bear."

My eyebrows rise. "Oh." I didn't need that visual. It's been awhile since I was with someone.

My expression must reveal my thoughts. "Stop it, perv!" she scolds and chuckles.

"What?" I feign innocence.

"Like your brain didn't go to some pervy cheap porno when I said that. I saw the look on your face."

"You two are grown women. You can do whatever you want. Want some coffee?"

"Yeah, I do, please. Your theory has a hole though because I have a boyfriend, a serious one, and neither of us swing that way."

"You don't?" Now I'm really confused.

"No. Marina hates being alone, hates the dark and gets scared in new situations so she likes to sleep curled up with someone. Like a human security blanket or something." Shrugging her shoulders and glancing at the floor, she continues, "It's how I can tell when shit's going on with her. I could've stayed with my boyfriend, but I wasn't going to leave her in case she had that issue last night."

"She couldn't stay with the boyfriend too?"

"She could. Reggie doesn't mind, but his roommate freaks Marina out so she'd never stay there and I won't put her in the bed with us. It would be too weird."

"She doesn't have other friends to stay with?"

"Not that I'd leave her alone with. As you've noticed, she picks up the strays. Not dogs, people. She doesn't like to be alone so she'll hang with anyone who won't send her away. I'm pretty much her only normal friend. I'll find us somewhere to stay. Just give me a day or two. Maybe the landlord will get off his ass and fix the door, then this will be a non-issue."

"You can stay as long as you need to. I'm leaving tomorrow for a trip and will be gone almost a week. The place will be empty anyway."

"You're not half bad. I kind of got the asshole vibe from you yesterday. I know you've got history with Marina but I hope you'll cut her some slack; she's a good person with a tad too much stuff in her past. She never had much of a chance. If you want us out of here, I'll work something out. I would put us in a hotel but she got fired yesterday and I don't have the extra cash to pay for it all."

"Do you think it's going to be hard for her to get a job?"

"No. She always finds something. Resourceful should be her middle name."

Before Dee can elaborate, Marina steps out of the bedroom and the world pauses for the second time in two days. Just long enough for me to notice it's no longer moving. Except for the tattoos, the woman standing in front of me is the 16-year-old girl I left standing in front of the foster home.

Tousled hair, fresh face, no piercings except for the little hoop on the side of her nose, which without the other stuff is sexy. Her wide eyes watch me hesitantly like she's afraid I'll say something mean to her.

This is the girl I lived to see every day when we were teenagers and it's blowing my mind, like we stepped back in time. All my teenage-boy angst and hormones come crashing through me as I take in the sight of the woman I wanted to protect and love so much more than I ever got a chance to. Circumstances and the fact that I was a late bloomer kept that from happening back then. But this Mari, standing right in front of me, is the same woman I wrapped myself around those couple of nights, wishing it would never end. She's stunning, almost angelic.

"Um, good morning." Her hesitant smile reminds me that I've been less than friendly when it's come to her and I'd like to kick myself in the ass. She may be a grown woman with a penchant for trouble but she's still the sweet, beautiful, young woman I stood up for. The one I secretly loved, but would never tell anyone about.

Clearing my throat and forcing myself back to the coffee pot, I reply, "Morning. Coffee?"

I can hear her tentative footsteps move around the counter behind me as she says, "I can get it. I don't want to put you out."

"It's fine." I pour the steamy liquid into the cup and hand it to her. Then I wave my hand toward the cream and sugar in case she wants to doctor up her brew.

"Dee and I are going to find somewhere else to stay today. Thank you for giving us a place to go last night. I'll be sure to clean up our mess before we leave."

My stomach flops unpleasantly. "I already told Dee before you came out here that you can stay longer. I'm leaving tomorrow to go out of town for a week. You'll have the place to yourselves. Hopefully during that time your landlord will fix your door. If not, we'll worry about it when I get back."

"Oh. You're leaving?" I can't help but notice the slight disappointment in her voice.

"Yes, vacation."

I don't elaborate about my trip. Only Quinn, Judson and Marv know where I go and why. I don't like answering questions about it. People always want to hear the gory details and I'm not in the mood for that, nor do I think Marina could handle it.

"Um. Okay, thank you." It's all she says and I'm a little taken aback by her quiet demeanor today. So far, every time I've been around this woman she's been full of chatter and life. Her sudden change is weird and leaves me feeling unsteady. I should be happy about it because it's what I've wanted since she reappeared, but now it feels strange and unnatural.

My phone buzzes on the counter and the caller ID shows it's Leslie. Both women glance down and see the name. They exchange a look as I excuse myself to take the call.

I close the door to my room behind me as I answer. "Hey, Les."

"You'll be here tomorrow, right?" Her voice is shaking like she's been crying for a while. She hasn't called crying recently so it worries me.

"Of course. Flight arrives at one in the afternoon. You okay? What's up?"

"Rushton is such a handful right now. I don't know what to do. I got a call from the school and they want a meeting with me, but I can't do it alone. Can you catch an earlier flight? I'll pay the difference. I don't know what to do with him and I need some backup. Please."

"Give me a few minutes to work on it, if I can't get an earlier flight I'll drive. Let me call you back."

"I know. I don't want you to have to do that, but I need you."

That's all she ever has to say to me. We hang up and I call the airlines. They can't move my flight so I buy a whole other ticket through a different airline in order to fly out this afternoon. I promised Larkin I'd take care of his family and I won't go back on that. When I'm done, I call Les back and let her know the new plan.

THAT EVENING I ARRIVE IN TAMPA. OTHER THAN GETTING THE call to get here early, I make this trek every year to do a celebration of life with Stu's family; this will be the fifth year. Then I spend the week taking Les and the kids anywhere and everywhere they want to go. I've never been called to come early so this must be bad.

An intimidating wall of books that reaches from the floor to the ceiling behind the principal's cheap desk dwarfs the little office. My chair is next to Rushton's, with his mom on the other side, and we're facing the principal. The school counselor is seated to my left, angled so she can see everyone. From everything I've been told, we're all sitting here because Rushton's grades have taken a nose dive and he's decided that fighting is the best way to handle his problems.

The principal clears his throat and glances between me and Les before he says, "We have to suspend him and if it happens again we'll be forced to expel him."

I can practically hear Les sizzle with anger and I wish she were closer so I could calm her down a little. "He's already having problems with his grades, missing school will only make that worse," Les replies.

"That's not our problem, Ms. Larkin. We told you the last time this happened what the punishment would be."

My head swings to her and then to Rushton. "Last time?" I ask, surprised by this information.

"A month ago. I'll explain later," Leslie tells me.

The counselor leans in and tries for a gentle approach, "Ms. Larkin, perhaps counseling would be a good idea. He's obviously not adjusting easily to the idea of you remarrying."

My eyes widen. *Remarrying?* Is that what she said? I glance over at Les to find her fiddling with a giant diamond ring on her finger that I know Stu didn't give her. The surprises keep on coming, this being the biggest. "Les?"

Her eyes are watery as she looks at me. "Can we talk about this afterwards? I can't do this now."

I feel like the air has been knocked out of my lungs. I didn't even know she was seriously dating. She mentioned a few dates but when I tried to ask questions she shut me down. I haven't even met the guy yet. What if he's a douchebag? What if he won't allow Uncle Dexter week every year? Will I lose the kids? The thought of not seeing them again is crushing. I breath deep. I need to lock down this rush of emotion that's so unlike me, to handle the situation at hand, which is getting him out of trouble.

My priority is Rushton. I ignore her plea and focus my attention on the counselor.

"I'll deal with him and make sure he gets counseling, but you need to give the boy a break. Kids fight all the time. When you were young, I'm sure you did too. He's had a lot to deal with over the last few years and it's not getting easier."

We go a few more verbal rounds with the principal and the counselor before I finally agree to work with Rushton while I'm here if they give him a little more time and a reduced sentence.

The ride back to Leslie's house is silent. When we pull into the driveway I don't get out of the car right away; instead I tell Rushton, "Go inside and change. We're going fishing but first I need to talk to your mom. Once you've changed, do the dishes and wait for me." The first thing out of his mouth is an excuse and I hold up a hand and say, "You're in no place to protest, dude. Go do what I say and I'll be there in a little bit."

He hops out of the SUV and stomps inside. As the front door slams behind him, Les says, "Dex—"

I cut her off. "Married? Why didn't you tell me Leslie? That was a shitty way to find out."

"I didn't know how." She fidgets with her ring and glances out the car window to the neighbor's yard.

"What does that mean? I didn't even know you were dating anyone seriously."

"Well I thought it was weird to talk about after...everything."

"Les. We aren't teenagers. I want you to be happy. I love you and Rushton and Skylar. If you've found someone that makes you happy then I'm happy for you. I do want to know what this mean for me, though. Can I still see the kids and have Rushton in Colorado every year? I was hoping to add Skylar soon too. I promised Stu I'd take care of you guys and I knew there would come a day we'd face this, but I had no idea it was this close."

"I just didn't know how to tell you. Joe and I've been dating since this time last year. Right after you left last year he asked me out. I introduced the kids to him a couple of months ago, but he proposed last week. I told him we have to let the kids get comfortable before we get married and he understood. It's not going to be next week or anything, but Rushton's grades dropped after he met Joe and the fighting started not long after that. I don't know what to do. As for your relationship with us, I don't want that to change."

"Hon, you've got a new man. He's not going to take kindly to another man coming around."

"He doesn't have a choice."

"You say that now, but when he puts his foot down you may feel differently."

"That's never going to happen, Dex. Once you meet him you'll understand. He knows you come as part of our package. Please trust me."

"I need to meet him. Did you plan to tell me while I was here or wait until I got home?"

"Of course I was going to tell you. But not right when you walked through the door, especially with Rushton's situation. There is only so much I can handle at one time."

I knew this was a possibility. How could it not be? Leslie's beautiful, intelligent and fun as hell. It would be a waste for her to grow old alone. I just wasn't prepared for it now.

STANDING ON THE DOCK OF THE LITTLE LAKE BEHIND STU'S parents' house, it's just Rushton and me fishing, and he's brooding. He got that from his dad. When his dad was pissed, it was the same face, same silence, same occasional growl. That's part of what worked for our friendship. I'm not a big talker, not a share-your-feelings guy which made it easy to keep quiet and wait him out until he was ready to talk or get over it.

"What do you think of your mom's new man?"

The look he gives me could scare a rabid coyote. I have my work cut out for me.

"So he's a jerk?" No reply, just the stare. "Is he rude to you and Sky? Because I can beat his ass while I'm here. No one's gonna treat you guys like crap." His little brow furrows but still no words.

"Your mom says he's coming over for dinner tonight. I'll take care of him. Can you tell me exactly what he did so I can make sure he doesn't do it again?"

Rushton glares at me before he answers. "He didn't do anything, exactly."

"If he didn't do anything, what did he say?"

"He didn't really say anything either," he mumbles.

"Then why do you hate him?"

He makes a big production of being irritated by my questions with an exaggerated sigh. "Connor told me Joe was gonna be my new dad and my old dad wouldn't count anymore and I wouldn't be able to see you and you wouldn't love us anymore because that's gonna be Joe's job."

"Hmmm." This makes a little more sense. I try to appear as if I'm contemplating what he's said. "Does Connor have an Uncle Dexter in his life?"

Shaking his head, he answers, "No. None of the kids do. Their dads didn't die in Afghanistan."

"Then how the hell does he know what happens to an Uncle Dexter if he never had one?"

"I don't know." His eyebrow raises like he never thought of that.

"Here's the deal, kid. Your dad was my best friend, almost like my brother, and I promised him I'd take care of you guys no matter what. I didn't say I'd take care of you until your mom has a new man. I didn't say I'd take care of you until you grow up. No. I promised him I'd take care of you guys for as long as I live and I plan on that being a really long time.

"Your mom told me today that you can still come to Colorado like you do every year. I still plan to come back for your dad's celebration every year. If you need me in between, I'm here. Stop listening to this Connor-idiot and start calling me when you have questions or issues. If you need a phone I'll talk to your mom and get you one, but I'll always take care of you."

"Why can't you be my new dad?" There it is. The puppy-dog eyes and quivering lip tell me this is his biggest issue. He looks back to the water while he waits for my answer. Time to clear this up.

"Turn around and look at me." Reluctantly he turns and squints up at me. "Because your mom needed someone who had nothing to do with your dad when he was alive, or she would always think of your dad while she was with the new guy. We both deserve better than that. There isn't a replacement for him, your dad was one of a kind, so no one should try to be him. Besides, you don't need a new dad. You need a friend and someone around to help take care of your mom and Sky. You already had the best dad that ever lived and he didn't stop being your dad just because he died. No one can ever take his place. Someday you'll better understand what I've said, but do you understand enough to give Joe a chance now?"

He appears to consider it for a second until he finally nods. I ruffle Rushton's hair and go back to casting my line. Within 10 minutes he starts talking again, about anything and everything, and I'm reminded of the times I spent with his dad, listening to him do the same thing.

When Joe arrives, I greet him in as friendly a manner as I can. After my talk with Rushton today I decided that even if I hated him I couldn't show it unless he was a complete douche. What I observe during our pleasant dinner is that Joe is good with the kids and sweet to Les. I almost wish I had something bad to say about the guy, but I don't. He owns a car dealership so he has money. He's a little on the nerdy side, but I'm glad he's not a replica of Stu; that would be weird. We talk football a little and he tells me about himself. Once dinner is over I ask to speak to him privately while the kids are getting ready for bed.

We step out into the muggy night air and sit on the cushioned chairs by the pool. Before I can say a word he looks up at the clear night sky and says, "I was nervous to meet you. All I ever hear about is Uncle Dexter this and Uncle Dexter that, from both Leslie and the kids. I see why now." He lowers his chin to make eye contact and asks, "Do I have anything to worry about with you? I know about you and Leslie and I'm not sure what to do with that information."

"She told you about us?" Why would she tell her future husband about the one night we had?

"Yeah, on a night when she'd had one too many." Joe's attention shifts back to the sky and I can tell by the way his heel is bouncing, this whole conversation is making him nervous. Granted I'm twice his size and more likely to beat someone's ass than have a conversation, but he shouldn't be nervous for this conversation. I kind of admire the balls it took to mention any of this.

"You've got nothing to worry about from me as long as you're good to them. I love all three of them and plan to stay in their lives, but I knew a long time ago that Leslie needed someone different than me in order to move on. We were never the right fit for anything other than friends. I only want them safe, happy and cared for. They deserve it."

"I agree. Though I realize Rushton doesn't like me and I'm not sure how to fix it."

"I spent some time talking with him today and all I can say is the kid will be okay if you don't try to be his dad. Be his friend with the understanding that you respect and will enforce the rules his mother sets, and it'll be fine. One day he may think of you as a dad but for now that freaks him out. After our talk today he's willing to give you a chance. He's a good kid, I'm certain he'll come around."

The rest of the week goes well and although the celebration of life seems to be more emotional this year than last year, it's still a good day. When it's time for me to leave, Leslie passes me the keys to Stu's fully restored red 1951 Ford F-100 pickup truck. When I lived with them she said she wanted me to have it when she was ready to give it up. I should have realized when she called about me taking it home at the end of this visit that bigger things were going on. Even though I knew in advance I was going to drive it back to Colorado, I wasn't prepared for the onslaught of emotion climbing behind the wheel of that truck would produce in me. Everything has been left the exact same as the last time he drove it. Folded up on the backseat is an old T-shirt he kept there in case he needed a fresh one after the gym. Two old lottery tickets sit faded in the corner of the dash. A picture of Les and the kids the day she brought Skylar home from the hospital is wedged in by the odometer. When I turn the key Tim McGraw's voice pours through the speakers. Because of Stu I know every word to every song the man released up until Stu died. Nights when we were off duty and had nothing to do, we'd sit around playing cards and he'd play this stuff until I begged for something else. A rare smile crosses my lips at the memory.

This old truck smells musty from sitting too long so I roll down the windows, ready to drive cross-country. Leslie has driven her once a week and made sure to have the oil changed so I'm certain I'll make it to Colorado with no issue. I glance around before I put it in gear and think about how I won't have moved a single thing by the time I turn her back over to Rushton when he's 16. I want him to have the same opportunity to experience his own memories he might have of his dad and this truck.

It takes two days to drive home. When I arrive, it's one in the morning and the only light on in my apartment is from the television. Marina is sitting in front of the TV with two big pillows propped next to her, one on each side and a blanket pulled up to her chin. She's watching a cheesy 1980s movie.

"Hey." I had too much time to think on my way back in Stuart's truck and most of it involved Marina. There was nothing specific. My thoughts ranged from wondering why she wears all that makeup and hardware to why she seems to still just barely be getting by at this point in her life. The thoughts drifted so far that I started to wonder dumb shit like if my apartment would smell like her when I got back.

"Hi. Did you have a good trip?"

"Yeah, but it was long." I twist my upper torso hoping to crack my back. The long drive has everything feeling tight.

"Oh." Her answer is quick and she doesn't say anything else for a minute. "Dee's hoping our apartment door will be fixed by tomorrow. The landlord said the door itself was damaged not just the lock and isn't easy to fix. So basically, he's being a dick about replacing it, but she lit him up yesterday. I'm sorry I'm still here. I was hoping I'd be back at my place by the time you returned."

I won't say it out loud but I'm glad she's not back at her place. "I told you that you could stay. I won't be here much; I work the next five days straight." She doesn't say anything else so I tell her, "I'm beat so I'm headed to bed."

"Okay, night," she replies to my retreating back. I lift a hand to wave and slip into my room. As I submerge myself under the hot flow of water from the showerhead, I think about how beautifully broken she is. And how I wish I could save her without losing myself. The more she's around, the more I feel, and riding alone for two days with thoughts of her hasn't helped my state of mind.

After my shower, I dry off and tug on some boxers and a T-shirt. Then I lie down and stare at the ceiling for an hour with too much tumbling around in my mind. As my eyes drift shut I hear a tentative knock on my door so I prop up on my elbows. "Come in."

Marina's head pokes in the door and she sniffles like she's been crying.

"What is it? What's wrong?"

She's quiet and hesitant as she answers, "I'm scared. I haven't slept in two days, I'm exhausted, but I'm scared. Can I please come in? I promise I won't bother you, but I can't sleep alone."

"Where's Dee?"

"She's at Reggie's. He was getting pissed because she wasn't with him so I told her to go. I thought I'd be okay, but I can't sleep and I'm so tired. I just need a couple of hours."

This is a bad idea for me, I know it, but Dee warned me this was an issue for Marina and she's a mess. It's the tears that get me, though. I'll do almost anything to make those stop.

"Come in." I lift the covers for her to climb in. I thought she'd roll right into me with the koala-hold that Dee was telling me about, but she doesn't. She curls up as far from me as she can get and covers up. Her crying is shaking the bed, but it's obvious she's trying to keep it quiet. The little squeaks are painful to listen to and I can't take it. The need to comfort her is so overwhelming that I reach out and pull her toward me. "Come on, Mari. Get over here next to me."

She sniffles loudly and lays her head on my shoulder as she curls into my side, fitting there perfectly like that spot was made for her. Her body shakes with muffled sobs as a stream of tears soaks into my T-shirt and even a few strays drip down my ribs. I pull her tight to me, doing my best to comfort her. I have no words of wisdom and don't quite understand what she's going through. The strange part for me is that I can't help but notice how normal it feels to be holding her and taking care of her this way. Because of my preference to be alone and have my own space, I never thought I would enjoy lying like this with someone. Once the sex is done I usually leave or usher them out. I've never lain like this with someone before other than when we were teenagers.

After 10 or 15 minutes of holding her tight to me, I feel her body relax and her sniffles slow to a stop. I think she's finally asleep. As tired as I am you'd think I could fall asleep, but the terrified beauty in my arms has my head all messed up. I want to rail against her closeness. I don't want to let anyone in, especially someone like her who seems to be a bottomless pit of need. Everyone I've ever cared about leaves or dies or gets pulled away by life, so it's simply easier if I don't go there. But her sweet little body fits so nicely into mine, so much like a missing puzzle piece that it's hard to ignore. Although I'm damp from her tears it feels good to have her next to me. Without thinking I kiss her hair and settle into the comfort. Maybe I shouldn't fight it. Maybe I should see how it goes.

THE NEXT MORNING, I WAKE UP WITH A RAGING HARD-ON. I get them from time to time but not like this. Mari and I shifted in the night and her sweet little ass is backed up tight against my dick—which is probably why I'm like steel—so I'm certain she realizes my state of affairs. Evaluating my position, I find that one arm is under her head instead of a pillow and the other is wrapped around her with my palm on her breast. Shit, I have to get out of this or she'll think I'm a teenage horndog who can't control himself. I don't want to be another person who takes advantage of her.

Wiggle, stop, shift. Wiggle, shift, stop. It takes a couple of minutes of this to separate myself from her. After a quick tiptoe to the bathroom, I close the door with a sigh of relief. I'm so glad I didn't wake her. A quick shower will take care of my issue and she'll be none the wiser.

Chapter Seven

MARINA

Oh, my God! He's huge! I woke up with his cock fully hard and pressed against my backside. Gone is the young scrawny kid I once knew. He's all man now in all the ways a woman needs. I just wish he wasn't so repulsed by me. Something about his quiet confidence draws me in and scares the shit out of me at the same time. I was terrified when I knocked on his door last night, but I was also desperate for sleep and a little bit of comfort. His prickly attitude should have kept me away but the few moments of tenderness I've seen from him were enough for me to chance it, and I was tired enough after two sleepless nights to ignore the fear and instead hope for his tender side. I have a job interview today and needed the rest so badly.

I was more than a little surprised by his response to me. When I climbed into his bed I hoped that merely being in the same room with someone would allow me to sleep, but it was so much better when he brought me close. The sound of his heartbeat and the warmth of his muscular body settled me. I haven't slept that well in forever. Even curled up next to Dee, I never relax like that.

If he wasn't so disgusted by me I could have taken care of the morning wood for him, but he hauled ass out of bed as soon as he realized I was in here with him. Well, he didn't haul ass, but his crazy little maneuver to get out of bed was so careful I understood he didn't want me to wake up. I guess I shouldn't be surprised since he can barely tolerate me. I don't know what cracked his armor last night when he pulled me in close, but if I figure it out, you can bet I'll exploit it in the future.

The last drip of coffee falls into the complete pot and I pour myself a cup adding three scoops of sugar with a splash of cream and prepare him a black coffee. As I'm turning to place them on the table, he appears in front of me like an apparition, scaring the crap out of me and I lose my grip on the cups. They drop to the ground and shatter, sending hot coffee and shards of ceramic all over the room, one of which jabs right into the instep of my left foot. Next thing I know I'm screaming from the burn of the hot coffee, which seems to be everywhere, and the blood...Oh God, the blood! I can't deal with blood and as soon as I see it rushing out of the gash in my foot I black out.

When my eyes flutter open, the first thing I see is the white ceiling of the living room. *What the hell?* Something wraps around my foot and as I glance down I see Jase tying a shirt around it and I remember what happened.

"You'll ruin your shirt," I squeak. "And I'm gonna get it on your couch." An attempt to sit up brings on a wave of dizziness I didn't expect so I lie back down. Usually he's in his uniform or a T-shirt and I notice for the first time that the front of his body is covered in intricate, beautiful tattoos.

"Mari, don't move." His tone is stern and my eyes snap to his.

"I need to. It's not only the blood, I'm covered in coffee too. I'm so sorry! I can't do anything right."

He frowns before he asks, "I don't care about what gets on the couch. Are you okay? Let me grab a washcloth and wipe you off."

"I hate blood. I can't see it in movies or in person and especially not from myself." As he walks away to get a washcloth his bare back is visible and unlike the front with its tattooed beauty, the back is a scarred mess of burnt flesh from his shoulders all the way down below the line of his pants. I'm so shocked that I can't help but gasp.

"Jasen!"

He glances back at me and then down. "Fuck!"

"Jase, what happened?"

"It was a long time ago." He continues his retreat to the bathroom and returns a minute later with a new shirt on and a washcloth in his hand. By the look on his face I'm afraid to say anything about the burns, but I want to know what they're from. How did he get burnt that badly? He didn't have them when he was young. Did he get them in the Army? I thought he was a sniper. Aren't those guys removed from the main portion of combat?

He cleans me up and luckily the coffee only left little red marks instead of my own full-fledged burns. The slice in the foot required some butterfly bandages and he said it may need stitches. I'm hoping it doesn't because I can't afford a trip to the ER. In fact, I need to find a way to get a shoe on for the interview today. Ugh. Oh well. I've dealt with and felt worse. It'll be okay.

"I've got to get ready for work. Are you okay?" he asks me.

"Yeah, I'm fine or I will be."

With that he nods and returns to his room, shutting the door. I go back to his spare bedroom on unsteady feet and figure I'll clean up the mess once he's gone to work.

When I come out after getting ready for the day, I return to the kitchen to find it's already been cleaned. He must have done it when I was in the shower because I didn't hear it at all. I'm grateful since I was dreading seeing the blood.

Before the interview, I take the bus to my apartment and pester the landlord about the door. He promises it will be done the day after tomorrow. It was awesome sleeping next to Jase last night, but I don't want to push my luck with him. He's kind of moody and I hate when he looks at me like he's disappointed, which seems to be all the time.

To test my tolerance for pain and my stamina on the injured foot, I cook dinner for Jase and I since Dee won't be here again tonight. I got the job at the bar and am supposed to start tomorrow, but my foot is sore and I'm nervous I won't be able to work on it yet. I need the paycheck so I'll test it out now.

When Jase comes through the door he pauses in the entryway and looks around in search of something. His eyes reach me in the kitchen, leaned over the pot, stirring, and his brow furrows.

"You cooked?" he asks, clearly shocked by this idea.

"Well, yeah, it's the least I could do since you're letting me stay with you. By the way, I can go back home day after tomorrow."

"You don't have to cook for me, but I'm hungry tonight so I'll say thank you and shut up."

"You don't have to shut up. I like when you talk. Your voice is soothing or something, all deep and strong. Most of the guys I know have normal voices…" I don't finish my thought because I realize that I sound like an idiot. Shrugging my shoulders, I go back to stirring.

Despite my declaration of the enjoyment his voice gives, he doesn't speak much during dinner. He only answers questions when I ask them. I smile to myself, pleased that I've done something right where he's concerned because he likes the food at least enough to go back for seconds.

When dinner is over he refuses to let me help as he washes the dishes. After that he sits in front of the television with a hockey game on. I've never tried to watch hockey before, but it looks kind of cool. I sit at the other end of the couch, so I don't make him uncomfortable, and ask questions, trying to understand what we're watching. After a while I don't care about the game, I only want to hear his voice so I come up with question after question.

If I had my way right now, my head would be on his lap as he runs his fingers through my hair and talks to me about anything. It could be the New York Stock Exchange for all I care. Just to hear the soothing sound of his voice would be awesome and to have those hands in my hair... Damn.

"Marina." I startle out of my reverie and realize I was probably staring at him with my mouth hanging open or something stupid.

"Sorry, what did you say?" I blink rapidly, trying to clear the thoughts from my head completely.

"I said game's over so I'm headed to bed. You okay? Need anything?"

I shake my head because what I want I'm sure he wants no part of.

"Okay, night," he says as he walks out of the room without a second glance. I'm so affected by him I don't know how to function with him in the room, and our history, although brief, is still meaningful to me. Why can't I find a guy like him? Stable, sexy, thoughtful and strong. He's everything I ever wanted in a man—minus the attitude—but I'm such a screw-up he'd never look at me for anything romantically. He probably only dates classy women with college degrees who work the pampered princess look. I've never seen a woman as eccentric as I am with a guy like him. You'd think I'd change my look to gain his attention, but even if you polished me up pretty that's not who I am.

I like the colorful streaks in my hair and the tattoos. The piercings are cool and although there are some I could live without, I like most of them so why would I change that? Whatever. I don't know why my brain has taken this path tonight. Maybe it's because we had dinner together and then sat and talked like normal dating people do.

I get up, brush my teeth, wash off my makeup, pull my hair up in a messy bun and put on my pajamas. It's late, it's been a long day and I should be wiped out, but the closer I get to that empty bed the more awake I become. I've had enough therapy over the years that it shouldn't seem like such a huge feat to get into that bed alone and sleep. But bedtime is the one thing I never could get past. Too much of the horror in my life happened in the wee hours of the morning.

It doesn't even have to be dark in the room for me to freak out. I've tried sleeping with every light on and it still didn't help. Before our stuff went missing I'd gotten to the point in my apartment that I could sleep alone for at least a couple of hours a night when Dee was gone or when Reggie was staying over. The sleep wasn't as good as when Dee was with me or when I was dating someone and they would stay over.

Leaving the light on in the hopes that it will help, I climb into bed and pull the covers up to my throat. Then I spend the next hour staring at the walls, wondering if I'll be awake again all night. I hear the front door open and close and figure Jase has gone out for a booty call. I mean, what does a guy like him leave the house at one in the morning to do? He did it the first night we were here too. Then he got a call from some chick named Leslie that he took in private. He even moved up his vacation because she wanted him there earlier. I wonder if she'll show up here before I leave. I'm curious about her enough that I want to see her, but I don't think I'll be able to hide the jealousy that's sitting just below the surface.

Now that he's gone I don't have to worry about keeping him awake with the television on so I can go back to the couch and find an old movie to watch. Maybe I'll doze off while I'm there. I trudge back to the couch and grab the blanket that's neatly folded over the back and flip on the television. I pull the cover up as I settle in to the super-comfy couch that's covered in chocolate-colored microfiber. It's nothing like our old threadbare pink and white floral couch that Dee's mom gave us when she got new furniture, but it's really comfortable.

About an hour later, Jase comes back through the door in running gear. Did he jog to his booty call? That's a little weird, but hey, I wouldn't turn him away if he showed up all sweaty on my front porch for that sort of thing.

"Couldn't sleep?" he asks, a little out of breath.

"Yeah. It's okay, though." I try to play it off like it's no big deal because I've been so needy in front of him up to this point, I don't want him to think I'm always this way. Inside though I'm silently begging him to invite me in. I haven't sleep as soundly as I did when I was with him since I was a little kid, before my family went off the rails.

He stares at me for a minute and strides out of the room. Guess he didn't like that answer. He's probably worried the noise from the television will keep him up so I lower the volume almost all the way down and do my best to focus on the movie.

Ten minutes later the door to his room creaks open and with the flicker from the television I can tell he's wearing a T-shirt and baggy gym shorts. Maybe he wants the TV off all the way. I guess I could sit here in the dark by myself, but I'd rather not.

"Marina, come on." He waves me toward the bedroom and it takes a second to register that he's inviting me in. I look around like there might be someone else here because I'm so surprised he's asking me.

A little more impatiently this time, he says, "Mari, if you want to sleep, come on."

I leap up and toss the blanket to the couch, afraid he'll change his mind. I could practically skip to his room for this. I know it's only so I can sleep and nothing more, he was probably with his chick a little while ago, but I can live the dream in my head where no one will know.

It's dark in his room but after being here last night, I know his bed is in the center so I climb in on the side closest to the door like last night. Before it can get awkward as I decide if I should stay along the edge or curl up to him, he spreads his arm across the bed and invites, "Come on, don't waste time lying over there."

My heart rate kicks up. I don't care if he was with someone an hour ago, I just want to be held close, to feel safe, to sleep in comfort with this sexy beast of a man. It sounds desperate because it is, but I simply don't care.

He's on his back so I crawl up and stretch out along his side with my head on his shoulder and my arm over his stomach. His arm wraps around me and his other arm lies across his belly under where mine is but close enough that I can feel the heat from his skin. Oh, God, this feels so damn good. "Thank you," I whisper in the dark, unable to keep my emotions in check.

With a quick squeeze, he replies, "You're welcome, get some sleep." And I do. It doesn't take long as I listen to the steady cadence of his heartbeat before I'm out for the night.

When I wake up the next day I'm sprawled out alone in Jase's bed. My face is buried in his pillow while the covers are pulled up over me and I grin as his scent brings me back to the night before when I fell asleep with a smile on my face.

That afternoon I stop by Reggie's to see Dee. I want to tell her about my night with Jase and see how she's doing. I'm used to seeing her at least once every day and I haven't been able to for the last several days. When I knock on the door, Ray, Reggie's asshole from hell roommate, opens it. Bloodshot eyes and the stench of pot stench surround him, alerting me to the fact that he's baked beyond belief. The guy always looks like shit. Dirty, sleazy and just plain gross, but he's got the nicest sneakers and ball caps in town. He hasn't figured out that it doesn't matter how sweet the gear is for your head and feet, if you're dirty and reek of pot while looking homeless, people are going to scatter when you enter a room. *Why does Reggie live with this dirtbag?*

"Marina," he greets, perusing me from head to toe. *Gross.*

"Ray, I'm looking for Dee."

"Yeah that bitch has been here so often she needs to fork over some damn rent. Come in. Now *you* could stay here rent-free. I even have a bed you can sleep in." His cackle that screams heavy smoker as he laughs at his own joke does nothing but annoy me. There's not enough money in the world for me to get in his bed. I'd rather sleep on the street with the homeless guys or have permanent insomnia than get anywhere near his bed.

I move quickly past him, calling for Dee. I need her to appear quickly. Ray sets off all the creeper alarm bells in my head so I hate to be alone with him even for a minute. Dee comes out with her hair in rollers and her makeup half on. "Sorry, getting ready for work. Come in." She pulls me to Reggie's room and I sit on the toilet with the lid down and tell her about the last couple of days.

"So you really slept in his bed? Like, cuddled with him too?"

I nod and give her a shy smile.

"Wow. Didn't see that coming. He doesn't come across as the cuddle type."

"I agree, me either. Maybe I was keeping him up with the TV noise. I don't know, but it was nice. I slept better with him than I even sleep with you."

"I bet." Her eyebrows rise to her hairline.

"No, you perv. Nothing happened. I mean, he woke up with morning wood the first day, but he was gone today before I knew it."

We giggle and chat for the next 15 minutes while she gets ready for work, and I feel light as I go to my new job. A good night's sleep next to a beautiful, strong man and some giggles with your best friend will do that.

My first night of work is an eventful one. The bar I now work at is rough, but they were willing to hire and train me quickly since they're short-staffed. It's a biker bar downtown and it seems the roughest of the rough come here. The clientele is loud, rowdy and wild, but luckily most of them seem harmless.

When I get back to Jase's apartment he's already in bed and my stomach sinks, realizing I have to go to my empty bed or the couch. I want to go crawl in bed with him, but I don't want to assume it's okay. I don't want to walk in on him if he has company either. I shower and prepare for bed. Then I return to my spot on the couch and turn on the TV. I haven't settled on a channel when the door to Jase's room opens and he calls, "Come on, Mari."

A smile is on my face before he can blink. I leap from the couch and haul ass to the bed. As soon as he lies down I curl up tight to him and breathe a sigh of relief. It feels so good to be here. I don't want to go back to my empty apartment tomorrow. I'd much rather stay like this every night.

"You cooked for me." It's a statement rather than a question that comes out of nowhere so I'm not sure what to say.

"Well, yeah. You've let me stay here this week. I'm just trying to repay the favor. I'll get the dishes in the morning before I leave. My apartment will be ready tomorrow supposedly."

"I already did the dishes. You leave tomorrow?"

"Yeah. The landlord said the door would be fixed."

Several minutes of quiet go by and the steady thump of his heartbeat is about to lull me to sleep when he says, "Never had anyone cook for me at home."

"I thought you ate with Quinn and Judson all the time."

"I do, at their house. I've never, not even as a kid, had someone make dinner for me, not outside of foster care and that didn't really count. It was nice the last couple of days. Thank you."

"Not even your grandma?"

"No, she wasn't in the best of health so she told me what to do and I cooked."

My heart warms knowing I've given him that. Not once but twice. Praying I won't freak him out I reach up and run my fingers along the short hair of his scalp. I've wanted to touch his hair and face so badly since he's reappeared in my life, so I might as well do it now. There won't be another chance because I'll be gone tomorrow, back in my apartment and he'll be here. As my fingers move over the silky strands, he nuzzles into the touch like he's trying to get closer.

"Mmmm. Feels good." Bravery rises inside me and I trail my fingers away from his hair, over his jaw, along the five o'clock shadow that darkens his jaw and down over his lips. When I pause midway across his lips he kisses my fingers softly and heat floods between my legs. Losing my fear by the second as my hormones kick in, I prop up on my elbow and search his face in the moonlight. The striking eyes that I love so much are shrouded in darkness, but I can tell he's watching me. I trail my fingers lightly down his neck and over his T-shirt. When I reach the hem, I slide my fingers inside and back up. Goose bumps spread all over his torso and I decide if I'm going to make my move it should be now.

My leg slides over his hips and I straddle him. Words can't describe the thrill I feel when I find him hard between my legs. I rock a little against him and a deep groan vibrates from within him. His hands adjust to rest on my hips and when he doesn't push me away I take that as the go sign. I shimmy my tank top over my head and toss it to the floor leaving me bare from the waist up and guide his right hand up to cover my exposed breast. *Don't lose your nerve*, I tell myself. When the warmth of his palm covers the cool skin, I rock against him again and whimper quietly. Without me prompting him, his thumb slides across the peaked nipple and I rock more, setting up a little rhythm. His other hand takes over the other breast and it feels so damn good. I shiver as he continues and cry out when he plucks the sensitive peaks.

When I can't take it anymore, I drop to the side and slip off my little sleep shorts and panties. As I hook my fingers in the waistband of his shorts, I ask, "May I?" I'm praying he won't stop me.

Instead of answering he hooks his fingers in the backside of the waistband and helps me to take them down. Normally, being this close to his cock with my mouth would prompt me to swallow him, but I crave something different tonight so I climb back up and over him. His hot flesh rests between the lips of my sex and I want to slide down on him, but instead I lean forward and place a tentative kiss to his lips. "Jase."

"Get a condom. Side drawer next to the bed." His deep, sex-laced voice could tell me to go get a machete and cut off a toe and I'd probably do it. When I pass it to him, he lifts my hips and fiddles around until the condom is on, then I lower myself onto him as slowly as I can, savoring each fraction of his enormous cock as it fills and stretches me until he's buried all the way.

"Mari," he whispers to me through the dark, not to get my attention, but more of a plea. I love when he uses the shorter version of my name and the little hint of Spanish comes out.

With one of his hands on my breast and one on my hip to guide me, the speed of my motion increases and it feels good, but I need more. Tilting forward I plant my hands on his chest the shift in angle allows me to go faster. I'm bouncing hard on him now, completely lost in the fullness and it feels so damn good.

"I'm almost there Jase, God, I'm so close."

The hand on my breast slips down between us and with very little effort his fingers find my clit and rub circles. My entire body seizes up as my orgasm consumes me. Every muscle, every nerve, every centimeter of skin is in the middle of a sweet fire overload. I've never felt anything like it before. I've gotten off before, but never quite like this. When everything begins to loosen up, he grips both of my hips to hold me in place and hammers into me until he groans and his hips jerk erratically with his release. Absolutely spent, I fall forward onto his chest and breathe a relaxed sigh. There's no awkward pause as he wraps his arms around me and holds me tight against him. My heart melts a little when I feel his lips press to my hair and his chest expand under me in a deep breath. I wish I could stay exactly like this with him buried deep, both of us sated, wrapped in his arms forever. But I know tomorrow I go back to my apartment and he goes back to whomever he's seeing. I turn and kiss his breastbone over his T-shirt, which I notice never came off, and lay my head back down.

After a minute or so he taps my right ass cheek twice and says, "I've got to get rid of this." I roll off to the side and start feeling around for my tank top. I can't find the damn thing in the dark.

"Can you hit the light so I can find my top please?"

"No."

"No?"

He climbs back on the bed and pulls me down into his arms like we started out a little while ago, only this time his shirt is gone and we're skin to skin. This is heaven for me. I could cry I'm so happy, but I don't want him to know how much the physical connection means to me. That would probably freak him out. I need to relax and play this cool. Forcing myself to settle it doesn't take long before I drift off to another amazing night of sleep.

The next morning when I wake he's gone and I want to cry at the loss. I hate that I won't come home to him anymore or ever get another night like last night. Before I leave I cook his dinner and put it in the fridge with a note on the counter so he'll know to look for it.

JASE,

Dinner is in the fridge. My apartment door is fixed so I'm going home and getting out of your hair. I bet you'll like having the quiet back. I appreciate all you've done for me. I'll drop the key off at the station because I need it to lock the door on my way out. Take care of yourself.

Love,
Mari

MY CHEST LITERALLY HURTS WHEN I LEAVE HIS PLACE AND IT only gets worse when I open the door to mine and remember I may have a place to stay but absolutely nothing in it. I need to take my tips from last night to the Laundromat to wash the stuff Quinn let me borrow. It'll take a few more days to be able to buy some clothes. I don't have rent money set aside yet so I have to get that before anything else. I forgot how bad this situation was while I was in the sweet little bubble with Jase. I wasn't going to sleep anyway, since I'd be alone, so I guess it doesn't matter that I don't have a blanket or pillow available to sleep on the floor with, which makes me wonder again who the hell steals dirty sheets and underwear? This person must be a desperate freak so I try hard not to think about it.

After an hour of doing nothing, because there's nothing to do, I leave for work. It's another night in paradise. The guys in the crowd tonight are rowdier than the first night and borderline overboard. If my ass gets smacked or groped one more time, I'm likely to lose my mind. Most of the time I can ignore it and keep moving, but after about the 25th swat my irritation hit an all-time high.

When I clock out and take the bus home, a strange dude with skinny jeans and a band T-shirt sits a few rows behind me and I can tell he's staring at me because the little hairs on the back of my neck stand on end. There's something familiar about him, but I'm not going to turn around for a better look because I'm so freaked out. Besides, when you ride the bus this late you see all kinds of special creatures around town, so it could be my overactive imagination.

As the bus reaches my stop, I stand and walk down the aisle. It takes everything I have not to glance back. The doors close behind me and I shuffle into my apartment building, cussing my shitty life and wishing I were wrapped up with Jase again. Why can't that be my life? Why can't he be my guy and my future? And what will I do when Dee gets married and I'm completely alone? It's inevitable. She can't stay single to live with me forever. I push that thought aside because I can't think of it right now either. It's too much to process—all that's happened and then to add Dee leaving me to the mix.

I shower and drip dry and throw on the tank top and shorts from last night. I hand-washed my panties during my shower so they're hanging on a hook in the bathroom, drying for tomorrow.

I turn up the heat and lie on the floor with all the lights on. My electric bill is going to be ridiculous this month but I can't even rest if I'm cold. I'm only lying here feeling sorry for myself for about 20 minutes when someone bangs on my door. I'm not expecting anyone so the abrupt sound scares the crap out of me.

Peeking through the peephole I find Jase standing there with his hands on his hips and a nasty scowl on his face. I tug my tank top down to cover myself and open the door. "Jase."

"Mari, what the hell are you doing?" He asks angrily pushing past me to get inside.

"Um. Trying to rest?" What's that supposed to mean?

"On the floor? Or did you get a mattress today?"

"You know I don't have the cash to replace my stuff right now. I'm fine."

"Where's Dee?"

"At Reggie's."

"Yeah, you know why?" He has the sarcasm down pat.

"Because she has a boyfriend?"

His scowl is fierce. "No, because she knows there's nowhere to sleep, no clothes to wear and nothing to eat. Get dressed."

"'What? Why?" Who's he ordering around? Has he lost his mind?

"Don't be stupid, Mari. You're staying at my place. I've got a washer and dryer, a blanket and pillows, and food in the damn fridge. Now get what little shit you have here and follow me back to my place."

"Um."

"What?" His impatience is obvious.

"I don't have a car to follow you."

"Shit! I forgot about that." He throws his hands in the air. "You're killing me. Get your stuff."

I probably should be mad with how condescending he's being, but I'm excited to go back to his place that I push the irritation aside and hurry to the bathroom to gather my wet clothes.

He's silent and brooding in the car on the way to his place and I can't stand it so I chatter the whole way. At one point, he looks at me like he'd rather shove burning onions in his ears than hear me talk anymore, but I can't help myself. When I enter his apartment I finally stop talking and shuffle toward the room that was mine before and to set my stuff down.

"When you get changed just come in my room; don't bother with the TV routine."

My eyes widen. Did I hear him right?

"I think we're past that, don't you?" he asks me.

I shrug one shoulder because I didn't want to assume anything, not with him. One minute he's yelling at me with that maddening condescending tone he gets and the next he's pulling me closer to snuggle him and thanking me for dinner. He shakes his head like he doesn't know what to do with me and disappears into his room. I change quickly, still commando, and go to his room. This time when I climb on his bed he flips me to my back in a move I didn't expect and hovers over me. His fingers thread with mine and shift above my head to rest on the pillow.

"You drive me insane, Mari. Always putting yourself in danger. Always making bad choices. Constant talking. Too much makeup. Too many holes in your skin. But damn it, I can't get enough of you either. I fluctuate between wanting to tape your lips shut and wanting to ask more questions." Leaning in close, he nips at my neck before continuing. "I don't know if I'm coming or going with you and it's making me fucking crazy. Last night you gave me something I've wanted for as far back as when I was 16 years old, and it was better than I ever dreamed it would be, but fuck, woman, you're driving me nuts."

Before I can reply to his rude and offensive thoughts, his mouth crashes to mine and it's obvious he's hungry for me. As much as I hate myself for being weak I can't help my body's reaction to him. My legs drop open, welcoming him. Our tongues battle, tangle and twist around each other in the hottest kiss known to mankind. Before it's over he adjusts his big body between my legs and they automatically wrap around him to lock at the ankles.

He pulls away just enough so that our lips brush as he says, "Mari, God, you're killing me."

I smile and tug on the T-shirt he's wearing. I'm pretty sure he's pulling away to protest, but I'm not about to let him win this one. I need the feel of his skin against mine, not the impersonal feel of fabric. "Take it off. Skin on skin, Jase."

"Mari." It's a warning and a plea all wrapped into one.

"Jasen, I saw your back the other day. It's no big deal. Take the damn shirt off or I'll hitchhike back to my place and sleep on the nasty floor."

His chuckle shakes my whole body and the sound is beautiful, amazing, and might be my favorite sound ever. It's sound-bite gold.

"You're going nowhere." He rises and sheds the shirt and I'm practically clawing at the air to reach his skin. When he gets close enough, my hands are all over him in seconds. I need to know this is real. I need to feel every inch of him.

My touch seems to ignite his libido and he goes into attack mode, devouring me with his kiss. His hands slide under me and grip my ass, pulling me tighter to him. We fuck like animals, rolling all over the bed, knocking stuff off the side table and dislodging the sheets. Tongues and teeth, fingernails and lips all work together to take us higher, preparing for the orgasmic dive off the cliff into ecstasy. I've never felt more connected to anyone than I do right now. Never felt more out of control from someone's touch. Every third or fourth kiss he breathes my name across my skin like he's worshiping every part of me. I've never felt so beautiful as I do at the mercy of his desire. By the time we find nirvana, he's spooned up behind me, connected to me from my heels to my head as we try to catch our breath. Once my heart rate slows, I pull the courage out of some unknown location and ask, "Are you seeing anyone else?"

He freezes, his muscles pulling tight like he's been caught doing something wrong.

"No."

"Not even Leslie?"

This time he holds his breath for a few seconds before he asks, "Leslie?"

"She called you before vacation and you left sooner so I figured, you know...she couldn't wait or something. Please don't make me spell it out when I'm lying here with you, naked."

He kisses my head and tells me, "No, there's nothing going on with Leslie." That's not a ringing endorsement, but I don't want to push my luck tonight.

"I just can't be one of many with you, Jase. Not with you. So if there are others, let me go this time. Please."

He buries his face in my neck. "No one else, Mari."

I love, love, love when he calls me that. My heart aches a little with want, for so much more of him, so I look for a distraction from the previous subject.

"You never told me where the Spanish came from."

"What?"

"The way you say my name, it sounds Spanish. You're obviously not Spanish."

"My stepdad was Mexican and most of his yelling was in Spanish. When he was pissed, he wouldn't let us reply to him in English at all. I learned to speak it quickly so I wouldn't get my ass beaten as often. Not good memories. Why are you such a chatterbox right now? I thought for sure the double orgasm would quiet you down."

I reach back and smack his ass, irritated at his comment. "You fucked me to quiet me down?" A little bit of hurt creeps in, but I do my best to ignore it.

"I was kidding. Well, sort of. It's not why I fucked you, but I thought it would be a side effect." I try to push him off me, irritated at his thought process, but the big ox won't move. In fact, he holds me tighter and chuckles into my neck. We stay that way for several minutes before he rolls away and disposes of the condom. When he returns to the bed he pulls me into his side like the last couple of nights.

I lie there unable to sleep, but now for a different reason. Why am I here? He doesn't like how much I talk or my crazy lifestyle or my tats, makeup or piercings, so what's the deal? He can have any woman he wants in his bed so why me? It's unfortunate that I have a comfortable place to sleep where I'm not alone and the freaking hamster is on the wheel in my head keeping me awake. Thought after thought after thought goes round and round and I can't shut it down. Tension settles back in my shoulders and confusion in my mind. It takes forever but I finally fall asleep. I wake up late the next morning to find he's gone to work, and I'm back to wondering what the hell I'm doing here. When I go to the kitchen I see he's left me a note that simply says,

Stay again tonight, please.
    Dex

He said please. Warmth spreads through my chest. Even if I'm a place holder for him, I'll take it. I've never craved a man like I do him. His voice, his arms, his bed, his eyes... Dear God, his eyes do it for me even with his silence. But more than anything, I feel safe when I'm with him. Like the bad stuff that's happened most of my life won't happen again. Like I'll live a life of roses and smiles and sunshine if he's my man. But I know I'm not a long-term thing for him. Like I said before, he's probably got his eye on some high-class chick with long blond hair and legs that go on forever. One with a college degree and an expensive SUV. I'm not delusional, just desperate for him and what he gives me because I've never had it a day in my life, besides with him.

Chapter Eight
DEX

God, that girl drives me batshit crazy. She has no regard for her personal safety. I can't believe she thought she was going to sleep on her apartment floor with no blanket and no pillow. Who does that? Did she think I'd leave her to that after the night before? I was so pissed when I realized that's what she thought. I was ready to throw her over my shoulder and carry her back to my place if I had to. There's no way in hell I could've left her to sleep in that place. She had to be scared and uncomfortable. Once I arrived though, and got a look at her in those little scraps of fabric she calls pajamas, I wasn't mad anymore. What I was has a whole other name. All I could think about was getting her back to my place and under me.

The chemistry between us last night was unlike anything I've ever experienced. The scent of her hair and the feel of her incredibly soft skin left me feeling drunk. I couldn't get enough of her and I've never felt that way before. I don't know what I'm going to do about her, though. She's not long-term relationship material and neither am I. The damage was done to me too many years ago and there is no reversing it. I prefer to be alone and quiet, whereas she never wants to be alone and couldn't sit in a quiet room for more than 30 seconds without filling it with some kind of sound. On a regular basis, we would clash like crazy.

If I was doing what's best for me, I would've left her in her apartment to figure things out on her own. Besides losing all conscious thought when she's around, I worry about her. It's not just that so many unfortunate things happen to her. Something about the burglary doesn't sit right with me. It's fucking weird that every single thing in their apartment is gone. The only thing left behind is a half roll of toilet paper in the bathroom. Every ounce of food, all the dirty laundry, the throw rugs, the pictures...everything just vanished. It doesn't add up. There is a piece to this puzzle that I'm missing and I don't have a clue what it is. When I spoke to the cop who filed the report, she said she ran the MO in the database, hoping other reports would pop up with similar findings. One woman from a town about an hour from here filed a similar report over a year ago and a month later was reported missing. According to the files, it's still an open case because she's never been found.

I don't know if that case is related, but I'm trying to keep an eye on Marina just in case. I may not want to marry her, but I don't want anything to happen to her either. I'd never forgive myself if something happened to her that I could've prevented by keeping her close. The fact that I crave her touch has nothing to do with any of this; maybe if I keep telling myself that, it will be true.

After two weeks of Mari sharing my bed and my apartment, you'd think I'd be ready for her to go, but honestly, it's been kind of nice. Every night I come home to a home-cooked meal, even if I have to pop it in the microwave because she's still at work, and every night she's warming my bed. Our chemistry is off the charts. Our first time together has nothing on every subsequent night since then. I've never been with a woman where the already phenomenal sex gets better every time. In fact, I didn't even realize that was possible. There's something about the two of us together that works beautifully. If I had one complaint it would be that there is no peace with her, though; no quiet moments where she relaxes. I wish I could teach her that, but I'm not sure it's in her nature.

Somewhere around four o'clock in the morning, my phone rings on the nightstand closest to Mari. She picks it up and mumbles as she's passing it to me, "It's Leslie."

I haven't told her about Leslie, Rushton and Sklyer yet. I don't know why. Maybe because I don't want to talk about Stu. It seems too intimate, too personal, and I know she'll have a thousand questions about him, what happened, and about Leslie. None of which I want to talk about.

"Les, hold on." I climb out of bed and move to the living room for privacy.

Panic carries in her voice. "It's Rushton. He's gone. There's an Amber Alert out for him. We've looked everywhere. I've had the police involved since last night. Dex, I need you. Oh, God, I need you here!"

My heart is racing. Where the hell could he be? "Did you check the dock?"

"Yes."

"Did you check the fort out in his friend Parker's woods?"

"Yes. Dex, we've been everywhere. All his friends and their families are involved in the search. I don't know where he is."

"Fuck! Okay, I'll get on the first flight out. Keep me up to date. I'll text you with my info. Have Joe pick me up. Did something happen to prompt this?"

"We talked about moving in with Joe after we get married. Not yet, but in a few months. I couldn't bring Joe to this house where I shared a bed with Stu. I thought it would be easier for them if we were in a different place that didn't belong to Stu, you know? God, I'm such an idiot!"

"No, you were right. Just calm down, we'll find him. I need to get off the call to get a flight." Her sobs grow louder through the phone and I hate that it's going to take me so long to get to her. "Hey! Calm down. It's gonna be okay."

"Love you, Dex."

"Love you too, Les."

I'M SITTING ON A PLANE THINKING ABOUT MARINA AS WE CIRCLE Tampa preparing to land. I fucked up and I know it, but I can't do anything about it now, at least not until I find Rushton and tan his little ass. I'm sure the kid is hiding. He's pissed and sulking and this has to stop. I can't jump on a flight like this at the last minute for crap that's easy to fix, but I can't leave Leslie to deal with it either. I promised Stu I'd be there and this is when it counts the most.

I close my eyes and my mind drifts back to this morning when I returned to the room after taking the call. Mari was sitting up in bed with the sheet pulled up to her chest and the light on, waiting for me. The concern in her eyes was clear and I should have taken the 10 minutes to give her an overview, but I was too busy freaking out. When you hear an 11-year-old is missing, you don't tend to be rational. Especially when an Amber Alert has been issued. Instead of explaining what was going on, I went straight to my closet, grabbed a duffel bag and started filling it with clothes. I'm not even sure what's in the damn thing except my sneakers and a pair of shorts. Mari asked, "What's going on?"

"I can't talk about it now; I don't have time. I'll be gone for...I don't know how long. You can stay here. In fact, I don't want you going home with nothing there. You have a key. I'll be back as soon as I can."

"Who's Leslie?"

"Not now, Marina. We can talk about it when I get home."

"So, you're leaving in the middle of the night after getting a call from a woman named Leslie and I don't get an explanation or an exact time you're coming back? Are you kidding?"

"Marina, I don't have time for this shit. I have to go."

She yanked the sheet from the end of the bed and stood, making sure she was covered. The tears were sitting on her eyelids, but she made sure they didn't fall.

"Fuck you, Jase. I may be a disaster most days but I deserve more than that load of crap you just handed me. I think it's funny that I'm good enough to warm your bed for over two weeks but not good enough to get an explanation when another woman is involved. I already told you I refuse to be just another notch on your bedpost, and when you're on the phone in the middle of the night, telling some woman you love her, that makes me a fucking notch!" She screamed the last of it. I didn't have time for that scene or to calm her down. That kind of shit is why we would never work anyway.

"Marina, I'll explain when I get home. I have to go now. Stay here where you have a bed and food. I'll be back as soon as I can." Before she could say anything else, I pulled the duffel on my shoulder and strode out of the room. The last sound I heard before the door closed is her dam of tears breaking. I'm such an ass. I didn't have time for it and I told her that. If she'd stopped talking long enough to listen to what I was saying, she'd understand that I didn't have time and she just needed to wait until I got back for an explanation.

Now that I look back though, I see her point and wish I would've at least given her the one-paragraph version of who Leslie is and why I was leaving so abruptly. It wouldn't have affected my ability to catch my flight. I was just annoyed that she was pushing me for an answer and that her opinion of me seemed to be so low that she'd think I was in love with someone else while I've had her in my bed for the last couple of weeks. I haven't had to explain myself to anyone for a long time and I don't feel like starting now.

The only problem with all of my excuses is I feel like shit about not telling her what's going on. I shouldn't, we've made no commitment to each other, but I do. I know what kind of life she's had and I should be making it easier while she's with me. Instead I added to her pain in an asshole sort of way.

When Joe picks me up at the airport, I'm in a shitty mood and being a dick. I don't mean to be but getting a call at o-dark-30 and having a fight with my sort-of girlfriend is not the best way to start the day. So, I'm quieter than usual on the way to the Larkin house. As we're pulling down her street, Les calls Joe to tell him they found Rushton at a bus station in Tallahassee, five hours away. He was headed for Colorado. How did an 11-year-old get a bus ticket to Colorado? The kid is conniving and smart enough to be dangerous, just like his dad was so it shouldn't surprise me.

We both breathe a sigh of relief that he's found and when Joe puts the car in park, he says, "I'm sorry, man. I'm doing my best to help them navigate this shit, but it's tough. Stuart is a tough man to walk behind and I don't know if I can do it. Not if every announcement is going to have the world in an uproar like this. I want to make their lives better, not worse, and when you see Leslie during this you'll know it's not better."

He's pissing me off. It takes me almost a full minute to remind myself that he's not used to fighting for everything so this has to be tough for him. "Fuck, man. You can't give up now. Les is happy, happier than she's been in a long time. The kids will be fine, but you've got to man up and roll with it. Rushton will eventually get it. Right now, he's in turmoil. He's 11 years old and caught between becoming a man and staying the little boy he's always been. Add to that a dead father and his mother moving on, and you should understand a little better."

"You don't think I should back off?" He looks shocked.

"Why would I think that? Because her son doesn't like the way things are going?"

"I know how you feel about them."

"Yeah, I love them all, but he's 11, man. When I was that age, I was living in foster home number eight and fighting off the uncle that liked to visit too often. That's an issue. Having too many people love you and want to take care of you is not an issue. He needs to get over it and I'm gonna be the one to tell him it's time. He needs some tough love for a change. The coddling isn't working. Just hang tight. They're worth it. I promise you that."

"I didn't hear you say this many words the whole time you were here last time."

"Not a big talker, but Leslie is happy and I don't want her to lose that."

"Why didn't you marry her?"

"Me? We talked about this. Because I would have been Stu's replacement, his surrogate. They never would have loved me like that for just being me. This way I get their love and I fulfill my promise to Stu. It wasn't in the cards for me, but you're a good fit."

"Thanks."

I climb out of the car and stride to the door as Skylar comes screaming out of the house, "They found him!"

"I know, baby. I'm going to take your mama and we're going to go get him. Can you stay with Joe while we're gone?"

"If you take me for ice cream when you come home."

Another born manipulator using those damn adorable missing front teeth as part of the ploy to get what she wants. "Yeah, I'll take you for ice cream, but it will have to wait until tomorrow. Now take care of Joe for me while we're gone, okay?"

"Okay, Uncle Dex." She places a sloppy wet kiss on my cheek and a tearful Leslie steps out the door.

I set Skylar down and wrap my arms around Leslie. "Let's go get your boy. Sky's gonna stay with Joe."

She nods and leaves my arms for his. He holds her while she cries and I leave them to talk while I drop my stuff in the guest room and go to the bathroom. When I come out, she's waiting with the keys in her hand.

The next evening, I get a call from Quinn. "Everything is okay, but I wanted you to know that Marina's staying with us."

"She wasn't sleeping well? Dee couldn't help?"

"No, not exactly." Something in her voice tells me I'm not going to like this.

"Someone tried to snatch Marina out of the parking lot at the bar tonight. One of the bikers was having sex in the parking lot when it happened and he saved her. Kind of a funny story since his pants were around his knees, but his woman called 911 while he was fighting for Marina. I was going to let her tell you about it but she said you guys aren't together so I thought I'd give you a heads-up."

"What do you mean snatch?"

"Grabbed her while she was waiting for an Uber at the end of her shift and tried to pull her into his car. Description sounds like it was Trent Reznor from Nine Inch Nails, circa 1995. A thin, black-haired, goth guy."

"Fuck! Does she know him?"

"Nope. Thank God he was scrawny or the biker with the pants down wouldn't have saved her. The guy got away, though. They found his car abandoned a couple of hours later. It was stolen with no prints. No surprise there."

"She okay?"

"Yeah. Shaken up. Dee's here and going to stay with her. She'll be okay. See you when you get home."

"My flight is for tomorrow. Do I need to come home tonight?"

"Nope, we've got it. Especially since you guys aren't together.

It'll send the wrong message to her and she's sweet. Don't dick her around."

"Quinn," I reply, irritated. The tone is probably too harsh to use with her since she's only being a good friend.

"You and I have never talked about women and dating so I don't know how you roll. I only know this is the first woman I've ever known you to have around more than once so I'm just saying, she's a sweet girl who has a shit deal in life. Don't make it worse."

Now my partner thinks I'm a douchebag.

"I won't. Take care of her, okay?"

"I will. Besides, my kids love her. Even with everything going on she got down on the floor to play with Lila and listened to Carlo try to impress her with football stories. I think Carlo has a crush on her. He told her that her nose ring was 'on point.' When I asked him what that meant it took him five minutes of belly laughter to tell me it meant it looked good. I guess I'm officially old."

"I'll be back to work the day after tomorrow. Call me if anything else comes up."

When I hang up the phone, Leslie's watching me with open curiosity.

"Okay, who is she?"

"Quinn."

"Not Quinn. I know Quinn. Who is the woman?"

"No one. Well it's someone I knew when I was young. I hadn't seen her in years and now she's everywhere with one problem after another. The lady is a train wreck. Someone tried to snatch her from the parking lot at work and this isn't the first crazy thing to happen to her in the last couple of months."

Leslie gasps and slaps her hand to her chest. "Is she okay?"

"Yeah, a biker saved her, but she's staying with Quinn."

"Is it normal to take a victim back home?"

"No, there's more to it than that, but I don't want to get into it."

"You never do, Dex. I love you, but you're so damn closed off. Don't stay that way. Growing old alone would suck."

"I'm doing fine the way I am."

"Except you're not. You run. You hike. You work. You do some things with the Rivers family and you take care of us. That's not a life, Dexter. It's an existence and if Stu were here he'd kick your ass. I saw your face when you heard about the girl back in Colorado. Whatever you aren't telling me is something big. Whatever it is, go home and face it. Love is worth the fight, Dex."

"I'm not in love."

"Keep telling yourself that and maybe you'll believe it too."

Before I can say something else, she sashays out of the room humming. *Damn it!*

RUSHTON IS SETTLED AND I FEEL LIKE I CAN GO HOME. WE HAD a long-ass man-to-man chat on the way home while Les pretended to listen to music on her headphones in the backseat. I could tell she wasn't though because her eyes would shoot to mine in the rearview mirror when she heard something that freaked her out. Rushton thought Leslie and Joe were trying to flush Stu's memory down the toilet. Thought they wanted him and Sky to forget their dad, so I had to be honest and explain why things were going the way they were and why it was important to accept Joe. By the time we got home he was okay. He's grounded for his disappearing stunt but he'll be okay.

Before I leave, I step into Rushton's room and close the door. He's sitting on the edge of his bed, staring out the window. "You wanted to talk to me?" I ask.

"Yeah. Can I ask you something?"

"Of course. Anything, any time."

"Did my dad ever get scared?" He bites down on his lower lip and shifts his gaze to the floor.

"Of course. He wasn't a wuss or anything, but he got scared. That's normal. Why?"

"Do you think he'd be mad that I'm scared?"

This is tough. I'm not sure where he's going with this, but I know this is going to get tricky. "What are you scared of?"

"I'm..." he trails off and I get the distinct impression he's fighting back heavy emotion.

"Say it. Whatever it is, say it. You'll feel better once you do." I sit down in the desk chair and scoot it closer to him.

"I'm scared I'm going to forget him. What if Mom marries Joe and we all forget him?"

"I thought we covered this in the car on the way home from Tallahassee?"

"I couldn't stop thinking about it and I think I'm just scared I'll forget him. It's already hard to remember some things. Like the sound of his voice and his laugh. I know he had a cool laugh but I can't find it in my head. What if all of that goes away? That's why I like it when you're around. You make me think of some of the things I forgot about him."

"You'll never forget him. Memories fade but they're always there. One day you may be walking through the grocery store and a memory, one you were missing, will come to you out of nowhere. Or you could be watching TV and someone will say something that triggers it. I get what you're saying about me being here. You do the same for me. You're *just like* your dad in all the best ways and it helps me too. That's part of the reason I want you to keep coming to see me in Colorado. It's selfish, but I don't want to lose him completely either. I never want to lose that either."

"Do you think he really loved us?"

"Is that a real question?" I ask as I tilt my head. He nods and waits. "Of course he did. When we were deployed, there wasn't a lot to do when we weren't working. We worked out, we played cards and we talked. He mostly talked, but I listened. You and your mom and sister were the number one topic of conversation. In his stuff, he kept this little pile of the letters your mom wrote, the pictures you drew and the photographs of you guys. Once or twice a day I'd catch him looking through that stuff with a smile on his face. Being away from you guys was the hardest part of being over there for him. He worried about you all the time and he missed you too."

He's thoughtful for a minute so I do my best to wrap up the conversation. "Rush, you're growing up fast and your life is changing so it's going to be hard, but you're Stuart Larkin's son. You have some of that same brave blood running through your veins. You just don't realize it yet. You have to face the changes coming your way head-on and see what they bring before you freak out. Your dad wouldn't want you losing your mind every time something new comes up. He'd want you to stand up tall and try to work through it. If you need me to remind you of that every time something comes up, I will, but be like your dad, call and talk to me before you run from it. Your dad was the bravest man I've ever known and you'll grow up to be the same, I know it."

"How can you be sure? I don't feel brave. I feel scared most of the time."

"Because you're so much like your dad it freaks me out sometimes. I'm sure as you get older it's going to get even weirder for me, but with your dad gone, if I had to trust anyone to stand by my side when the shit hits the fan, it would be you."

"I'm only 11."

"Age has nothing to do with it. Who you are on the inside and who you're working to become are what counts. I know a lot of great men and I know a lot of dirtbags. You're going to be one of the greats. I don't say it much because it just isn't my way, but I want you to know I love you and I've always got your back. You need something, you call me. When we stand together nothing can take us down. With all these changes going on, if you feel like you're forgetting him, pull out the pictures, the videos, the notes, whatever you need to help you remember, and if those don't work, call me and I'll tell you some stories about him." He smiles so I hug him one last time and walk back out the door.

As I pull up to the Rivers' house, my stomach is knotted up with nerves knowing Mari is in there and our last conversation was tough. I haven't had that problem since I was a teenager. When I approach the back door, which is the way they like everyone to enter their house, I hear Marina's musical laughter float through the door. I peer in through the window to see her nuzzling Lila's stomach as she cracks up laughing.

Judson's on the couch next to Quinn with his arm around her, laughing too. Carlo's staring at Marina like she's the sun and moon rolled into one. I agree with Quinn; just by the look on his face I'm certain he has a crush. I'm not sure how long I stand there before I finally get up the nerve to knock on the door, but when I do Quinn answers and ushers me in. Marina stops what she's doing and faces me. She has a bruise on her cheek and scratch marks down her neck. I wonder what other marks are on her, but I know I won't get the answer to that question because her smile fades as I approach. She's not happy to see me.

"Hey bud," I say as I touch Carlo's hair on the way past. Carlo stands and mumbles something about being an idiot and Quinn sends everyone out of the room. Judson stands and announces, "Bath time. Glad you're home, Dex. Good to see you."

Distractedly I reply, "Yeah, you too." I haven't taken my eyes off the beautiful woman in front of me. She's makeup-free with only three piercings visible and the red streaks she had in her hair before I left are fading to pink.

The room empties and we're left staring at each other. I step in closer, probably too close for the way we left things, and sweep her hair over her shoulder to examine the scratches. She doesn't move. Her eyes are wide as she watches me in silence.

I lightly stroke over the bruise, "Mari..." I pause in my perusal. "You okay?"

She nods.

"I'm sorry I wasn't here."

She rolls her lips between her teeth and I can tell she's getting emotional and fighting it.

"Come sit on the porch with me so I can explain."

"It's a little cool and I don't have pants."

I snatch the fluffy blanket off the back of the couch and hold it up. She wraps herself in it and follows me out the door to sit in the swing. I sit next to her.

I don't waste any time before telling her about Stuart and the promise and about everything. The only thing I leave out is the one-night encounter with Leslie, because it's irrelevant considering it was forever ago, meant nothing and only going to hurt her.

"I'm sorry I couldn't explain. I was in a panic, something you know is not normal for me, and I knew you'd have a million questions. I should've taken the time to at least give you the basics, but I'm not used to having to explain myself or talk about this kind of shit. I wasn't trying to hurt you, I just needed to get to them."

"Did you sleep with her while you were there?"

"What?"

"Leslie. Did you sleep with her?"

"No, I told you Joe was there and they're getting married." It's a little white lie, skirting the truth because there is no need to bring up things from so long ago that have no bearing on the present, besides she asked if I slept with her while I was there. I did not.

"I know this isn't a relationship and it isn't going anywhere, but I appreciate you coming to talk to me. Our paths will probably continue to cross on occasion since I'm taking a job here on the ranch with Judson. They were planning to hire someone and I'm willing. It'll mean I don't have to go back to the bar more than one day a week. The patrons are a little rowdy but they turned out to be good people; I'm just ready to move on to something new."

"You'll be working here? Do you know anything about horses? Had you ever even seen a horse before coming here?"

"Nope. But Judson's going to teach me. I love animals so I think I'll be fine. I'm going to stay with them for the next week while I get acclimated to the job and then I'll go back to my apartment. By then we should have at least a mattress and some clothes. I already went to Goodwill while you were gone and grabbed some clothes to get me through."

"You aren't coming back to my place?"

"No. We don't want the same things and I don't want to be a placeholder for the blond Barbie doll with perfect makeup and an SUV that you're probably waiting on. You don't love me and I need that. I deserve it. I want a home, a family, and a man who loves my constant chatter, who can't get enough of me and my unconventional ways. We both know that's not how you feel and it's okay. It was nice while it lasted." By the set of her shoulders it's obvious that's she's serious even if the tone of her voice rings with sadness.

"You want a family? Most suburban moms aren't running around with lip rings and pink hair."

"Well then I'll be the first and there will be someone at my side who's not embarrassed by that. You're a great guy, Jase, but we both know you're not *my* guy and for once in my life I'll be strong enough to walk away."

She's right. I know she's right, so why does it feel like someone took a sledgehammer to my chest? I don't get the chance to say anything else. She stands and places a kiss to my forehead before she returns inside without another word. I sit for a long time before Judson comes out and hands me a beer. When did she get so strong? I was only gone a couple of days, which doesn't seem long enough for the changes I've witnessed in her tonight.

"Want to talk about it?"

"Nah. She didn't say anything but the truth. I'm not the guy for her. She deserves the pierced, tattooed version of Mr. 2.5 kids. Most of the time she drives me batty with her constant talking anyway. I just wish I understood why I feel like shit now."

"I can't tell you that. You have to figure it out on your own. I hope you get your head out of your ass though because she's pretty damn great." With that parting line, he leaves me sitting there alone with only my thoughts to keep me company. When I finish my beer, I return to my apartment and am struck stupid with how quiet it is. After the crazy last week and the previous weeks of having Marina here you'd think I'd relish this, but instead it's rubbing like burlap against soft skin, chaffing and mocking me.

Over the next few days I take more runs after midnight and shoot the shit with Marv. The nightmares are worse than ever, taking on elements fit for a Stephen King novel, not my dreams. The first two nights they felt so real I could smell that last battle where I lost Stu like I was standing in the middle of it again, even after I was awake for a few hours.

On my day off I go hiking and try to remind myself why I love to be alone. I think my problem is a matter of wanting what you can't have. Because when I had Marina, her constant talking made me nuts. She did make a great dinner and the sex was dynamite, but I can get both elsewhere, with a quieter person, and minus the crazy baggage. In fact, there's a gorgeous blonde at Starbucks every day when I roll through that I was eyeing before Marina blew through my life. Maybe I'll ask her out tomorrow.

By the weekend I have a date with the blonde, whose name is Catrina. We end up having dinner at a local chain restaurant per her suggestion. This woman may be beautiful, but she's not very intelligent and we have nothing in common. In fact, we're struggling through conversation when the Rivers family, accompanied by Marina, comes down the aisle where we're sitting. *Son of a bitch.*

Quinn introduces everyone as Carlo stands in the back shaking his head and avoiding eye contact. I know he thinks I'm an idiot, but he's not a grown man who knows what I know about Marina, so he can be pissed all he wants. Someday he'll understand. Mari excuses herself abruptly and Quinn follows. I realize seeing me on this date probably hurt her and I didn't want that, but we aren't together so there isn't much I can do about it. Judson gets the hint that this is awkward and leads his family to a table a little farther back than ours.

Catrina, on top of being unintelligent also proves to have a vicious streak. I find this out when she says something snotty about the now turquoise streaks in Mari's hair and it's that cue that ends the date. In an instant I felt the need to defend Mari. Surprisingly I like the turquoise and thought it was rude for Catrina to say something so nasty.

I thought a date would help take my mind off the hole Mari left behind. There wasn't a hole in my life before she came back into it, so I don't understand why there is now. Going out with a woman like Catrina was a huge mistake. She's certainly not the woman for me if she'd bash someone right in front of me who's obviously a friend. I don't want a woman who's quick to judge based on appearance, especially when the person she's judging is someone I care about.

Like a meteor out of the sky it hits me; that's what I've been doing all this time, judging her. I'm such a dick.

Once I get rid of Catrina I try to call Mari but she won't answer. I even send a text that she never answers. The hours and minutes of the night creep by at a snail's pace, giving me even more to think about. By the next day, I'm exhausted and desperate to talk to her so I approach Quinn about it, and for the first time since we met she freaks out on me.

"Nope. You don't get to do this, Dex. She's not a toy you can take down and play with at will. She's a sweet girl with a world of hurt and rejection in her heart and she doesn't need more. I love you, Dex. You're my best friend, but if you push me I'll push back. She spent the rest of the night crying after seeing you with the Colorado beauty queen last night. She knows that's your type, so let her go. Quit pushing and pulling at her. You've confused her with this game you have going. She's got a lot of armor on with all the outward appearance stuff, but that's all protecting a soft underbelly. Don't make me wrong about who you are."

I sit, stunned by what she's said. Is she right? Am I playing games? I never thought about it that way but if I analyze it, I probably have been. Even knowing she was vulnerable, I brought her to my bed. I also knew I had no intention of keeping her around for the long term and I still slept with her. I don't want to be the kind of guy who would do that to her. I guess it's time to back off. It might be different if I saw a future with her, but I don't. She's right. She's not my type and I don't want the whole family-soccer-dad thing she wants. I never have. I would have no idea what to do with all that. I don't exactly come from a place that's a good example of family, love and togetherness. It's time to finally step up and be a real man and make the hard choice to leave her alone so she can get on with her life.

Chapter Nine
MARINA

Walking away from Jase was so hard, but after a long talk with Quinn about my life goals—wanting a husband who loves me for me, a family, a house—I decided to start taking things into my own hands. So much happens to me because I follow someone else's lead or I'm careless or lonely or bored. I have to learn to deal with being alone until I can find the right guy to start a family with. I have time. It's not like I'm an old maid with a clock ticking away too fast for me to reach my goals.

I don't want a family like the one I grew up in so why I keep settling for guys who don't love me, are lazy or flat out aren't good people, I don't know. It's amazing that Dee's been trying to tell me this exact thing for years, but I never got it until I sat next to Quinn and watched her husband roll around the floor laughing his ass off with their wonderful kids, in their beautiful, comfortable home. She's living my dream so it makes sense for me to believe that she knows what she's talking about.

I think Jase—crap, I should stop calling him that, he goes by Dex now. I think Dex is the perfect guy, but not for me. I want someone who's madly in love with me. A man who can't live without me and can't wait to get home to me at the end of the day. Someone who wants to tell me everything in his heart and everything he fears. I want someone who'll be as consumed with me and our family as I am with him and them. Not someone who will look at me like I'm a freak when I try a new shade of color in my hair, but someone who'll think it's cute. That may be to much to ask, but I'm willing to wait and find out.

Judson offered me a job as a stable hand and I took it. It gets me out of the bar, other than the one day a week, and I'll get to work with animals all day. I know it's not glorious. I followed him around all day today getting an idea of what they do and some of it was gross, but in the end, I'll be nurturing life, and making a difference, not just allowing the world to pass me by while I sling drinks in a bar. I can imagine at the end of the day I'll be exhausted, but I'll feel better about me and what I'm doing. I still have to keep Saturday nights at the bar for a little while to be able to make my rent without a problem, but one day a week, as opposed to every day, is a much better situation.

The only issue for me will be when Dex is around. Quinn and Judson are his best friends so I imagine he's around a lot. I need to figure out a way to avoid him or deal with him. I'm thinking avoidance is the best bet for now. Sleeping with him was a bad choice for me. He quickly became an addiction that I'm now fighting. That level of physical intimacy makes it hard for me to not make more of our time together than what it was. I was so caught up with him that I really felt like we connected on a deeper level. I guess this is a good example of me living in a fantasyland where everything is perfect. I'd give almost anything to have him feel the way I feel and not just because I want someone, but because I want him. I've been with several guys over the years that I knew I didn't want to marry and start a life with, but I settled because I didn't want to be alone. Of course, now that I've found one I want to build a life with, he doesn't see me in that light or want that particular future. Although I want a family and a place to belong, I also want the right man, and I was certain it was him. I hate when I'm wrong. The man I want for the rest of my life would never say the hurtful things Dex said to me.

My plan was to go back to my apartment while Dex was in Florida since I now have a crappy mattress and some clothes and towels, but after that guy grabbed me and said a bunch of weird shit to me, Quinn doesn't want me to go. She was freaked for me, and it was nice to have someone besides Dee worry about me for a change. Dee stayed with me the first night here, but then went back to Reggie's. I can see the writing on the wall. She'll be moving in with him before the year is over and I'll have to find a new roommate. I'm not sure anyone will understand me like Dee does, but I guess everyone needs to grow up and let go sometime. I'll have to become less emotionally dependent on my roommate and just move a warm body in to help with expenses. I have no idea how I'll pull that off.

THE NEXT WEEK IS FILLED WITH A LOT OF MUCKING THE STALLS, brushing and feeding the horses, and sore muscles for me, but also a great deal of fulfillment too. I can't remember ever having a job that meant something to me beyond bringing in a paycheck. I'm finding that I love nurturing the animals and taking care of something other than myself for a change. This job is healing some things inside me that I didn't realize needed healing and I'm feeling stronger every day. Although I'm absolutely exhausted at the end of the day, my brain still goes into freak-out mode when I'm alone in my room. So every night after everyone goes to bed, I sneak out to the couch and lie down with the TV on low, and I'm able to catch a couple hours of sleep that way. The last two nights, Carlo has come out around one with sleepy, droopy eyes and plopped down in the chair near the couch and gone back to sleep. Sadly, I think this 12-year-old kid might be part of why I'm able to sleep for short periods of time. Having someone nearby that I trust helps so much.

After the first night Carlo came out, I heard Judson ask him about it when he thought I couldn't hear, and his reply made me tear up. "Dex told me she was in foster care too. I think it's why she can't sleep alone. If I sleep out there with her, maybe she'll be able to sleep. It doesn't bother me. I can sleep anywhere, so why not sleep out there so she can sleep too?"

What 12-year-old boy thinks like that? None. He's such a good kid, but it makes me feel bad that he feels like he should be the one to help. I mentioned it to Quinn and she told me not to worry, that they think it helps him to help me. I did see Judson check on us last night right before I fell asleep, so at least I know they're keeping an eye on things.

Today is the first day that my whole body doesn't hurt, like it's finally adjusted to this kind of physical labor and I'm loving every minute of it. Of the six horses they have on the property now, Trooper has taken to me the best. The giant chocolate-colored beast weighs about 1600 pounds, Judson said, and at first his size scared me. But he's such a flirt it didn't take long for me to warm up to him. It started when I wasn't paying attention and he leaned in and nuzzled my neck. I didn't realize horses did such things. I jumped about 10 feet in the air and Judson, who was in the stall next to me, died laughing. He thinks Trooper likes women better since he does the same to Quinn but not him. I don't care why, I'm just thrilled by his response. Besides, there's something so calming about spending time with this big, beautiful beast.

Because of our budding relationship, I tend to take a little longer with Trooper, and as I'm stroking his nose and having a perfectly long conversation about life with him, I hear someone's throat clear behind me. When I turn toward the sound I find Dex watching me. Being around the Rivers family has helped me to transition to calling him Dex, which I think will help me to let him go. I remind myself every time his name comes up that the person called Dex is a stranger. He's not the Jase that saved me so long ago, or the one with sweet unguarded moments during and after sex with me. He's just a guy who's friends with my new boss.

That strategy was working well until I turned and saw those eyes. Dear God, they could stop traffic and probably bring world peace if everyone took a few minutes to stare into their depths. Too bad he's kind of a jerk.

"Hey, Dex," I greet, aiming for nonchalance.

His head jerks back a little. "Since when did I become Dex?"

"It's what you go by now, right?" Now it's time to play innocent. Why does he care what I call him anyway?

"Well, yeah. But it's not what *you* call me."

"It is now. Sometimes you have to let go of the past and embrace the present." I turn away and go back to brushing Trooper even though I'm supposed to be done so Dex won't notice my shaking hands. I don't want to see the confused expression on his face and read into it more than I should.

"I like that you aren't like everyone else," he says softly and it feels more like a confession than a statement. I close my eyes, hoping to settle my racing heartbeat and control the flare of anger his words cause.

"That's not what you said before and really, what does it matter? I won't see you very often—if at all. I don't think you're here during working hours most of the time and I plan to go back home soon, so our paths won't even cross for me to call you anything."

"Why are you going home? Did they catch the guy who grabbed you? No one said anything to me about it."

"Nah. I'm sure the guy is long gone. I'm going home because this isn't my home and they have a family life they need to get back to. They don't need to be worried about some random stray girl."

"Mari—"

"Don't, Dex. Just let it go. I've made it this far in life without you or anyone else really. I'll continue to make it."

"I never meant to hurt you, Mari."

"Yeah, I know. I'm fine." I set the brush down and let myself out of Trooper's stall. Then I step in front of Dex and place my hands on his chest before I rise up on tiptoes and kiss his cheek. "Thanks for everything, Dex. But there's no need to worry about me. I'll be fine. I always am. Now if you'll excuse me, I need to get cleaned up for dinner."

Then without looking back, I stride to the house with my shoulders back, projecting strength and resolve that's all fake. When I take my shower, I stay in a little longer than is normal to allow all the tears to flow in private. At dinner, I try to keep my conversation light and aimed at Carlo. Luckily the kid is smart and has tons to talk about so it's easy. When dinner's over, I insist on cleaning up. Once the task is complete I retreat to the guest room so Dex can hang with his friends without the awkwardness of having me there. I hate being alone so it's pure torture to sit in the room and wait for him to leave.

I DECIDE THE NEXT DAY I SHOULD PROBABLY LEAVE AND attempt to get back to normal. I called Dee to pick me up and figured I'd Uber back and forth the rest of the week. I just feel like I'm wearing out my welcome and I don't want to do that considering they're my new employers and I love my job. After I make the rent for the month, I can probably get an old junker car to get me to and from if I pick up a Sunday night shift at the bar.

ALL IS WELL FOR THE FIRST TWO NIGHTS I'M BACK HOME, EVEN though I'm not sleeping because I'm here alone. I've dozed off a few times and that seems to be sustaining me as far as sleep goes, but I'm not sure how long that will last. Dee never comes here now that our stuff was stolen so I'm alone in a virtually empty apartment all the time. Tonight I decide I can't sit here alone with nothing to do again so I take a walk down several blocks to the local grocery store. Thank goodness it's a 24-hour establishment. I roam the whole store, slowly, aisle by aisle, for something to do. I'm almost to the last aisle when the hairs on the back of my neck rise. I turn to see who has my radar going off and I get a glimpse of black fabric turning the corner to leave the aisle, but that's it. Nothing else and no one else is near that I can see. I've got to get a grip and quit freaking myself out. When I've exhausted all the aisles and talked to every store employee I could find, I'm beyond bored. I splurge on a bag of peanut M&M's on my way out, thank the clerk and stroll out the door.

When I'm about a block from home and the streetlights seem farther apart, I hear the cadence of someone's footsteps behind me so I step to the far side of the sidewalk, thinking someone wants to pass me. The footsteps stop when I do so I turn to see if someone is standing back there and see no one. God, I've got to get a grip! I resume walking and as I pass through the door to my building, I hear the footsteps moving faster now like someone is running at me. Panic sets in and instead of running toward my door, I freeze. The fear literally locks me in place. What if it's the guy who tried to take me? What if it's a crazy rapist? Oh, my God! I should've stayed at the ranch a little longer. I'm in full meltdown mode, running every horrible scenario over in my head at warp speed when a jogger flies past the entrance, not even sparing me a glance.

I almost slide down the wall as my legs turn liquid with relief. Before I can freak out any more, I hustle to my apartment and lock the door behind me. After that little scare, my overactive imagination has me wide awake all night long.

The next morning my Uber driver is late because he took a

wrong turn and then he refuses to drive me up the gravel portion of the driveway to the ranch, so I hike the three quarters of a mile up the gravel road to their house. If I'd had some sleep last night the hike wouldn't be an issue, but of course I didn't get any. Judson had to take Carlo to school this morning and drop the baby off at his mom's house because of Quinn's schedule so he doesn't get back until I'm an hour into my shift.

"Hey, Marina!" he calls to me from the doorway as I'm mucking Comet's stall.

I pause and glance up at him. "Hey Judson. I'm moving a little slow. I'm sorry, long night."

"You okay?"

"Yup. Just freaked myself out, but I'm okay. Not all the way awake yet."

"If you need the day off, it's okay."

"No way. I need to be busy. It's no big deal." I provide him with a smile so he'll understand that I'm okay. I know he doesn't believe me, but I can't go there. It's better if I don't feed into the crazy shit that goes on in my head.

At the end of the day Judson offers to take me home, but I decline and instead walk back down the driveway to meet a different Uber driver. Thank God these Uber rides are so cheap or I'd be screwed.

When I get home, the light is on in my bedroom, which wouldn't be a problem except I don't remember it being on when I left. In fact, I'm certain I went back in there to turn it off right before I left. With my heart pounding, I search the place and find nothing. Not many places to hide since there still isn't any furniture here. I must have imagined turning it off. I was tired so it's possible I forgot.

AFTER ANOTHER NIGHT OF NO SLEEP, I TREK UP THE HILL TO

the ranch slower than yesterday. This time I didn't even ask the driver to take me up the driveway; I just assumed the answer would be no and I'm too tired to argue about it. In fact, I don't think I said a word to the driver about anything. That's the good thing about that Uber app, you type in where you want to go, before they even pick you up, and pay through your credit or debit card on file. It's perfect when you're not in the mood to talk.

Judson's concern is greater today as I stumble one time in front of him, landing on my knees in a pile of horse crap. I brush off his concern and blame it on being klutzy at times. I'm beyond exhausted, but I want to keep this job and prove I can make it on my own. It's time for me to put on my big-girl panties. Hell, at 28 years old I should be able to do it. Dee hasn't been around since I've been back and my feelings are a little hurt by her absence. She checks on me via text every day, but I think maybe she's a little tired of my needy bullshit so I refuse to call her for help.

At the end of the day I order my Uber and trudge back down the hill. Almost as soon as the Uber car pulls back onto the road after I get in, the hair on the back of my neck stands up. There's something familiar about the driver, but I'm unable to see his face in the rearview mirror to see if I know him. His baseball cap is pulled down too low on his head and the only thing I can see of his is straight, black hair sticking out the bottom of the hat.

I pull up the Uber app to see what the driver's name is and realize, to my horror, that my real driver hasn't arrived at the pick-up point yet. Shit! I wasn't paying attention and got in the wrong car, but who the hell else is out here picking up chicks on the side of the road? I could see if I were downtown and the wrong Uber picked me up, but out here in the middle of nowhere? Not possible. Alarm bells clang loud in my head.

Chapter Ten

MARINA

"Sir." Please let this be a mix-up. "Sir. I'm in the wrong Uber. Can you drop me off? I'll tip you for your trouble."

He doesn't respond and a chill dances down my spine. Why doesn't he respond? I decide I'll jump if I need to, but I'm getting out of this car now. Something about this whole situation is wrong.

I reach for the handle and he finally speaks. "Locks from the outside. Added that feature yesterday. You can try all you want but you aren't going anywhere. I've been planning this date for a while and you're going to enjoy it."

My heart thumps in my chest so hard I feel like you could hear it outside of the car. A fine sheen of sweat breaks out along my forehead and collar. *What am I going to do?*

"You've got the wrong girl." My voice is shaking and my brain is telling me it's a good idea to talk my way through this so the babbling begins. "I'm a lesbian. I don't date guys so I know you have the wrong girl. Besides, I've been mucking the horses' stalls all day. Don't you smell the manure on my knees? It's pretty stinky. My girlfriend is going to be so pissed. I'm not into guys and she's waiting for me at hom—"

"Enough. Lying will only piss me off. Dee is not your girlfriend and she's not at your apartment. She's at Reggie's house. I know she's there because she's moving in with him, she just hasn't figured out how to break it to you yet. She was worried about how you'll take it considering you hate to be alone and all."

Oh, my God! This guy knows Dee and an awful lot of information about me! How does he know this stuff?

"How do you know about Dee and Reggie?"

"I know everything. I've been watching you for a long time now. Don't worry, I'm going to make you comfortable. You'll feel right at home as a matter of fact. Once you're ready, we can have this date I've waited so long for. You've been a busy girl with Jasen Dexter, but that's no longer an issue."

"What do you mean?"

"About Dexter or it not being an issue? You and Dexter broke up and I've cleared your schedule for a very long time. That should answer both questions."

My phone! I can't believe I didn't think of it before, but my phone is in my hand. Sometimes service is spotty up here but it's worth a try. I slide it on and dial 911. Before I remember to lower the volume, the emergency operator comes on the line and is loud enough for him to hear.

Oh God! Oh God, he'll be able to hear it!

I fumble with the phone, trying to drop the volume. He slams on the brakes, throwing me forward, and the phone flies out of my hand, lodging between the front seats. I can hear the operator, but I can't reach it to do anything so I scream as loud as I can.

"I'm being taken! Help me! Please someone help me!"

The driver's cussing grows louder as he jerks the car off to the side of the road as I try to wiggle myself from my spot on the floor between the seats. He can't find the phone and I keep screaming the same thing over and over. He gets out of the car and yanks open the back door. I learned a long time ago not to be a victim when I'm being attacked. I can fight back now and that's what I plan to do.

As soon as he's within reach I kick my leg out as hard and as fast as I can, catching him in the nuts. "Argh!" he yells as he stumbles back, dropping to the ground. I wiggle myself out of the car as quickly as I can. This time, while he's still writhing on the ground in pain, I kick him in his side by his ribs as hard as I can and he groans and cusses at me louder.

I turn and run as fast as I can down the incline of the road toward town. It's just past dusk and I'm praying that helps to hide me. Once I hear his footsteps following me, and him call my name, I do the only thing I can think of. I drop to the ground on my side and roll down the side of the huge hill we're on into the darkness of the trees. Sticks, twigs and rocks tear me up, ripping my long-sleeved shirt and jeans, all the way down, until I'm stopped by the trunk of an enormous tree. I cry out and immediately cover my mouth to keep from saying anything else. *Shit that hurt!* I do my best to move so I can scramble further down the hill, but the pain in my ribs is excruciating and I can't breathe. I'm terrified I broke my back or a hip so I give up on changing locations and lie there, listening to him scream my name from above. My body shakes from fear and adrenaline overload.

How the hell am I going to get out of this one? I can't catch a break. My mind is spinning with crazy thoughts and a nauseated dizziness rolls through me. I turn to the side and puke, but I can't move enough to get away from it so I'm half in it. Something warm, other than the tears that started a second ago, drips down my cheek and over my nose so I reach up to swipe at the source and the heavy copper scent of the substance has me vomiting again. Thank God I can't see it. My ribs hurt tremendously and I can't move even a fraction of an inch more so I lie with tears, blood and vomit dripping down the side of my face. I wonder vaguely if I'll die here.

The days have been warm but the nights are cold and the torn long-sleeved shirt and jeans I'm wearing won't cut it if the temperature gets too low, although I'd rather risk hypothermia than face that guy again. His voice is fading and before I can think of anything more, another wave of dizziness hits and my world goes black.

Sometime later—with no concept of time, I'm not sure how long—I come to in the same position as I was in. Everything hurts, especially my ribs and my head. I can smell the blood and vomit mixed together and my stomach revolts. I fight it though. If I puke again it'll cause more pain.

White, blue, and red lights flash through the darkness up by the road above me and I wonder if I've lost my mind. I close my eyes to steady my spinning head and think when I open them again it'll be dark and I won't be hallucinating. I'm somewhere on the side of the large hill leading to Daisy Rivers Ranch, lodged against a tree trunk. It's the low side of a large hill, but still it's a hill. What the hell am I going to do?

Within a minute I hear voices yelling, "Marina! Marina!"

Is this real? Is that the crazy driver? I can't answer in case he's coming for me so I lie there as quiet as my shaking body will allow. I'm so scared that it's hard to stay still enough not to rustle the leaves under me.

This time the shouts are louder and coming from several places. A woman's voice rises above them all and I'm filled with hope. Oh, let this be help! Please! The woman calls again, "Marina!" I roll a little to sit up and cry out at the pain. When I flop back, trying to avoid the pain in my ribs, I land in my own vomit again. It smears down my face and neck as I fight to get up. My body protests at the pain and effort. "Here," I cry out weakly. "Here." I get a little louder this time.

As the white lights move farther away I panic and scream as loud as my lungs will allow, sending daggers of pain through my midsection. "Here!"

All noise stops so I scream again and drop back to the ground as the excruciating pain spreads all over my battered body. This time the white lights all swing toward me. I yell out, but not as loud as before. "Here!"

The next thing I know, someone is sliding down the hill on their backside with the flashlight bouncing along. A police uniform comes into view and I yell again. The man in the uniform scrambles over to me and yells, "I've got her! I've got her! I need help!" His light is right in my face and I can't imagine what he's seeing right now, nor do I care.

"Did you catch him? Do you have him?" I croak.

"What?" he sounds confused.

"The guy who took me. Do you have him?"

"No, he was gone when we got here. They were tracing him with your cell until the signal disappeared, but we're here and we won't let anything happen to you." His voice is sweet and comforting and I breathe a sigh of relief that help is here.

A COUPLE OF HOURS LATER JUDSON AND QUINN ARE TAKING ME back to their place from the hospital. I can't afford the bill staying will create so I request to leave. When Quinn was on her way home from work, she came across the scene and stopped to help. It was then she found out it was me they were looking for. With my cell phone long gone, I can't call Dee because I never memorized her number. That's the bad thing about technology, it makes you lazy. I feel so bad that Quinn and Judson are stuck with me again. I should call some other random friend to pick up the slack, but I don't have my damn phone!

While I'm getting settled on the couch, Carlo wakes up from all the commotion and comes out. The fear in his young face makes it all worse.

"I'm okay, Carlo. Really. I'm a survivor, I'm still kickin'." I try to make light of the situation for his sake, but the kid comes from the same kind of life I do and he knows without me saying it. I'm okay but not for any reason other than I have to be.

After studying my expression and my torn-up face for a minute, he sits on the floor and lays his head by my hip before he drifts back to sleep. Within half an hour of Carlo falling asleep beside me, the back door flies open and Dex's deep voice booms through the house, startling Carlo from his sleep again. "Mari!"

Quinn steps out of the kitchen and growls, "I will kick your ass if you wake my kids."

"Where is she?" he demands in a loud whisper that wasn't much of a whisper.

"On the couch. You know she won't sleep alone in a room."

Loud footsteps precede him. "Mari."

Carlo grabs my hand and says, "I'm going to bed until it quiets down, then I'll be back to keep you company."

"No, Carlo. Get some sleep. I'll be okay. If I need you I'll call for you. Thanks." He stares at me for several seconds then nods and disappears to his room.

Dex drops to his knees as his forehead wrinkles, eyes squinted. He's close enough I can see the pulse point in his neck fluttering like the wings of a hummingbird.

"What happened? I only got bits and pieces. I wasn't home yet when it all went down."

That was hours ago. Oddly, I wonder who he was with in the hours since he left work. Probably the blonde he took to dinner, the one with the sour look on her face. Like I should even care right now. It should be the farthest thing from my mind.

"Some guy acted like my Uber driver and picked me up from their driveway. It didn't take long to realize it wasn't my Uber driver. I tried to call 911 when I figured out what was happening. He heard it and slammed on the brakes and then all hell broke loose. I knew the only hope I had was going down the side of the hill into the trees."

"Are you crazy?"

"No, I was in survival mode."

"You could have killed yourself or been stranded out there with the wildlife for who knows how long."

"But I wasn't. If you came here to give me a bunch of shit, then go home Dex—"

"We're back to Dex?" *He's irritated about that?*

"That's your name. It's what everyone calls you. We established this already when I saw you the last time. But my point was to say I've been through enough without you yelling at me. Yes, I know I'm a mess. Yes, I know I end up in shitty situations more than the average person. I'm working on fixing that, but Rome wasn't built in a day, so give me a damn break. If you want to help, see if you can find Dee's phone number because the only place I had it was in my cell and that's gone. I need my best friend."

The tears I've been holding in for hours leak from my eyes, half out of frustration and half from embarrassment.

"God, Mari. You're killing me! Come here." He leans over me and pulls me in to him gently as I fall apart. "I'll get her number. If I can't find it, I'll go to your place and get her."

"She hasn't been at our place. She hasn't been back since everything happened. She's been staying with Reggie," I squeak.

"How've you been sleeping?"

"I haven't. That was part of the problem with the Uber situation; I was tired so I wasn't paying attention. That and who would've thought to check to make sure the Uber your app says is coming is the one who picks you up when you're in the middle of nowhere and no one else is waiting for one?"

"This guy obviously knows your schedule. He's watching closely if he caught on this quickly."

"I can't even think about that right now or I'll lose it. The whole thing freaks me out. It's something out of a thriller movie and I can't deal with that."

He holds me a little longer and finally says, "Let me go make some calls to find Dee."

"Okay." I rest against the back of the couch as Quinn comes out of the kitchen with a couple of pain pills and a small cup of water.

"Take these. You can have more around seven in the morning if you need them."

I thank her, swallow them down with a sip of water, and then relax against the back of the couch the best I can.

The medication and exhaustion from the whole ordeal must take over because I fall asleep and don't wake up until the next morning when the pain in my ribs forces me out of sleep.

When I try to stretch my legs, I can't and when I look up to see why, I find Dee asleep at the other end of the couch and my whole body relaxes. Sometimes you just need your best friend and right now is one of those times. I have a ton of friends. Some good, some not so good, but only one best friend and I've missed her. I was afraid she was tired of me. I was hoping to be a little more stable before I had to see her again. My crazy fear of being alone has never included fear of losing Dee too until recently when it seems my bullshit has escalated to be a constant in our lives. I know there's only so much of that she can take before she runs from me too. I adjust, trying to get up for a trip to the bathroom without waking her when her eyes pop open.

"Marina." Her eyes are soft but convey her feelings of guilt. "I'm sorry."

"For what?"

"I wasn't there for you. If Dex hadn't called me I'd never have known anything had happened. I'm sorry. I've been pretty self-absorbed lately."

"You have to be. Everything is always about me. It's why I gave you the space. I'm sorry I had him call you, but I needed you."

"Oh God, Marina. If you didn't call, I'd be pissed. I love you.

You're like my sister. I'm so sorry this happened. Where do you hurt? Are you okay? You look horrible."

"Yeah, I know. Everything hurts. Right now, I have to use the bathroom; can you help me get there? I'm pretty sore and I don't want to fall in the process."

Ten minutes later she's helping me back to the couch when she says, "I'm taking you back to Reggie's with me. Ray is out of town for a few days. There's nothing at our apartment to go home to. At least this way I can take care of you. Reggie suggested it."

"Ray's gone?"

"Yeah, I think Reggie's gonna kick him out anyway. The guy is disgusting and he hit on me last week. Thank God Reggie walked in on it and I didn't have to tell him. Girl, he lost his mind! Freaked out on Ray. So anyway, I'll take you back with me. I just wanted to get another dose of pain meds in you before you had to ride in the car again. Quinn told me you're due for more at seven and we're almost there."

With Ray gone, I could stomach going to Reggie's. I've always liked him, just not his nasty roommate. Besides, I'm hoping to only be there for a few days before I can go back to our apartment and hopefully get back to work out here. That is, if Judson wants me to. He seems like a pretty put-together guy so I'm sure he's having second thoughts now that he's gotten a belly full of my life. It'll be hard with the broken and bruised ribs. I hear they take forever to heal, but I can't go without a paycheck so I have to get back to work somewhere, and something about this place is calming. Especially Trooper, who I'm hoping to see before I leave today in case it's the last time. Dex comes out a few minutes later with sleepy eyes and lines on his cheek from his pillow.

Dee addresses Dex. "We're gonna take off as soon as I feed her and give her the meds. Don't you have to work today? I know Quinn already left."

"Yeah, but I didn't want to leave until I checked on Marina."

"I'm fine." I reply so they'll stop talking about me like I'm not in the room.

Judson comes through the hallway, chuckling as baby Lila cuddles against his chest with two fingers in her mouth.

"Fine?" He levels his laughing eyes at Dex and continues, "Yeah, take my advice. Fine is not a word you want to hear. It's also never the truth." I narrow my eyes at him and he laughs all the way to the kitchen. He has apparently broken the ancient woman code about using certain words. Fine is at the top of that list. Damn the enlightened man!

"How are you really?" Dex asks as he towers over me.

"Sore, but okay. I could be so much worse."

"Well, I'll be back after my shift to help take care of you. I have to go in after missing all that time a couple weeks ago."

"You don't need to worry about me. I'm going to stay with Dee at Reggie's. I have to rest for a few days. Dee can help me shower and take me to get my stitches removed when it's time. I appreciate what everyone has done for me but it's time I go back to my life."

I pause and look to Judson who has returned from the kitchen with Lila, who is gulping a bottle at a record pace in his arms. "You don't have to tell me now, but I'd like to come back to work in a few days. Do I still have a job? I understand if my brand of crazy has been too much for you, but I need to know if I'm coming back here or getting a new job."

Dex speaks up. "You can't do manual labor with messed-up ribs, Marina. You'll never make it and they take forever to heal."

"With all due respect Dex, I *have* to do manual labor because I don't have the option of not working. I've backed myself into a nice little corner here with no education and no vocational training, so my options are limited. I'm also in the special position of having no savings and being broke as hell. No matter what my body wants, I don't have a choice. This is the life I've created for myself, no matter how messed up it is. It's called sleeping in the bed you've made and that's what I have to do. What I need to know is if it'll be here or elsewhere. If it's not here, I understand. They have a family and a ranch to worry about and who knows what will happen with me next, but I love it so I don't want to walk away unless I'm told to. I won't hold any ill will if that's the choice. I just need to know."

Judson's expression is soft and sincere when he responds. "I understand what you're saying, and because this is a family-run ranch at my home, I need to talk to my wife about it. If you give me Dee's number, I'll call you tonight and let you know."

"That's fair enough. I appreciate it." I'm grateful he didn't say no outright.

Dex turns back to me and asks, "Why are you going to Reggie's? I thought he had a scumbag roommate you hated."

Dee joins the conversation and says, "Ray's out of town for the next couple of days so she should be fine until then."

Dex nods and says, "I need to get to work, but I'll check on you later."

"I'll be fine, Dex. Get on with your life. Thanks for checking on me last night and finding Dee. It's exactly what I needed."

He doesn't say anything because there's nothing to say.

I DON'T HEAR FROM JUDSON THAT NIGHT OR THE NEXT DAY, BUT the following morning Dee shows me a text from him asking if he can come by to talk to me and bring me my paycheck. I have nothing else going on and would rather have my final paycheck in my hand when he tells me he doesn't want me to come back, so I tell her to say yes.

Judson is due to come over at three o'clock, so when I hear a bunch of noise at the front door around that time, I think it's him. Without looking through the peephole, I open the door ready to greet Judson and instead am faced with Ray. He's got a duffel bag over one shoulder and two bags in his arms. That must be why he didn't open the door himself. Bloodshot eyes greet me and a slimy grin spreads across his scruffy face. *Gross!*

"Marina," he says as he strolls through the door. There's something about the way he says my name that makes me want to boil my skin in a scalding hot shower. He's disgusting, obnoxious and rude. What I don't understand is how the guy can have expensive, pristine sneakers and ball caps but have the dirtiest hair and clothes. He'd look homeless if it weren't for those two items. His yellow-tinted grin sets me on edge and I realize if he tries anything I'm screwed because I can't move fast enough to get away. Every time I turn a certain way I get a shooting pain in my abdomen from the rib injury.

"What's up, girly?" he asks as he sets the bags on the table. "You're looking a little rough. Fight?"

"No, I jumped out of a car and rolled down a hill into the woods."

His bloodshot eyes widen for a second before he busts up laughing. I have visions of hitting him with a crowbar over the head. *What a jerk!*

Stepping up to me, way too close for comfort, he pushes the chunk of hair that's lying across my chest over my shoulder and I catch the distinctive smell of pot on his breath. He needs to brush those teeth, but because I'm at a disadvantage in this situation, I keep my trap shut.

"So, are you here for a little comfort? 'Cause I can surely provide." Rubbing his hands across his chest and down over his belly, I cringe. His laugh is slow and forced and just plain ew.

"I've been staying with Reggie and Dee the last couple of days. I go home today when Reggie gets here, which should be anytime." I don't know what time Reggie will be home, but he did promise to take me back to my apartment when Ray shows his face again. He's been getting home around four, but I have no idea what today will bring. My only hope is Judson arriving on time.

I step away from him and begin to walk away when there's a knock at the door. Thank God Judson is here! A sigh of relief slips out as Ray grabs his duffel and scurries off to his room. He could have body parts in that thing for all I know. I open the door and usher Judson inside. Oddly enough, Dex and Quinn are with him and both are in uniform.

"Um...hey everyone. Come in. Reggie's roommate got home a few minutes ago. I should be going back to my place in a little while so it's a good thing you got here now."

Judson's the first to speak and his eyes narrow. "I thought you said his roommate was out of town for a few days."

"It has been a few days. He came back a few minutes ago."

I motion to the couch for them to sit and I rest on the edge of the recliner. Leaning back hurts so I'm avoiding it. Just as Judson opens his mouth to say something, Ray comes out of the bedroom. The strangest expression moves across Judson's features about a half second before he jumps to his feet. "What the fuck are you doing here?"

What did I miss? Does he know Ray?

Ray replies, "This is my apartment, motherfucker! You don't like it, get the fuck out. What are the police doing in my place anyway? Get the hell out!"

Dex jumps between the two as Quinn grabs on to Judson's arms, doing her best to tug him backwards as he approaches Ray. I get up from the seat faster than my body is happy with and flinch. No one notices because the tension is thick in the room.

"How do you know Ray, Judson?" I ask, because no one that knows Ray likes him, but I can't figure out how Judson would possibly know him.

"That asshole's a drug dealer. I'm in recovery, but I bought a bunch of pills off him that almost killed me a couple of years ago."

He turns to me, furious. "Get your shit. You're not staying here with this degenerate, drug-dealing dickhead."

"What're you talking about? He's a sleazeball...but drug dealer?" I never thought he was smart enough to deal drugs. I didn't think he could count, much less add up money.

"Yes! Now get your shit!" Judson has been nothing but laid back and kind since we met, seeing him pissed is a little scary.

"This is my home and I told you to leave so get the fuck out!" Ray yells, pissing Judson off further as is evident when he pushes against Dex again, ready to go after Ray.

Dex turns to me and says, "Get your shit, Mari. You're out of here. I may not be able to arrest him, but I'm not leaving you here with this scumbag."

Quinn's glaring at Ray now and I think if the guys weren't already fired up she'd be on his ass.

"Okay, give me five minutes, but I need someone to help me carry it. It won't be heavy. I don't have much, but it still hurts to lift anything."

Dex nods once and tells Quinn, "Go with her. I need to make sure your husband doesn't get assault charges tonight."

Fifteen minutes later I'm in Judson's truck with Quinn and Dex following us in the squad car.

Judson finally asks, "What is Reggie like if that guy is his roommate?"

"Reggie's great. He and Ray were friends growing up and he says Ray did a lot for him when they were young so when he needed somewhere to stay, Reggie let him move in. Apparently, the idiot hit on Dee last week so Reggie's going to kick him out. Ray came home right before you guys got there."

"He's trouble. You need to stay away from him."

"Yeah, I know. I can't seem to stay away from trouble and I'm afraid that even if I'm locked in a prison yard alone, surrounded by barbed wire, trouble would still find me. That's the story of my life. I don't enjoy it, that's for sure." There's a long moment of uncomfortable silence before I get up the courage to ask, "You bought pills from him?"

Glancing at me he sighs. I'm guessing he didn't want me to know.

"You don't have to answer," I tell him as I shift my focus to the city landscape moving past my window. I take note of the few trees that have started the autumn color change and wonder briefly how pretty the ranch will be once it's in full swing.

"I was coming over today to talk to you about everything. There was a time in my life not too long ago that I needed a second chance. I was in a bad place, but luckily a few people believed in me enough to give it to me. I want to pay it forward and give you another chance, but you've got to make some changes. I know the abduction wasn't your fault, but you put yourself in too many situations where shit can happen. Case in point, Ray the drug-dealing asshole. If you want to stay away from trouble you don't stay at the apartment of a guy like him."

"First of all, I avoid Ray at all costs. Reggie said he'd take me back to my apartment when Ray returned. I had nowhere else to go. As far as staying away from trouble, I'm not sure that's possible. I don't want to be in trouble or in questionable situations, they just happen. If you're basing your thoughts on giving me another chance on a big change in my life, you should probably put an ad in the paper to find my replacement now. Besides, I can barely shower by myself I hurt so bad. There's no way I can muck stalls or help with the horses for a little while longer."

Judson and I remain quiet for the next several minutes until he breaks the silence by telling me, "You know he cares about you, right?"

I look over at him, my eyebrow raising. Where did that come from? "I know you'd like to believe that about your friend, but I don't. He barely tolerates me when I'm around." I turn my head to look back out the window and am surprised when he continues to talk.

"You're not a stupid woman so I think if you open your eyes and pay attention you'll see what I'm talking about. Quinn said since they've been partners, they've run across a hundred or more women that need help and he's never gone this far with it."

"He probably feels some kind of obligation since he knew me from way back."

"Quinn said he arrested two girls from his foster care days the first year he was on the force here and never looked back. You're right for Dex, don't give up on him yet. He's a good guy and I think you have the key to open up a very closed man."

I open my mouth to say something, but am not sure what that would even be so I close it again until we arrive at my apartment. Once he's parked and out of the truck, he grabs my bag and follows me up the stairs. When we enter my apartment, I'm struck with how empty it is. I guess I keep expecting my belongings to show up or to realize the robbery was a bad dream. I still only have a mattress, some clothes and a few pots and pans I picked up from the thrift store. I'm going to go crazy without a television here and nowhere to sit. This ought to be fun.

Judson, Dex and Quinn file into the apartment behind me and Dex surprises me by dropping a string of cuss words in rapid succession before he says, "You cannot stay here, Mari."

"Yeah, I can. Not much choice considering Ray's back at Reggie's."

"Get your shit. You're coming to my apartment."

"No."

His eyes widen. He didn't expect defiance from me. If he's trying to embarrass me in front of other people, he's doing a good job. I'm not his child so he needs to quit talking to me like I am. "This is a jacked-up situation, I get that, but I can't do anything except live through it."

"Don't be proud, Mari. Just—"

"No way. I'm tired of being your charity project. I'm tired of being everyone's charity project!" I'm so angry at him and at the situation I've put myself in. I'm an emotional tornado, spinning out of control, ready to wipe everyone else out with me. I don't want to be alone but I don't want to stay at his apartment where I'm not wanted either. With a man like Dex, I don't want the handout. I want the real deal, the relationship with a man who wants to protect me because he loves me. Not a man who protects me and makes me his charity case because he pities me. I'm not like the family dog who'll be happy taking the leftovers from the big spread of food on a Thanksgiving table. What's strange is that I never had a problem taking the scraps of attention before, but I refuse to be that person any longer.

I don't want him to look at me like the victim I always seem to be and I'll avoid putting him in the position to do that, if I have another option. Lucky for me I have the option. It's not the best one, but it's still something. I can always have Dee call one of my random friends to come hang out. I need to get another phone, but I need to make rent first.

"So I have to ask, why did you guys come in a posse today? Judson could have come alone if you gave him the address."

Quinn answers this time. "We just wanted to check on you and update you on the case. They found the car you were taken in. It was stolen two weeks prior from a lot in downtown Denver. A traffic camera gave us a glimpse of dark hair but his head was turned. The guy abandoned it on the side of the road, not far from where you jumped from the car. The front was wiped clean but your prints are all over the backseat. Your phone was lodged between the seats. It's in evidence right now and it's possible you won't get it back. We have no idea who was driving the car. I'm sorry I don't have more."

My shoulders sag. I can't catch a break. "Whatever. It's the story of my life." I turn away toward the kitchen, not wanting to face any of them. In fact, I wish they'd leave. It's a rare moment for me to want to be alone, but they're killing me. I want to wallow in my self-pity while I wait for a friend to come over and entertain me. I'm pretty good about doing that and bouncing back, no matter what I get myself into. Thank goodness I'm resilient or my life would be pure hell.

"You can't stay here. Don't ask me to explain why but my gut says for you to stay away from here and you shouldn't go anywhere alone, it's not safe," Quinn implores.

"No offense but nothing in my life is safe, not since I was six years old. I've gotten used to living like this. You guys don't need to worry about me." I turn to face Judson. "I appreciate you wanting to give me another shot at working for you, but I don't think I can be what you want me to be, what you need me to be. I love working there but getting what I want is not what my life is about. Thank you for the opportunity. Now, you guys can get going. I'll have Dee call one of my friends to come hang with me for a little while. It'll be fine."

As soon as I finish my sentence, I realize I have no way to call Dee and I don't know if she'll come here at some point or go to Reggie's. I hate being without a phone.

Dex growls and moves past me into my room. *What the hell is he doing?* I follow him in there and find him staring at my almost barren closet.

"Where are your clothes?"

"All but that shirt are in my bag in the living room."

"You don't have any clothes?"

It's like he's trying to piss me off. "Damn it, Dex! You know all my stuff was stolen. I got the rest of this at Goodwill. I didn't want to spend a bunch of money on used stuff when I needed it for rent. It's no big deal. I've had a lot less at different times in my life."

He turns away from me and in an uncharacteristic move, smashes his fist into the drywall, leaving a huge hole. Startled, I jump back and flinch in pain. *What the hell?*

"Dex! I have to pay for repairs. I can't afford food, much less new drywall!" I cry.

"Get your stuff, Mari. You're not staying here. You can fight me if you want, but I'll drag your ass out of here despite the achy ribs. You're going with me."

"Why? It doesn't make any sense! You don't even like me, half the time you can't stomach looking at me. I don't understand why you won't leave me to deal with this alone."

"Mari, I can't leave you here. I can't do it. Don't ask me questions that I don't have answers to. Please just understand, I can't leave you here like this. Let's go."

The look on his face is one of steely determination and I know if I don't do as he says he'll probably drag me out of here. My palms itch with anger because I want to slap his face for being such a jerk. Why can't he let me deal with this on my own? I'm not his responsibility.

"I can't fight you, I'm in no shape for it. You win, but as soon as I can, I'm out of there. I need someone to call Dee and tell her what's going on so she doesn't freak if she comes looking for me." I stand by the door while the heat from my anger simmers on my skin. I refuse to make eye contact with them.

Quinn sighs and asks Judson, "Can you take her to Dex's apartment? We still have a half hour on shift."

BY THE TIME I GET SETTLED AT HIS PLACE, MY BODY IS WIPED out and my emotions are on overload. Does Dex not realize that even the minimal amount of care he's shown is like crack for a girl like me? I'm the girl who is starved for love and attention and will cling on to every ounce that's offered, even if it's far below the amount I deserve. I hate that about myself and have been working on it, but so far it seems to be a reaction I can't control. For the first time ever though, I can see it as it's happening and it makes me angry and sad, probably because he's made it clear what he thinks of me. When he shows up acting like he cares, I spiral down and ignore the warning in my head that this isn't real. The need for someone to care appears to be greater than self-preservation.

Sitting on the edge of the bed at Dex's apartment, I wonder what happened to the crazy but carefree life I was living a few weeks ago. It wasn't perfect but I was surviving. Sometimes it was even fun. I shake my head, annoyed that I'm trying to make sense of anything right now. I need sleep before I tackle this subject, but even as tired as I am, I still can't be alone in his spare bedroom bed so I curl up on the couch the best I can, take my pain pills and doze off, thankful Dex isn't home yet.

I'm not sure how much time has passed, but I hear the lock turn and the front door open. Dex steps inside, eyeing me warily. When he doesn't say anything neither do I, instead I close my eyes and pretend to return to rest. He doesn't have to know that his mere presence tilts my world on its axis.

The door to his room closes and I hear him moving around inside. Afterward he comes out dressed like he's going jogging. Quietly he slips out of the apartment and I'm left to wonder where he goes when he leaves like that.

Several hours later Dex returns. The apartment is quiet except for the soft hum of the fridge and the murmur of the television on low. I only have it on so I won't get freaked; there's nothing on worth watching. For me, part of hating to be alone is the fear of silence. When I was a kid, the extreme silence always preceded the seriously bad stuff. The counselor says eventually, if I keep fighting it and working through it, I'll be able to sit in a quiet room and relax, but with the horrors in my head I don't think that's possible.

Dex doesn't say a word to me, he just continues to his room. I wonder how long we can coexist without a word said between us.

I want to be mad at him for strong-arming me into coming here. I don't want to be his pet project, but I'm also thankful that he did. Alone in that empty apartment is not where I wanted to be. Not that I'll admit it, but after everything that's happened, my fear of being alone is bigger than ever. I don't want to think about all the reasons why, so I focus on the cheesy movie flickering in front of me.

Dex's door opens a little while later and his shadow appears in his doorway. He's wearing a white T-shirt that pulls tight across his shoulders and chest while red basketball shorts hang on his narrow hips. His feet are bare and I can only see one side of his face with the light from the television in the room. God, I love the rugged beauty of his face, even if I want to slap it at times.

"Can't sleep?" he asks, his deep voice low, but louder than the television.

"No. You know me. Nothing's changed." I try to sound unaffected as I shift my focus back to the television. I'm telling myself to ignore him but my dueling needs are having a battle. The weak side of me wants to beg him to let me sleep with him because too much has happened and I don't want to be alone. But I also don't want to be the needy girl anymore. Quinn and Judson are right; if I want my life to turn out differently, then I need to act differently and make different choices. My pride is winning this battle as I stay quiet and suffer in silence. Eventually, especially with the pain pills, I'll get tired enough to pass out.

With casual grace only a man like Dex can have, he saunters to the couch and holds out a hand to me. "Come on Mari, come lie with me. You need sleep to heal."

His tone is gentle, so much different than the one he used on me earlier this evening. "Come on, Mari, please don't be stubborn." The rumble of his voice is even lower than usual, triggering all the things that make women like me stupid around such masculine men, and the anger and irritation from earlier don't seem so important now. Without even trying, he's as effective as a snake charmer with a magic flute and I can feel my defenses lower.

I'm fighting a full-fledged battle in my mind because I want sleep and the feeling of safety he provides, but I also want to make changes in my life for the better. So far he's not proved to be the best choice for my future and I keep getting hurt, but losing the loneliness for a night, even at the expense of my new-found determination is what feels right.

Stepping even closer, he wiggles his fingers and says, "Come on. I won't be able to sleep if I know you're struggling. You can say you're not but I know you are."

He's right, even if I don't want him to be, so I stop fighting against it. I simply melt into his request and take his hand as he helps me up. My ribs scream in protest and I flinch.

"Take it easy, baby."

Baby? Why would he use a term of endearment with me? Doesn't he understand little things like that make keeping my emotional distance harder?

As he leads me into his room, my body temperature rises from the inside out, almost as if my mind connects the moments between his sheets with the mixed scent of his skin and cologne that seems to linger in his room. My aching body and traitorous hormones hum to life with very little effort from him. My mind knows what kind of magic happens in here and wants to make sure I acknowledge it. Why isn't there an off switch for olfactory senses?

Dex slips his shorts off but leaves his shirt and boxer briefs on and climbs between the covers. I'm wearing a giant AC/DC T-shirt I found at the thrift store for 50 cents that fits like a dress on me, hiding the pink bikini panties underneath. I join him under the covers but don't touch him. That could be bad news. I may not affect him in any significant way but he sure as hell affects me. It's not even just the sexual attraction with him, it's the sense of safety that I haven't felt anywhere else that's an issue.

I lie quiet for a few minutes before I ask, "Do you remember those two nights you held me in the foster home?"

"Yeah, I'm surprised I didn't hurt you with my bony body." His chuckle shakes the bed a little. "Why?"

"I just wondered. I think about it sometimes," I confess.

"You do? Why? I figured you'd want to forget." I can hear the confusion in his voice.

"I try to forget the things that Freddy did. I'm not a fan of being helpless. But up until recently, those were the only times in my life I felt safe. It's a nice memory," I tell him quietly.

"In the arms of a scrawny adolescent boy?"

I'm quiet for a second. I shouldn't share these things but I can't seem to help myself.

"Yeah, I'd never had anyone hold me with tenderness before, at least not that I could remember. I'd go through that night with Freddy a hundred times over just to have you hold me like that again. It made it worth it. I know that sounds sad but when you've lived my life, it makes sense. I'm comfortable when I sleep with Dee but that's different. With her I'm still a little on edge. So, thanks."

He says nothing. In fact, it's so quiet I can't even hear him breathe. It's kind of freaky and I almost want to go back to the living room and turn the volume on the TV back up. I've probably made him uncomfortable with my random confession. I need to learn to keep my mouth shut. "Dex, I'm sorry you found me in the parking lot that night with Gino. Once I heal, I'll be out of your hair and I'll find a way to stay out of it. I know you never asked to be my babysitter and even as embarrassed and mad at myself as I am about it, I'm also thankful that you've been here to help me. I don't know what I would've done without you. I couldn't stay in that place with Ray tonight and my apartment freaks me out. I feel like someone is always watching me. So, thanks and I'm sorry."

The heavy silence in the room continues and the paranoia I

get with that kind of silence jumps up two notches. I'm preparing myself for fight or flight. It's definitely a learned response to the lack of sound and just when I think I can't stand it anymore, Dex rolls to his side and gently places his arm across my hip like he's not exactly sure where he can touch me.

My eyebrows draw together as the confusion sets in. Why is he touching me? He practically hates me.

"Mari, I don't know what to do with you. We're polar opposites. You never stop talking and I never start. My life is controlled and calm and quiet. I only have a few friends and try to keep a low profile. You're a whirlwind of unpredictability. You and I couldn't be more opposite if we tried."

"I'm trying to keep a low profile, but I suck at it."

"I've never met anyone worse at it than you. I don't think it's even possible for you, but as much as I fight it, I'm drawn to that." There is a pregnant pause before he continues, "Drawn to you. I have been since we were teenagers. I used to watch you like a lovesick puppy and wish I were bigger, faster and stronger so you'd notice me as something other than a friend. I knew it was against the rules in the house, but I would have done anything just to have your hand in mine. The nights I could hold you meant the world to me. Does that make sense?"

"Then why do you act like you hate me all the time? Sometimes you look at me like I'm the scum on your shoes and it hurts, Dex. Especially since I know you're capable of tenderness with someone like Leslie. I heard it in your voice."

I can feel his weight shift in the bed and his lips press against my temple. Automatically I turn a little, moving toward the tender gesture and he bends his head toward me and places his lips softly against mine. My fingers thread into his hair of their own accord and I hold him to me, opening a little, hoping he'll take the invitation. Thank God he does. His tongue slips inside and dances with mine softly, sweetly. My heart is pounding so hard I'm certain it can be heard echoing around the room.

"Mari," he whispers, the Spanish accent stronger, his voice a rumble. He nips at my lower lip then swipes it with his tongue to soothe the slight sting and covers my mouth with his again. This time his hunger is obvious, his desire more acute. He moves across my cheek and down my neck with soft kisses and my body demands a reaction so I arch my back, forgetting about the damage I've sustained until the stab of pain hits me. I whimper and flinch and Dex pulls away.

"I'm sorry, something about you being this close, sharing my bed with just a little bit of fabric between us, started this. I forgot."

I don't want him to stop, afraid I won't get this again. It's part of what I crave, the intimacy, the contact, the warmth. I don't want him to stop. "Dex." It's almost a plea but for what, I don't know.

"Don't call me that, Mari. To you I'm Jase. I don't want to be Dex with you. I want to be the teenage kid madly in love with the gorgeous girl down the hall."

"But we're not 16 and 17 years old and you're not in love with me."

"No, but I don't like the 28- and 29-year-old versions of us. Not together. I want you to look at me like you did the night you crawled into my bed when we were young. I want to be that guy for you."

"Then you have to treat me like that's what you really want. I may be a mess but I'm trying to take my life back and part of that is keeping anyone out of my life that doesn't put in the same effort as I do."

"I know."

Chapter Eleven
DEX

Did I say all those things to her out loud? Holy shit! What is it about this woman that makes me lose my mind? All she has to do is look at me with any number of expressions and I lose all the control I've spent so many years crafting. I want to hold her, kiss her, take care of her and touch her in ways that no man ever has. I want to trace all her tattoos with my tongue and suck on every single piercing. I want to thread my fingers through her thick, wild hair and hold her to me as I sink inside her.

Most of all I want to protect her both physically and emotionally. I don't want anyone to hurt her again and the thought of her jumping out of that car and rolling down the side of the hill in the dark freaks me the fuck out. When I drove past it the next day, I got out and looked at where the incident took place. I'm surprised she didn't break her back or neck or get impaled by a stick. Once I realized a bear or a mountain lion could have gotten ahold of her, I almost threw up.

Who knows what else is out there, not to mention the fucker who grabbed her. I haven't told her, but Quinn and I approached Detective Sharpe about the possibility that she's dealing with a hardcore stalker. We both believe that her abductor had everything to do with the burglary of her apartment. It was something she mentioned in her interview, something he said to her in the car, that tipped us off. Of course, we can't prove it, but Sharpe at least listened and said he'd look into similar cases and see what he could find.

Mari brings me out of the heavy thoughts plaguing me. "Dex, don't say that kind of stuff to me. I don't want to get attached if you're going to change your mind in a week, and that's what I know will happen. We're so different and I'm not the kind of girl that will conform and be a 'normal' person, no matter how badly you or anyone wants me to. It's also not likely, given my history, that chaos will stop following me. You won't be able to tolerate that. If all of that isn't reason enough, you said you don't want a family and that's pretty much the only thing I want."

"Jase. Call me Jase. Please."

"Please don't ignore what I'm saying," she pleads.

"I'm not ignoring you. I just don't agree. I think with some of the changes you're making, things will settle down in your life, and the more I think about it, I like that you're different than every other woman I've been with. Please let us try this. Not just you in my bed. I mean really try."

"Why? We're so different. If it's just for sex, I can't even do that right now." I can hear the hesitation in her voice. This is a time when I wish I was better with words.

"I can get sex anywhere, Mari. I only want it with you. I'm tired of trying to think about something else. I'm tired of trying to stay away from you, of worrying about you and wondering if you're safe all the time."

Softly her fingers graze through my hair. "Give it until morning. You may not feel the same when I'm not half naked in your bed. Right now, I think my vulnerability is like catnip for you. You're the kind of person who wants to handle things. You like the white knight role. Couple that with a half-naked woman in your bed and it's a recipe for morning-after regret."

I can wait until tomorrow to tell her these things again if it'll reassure her. "I understand what you're saying and I'll respect that. Get some sleep and we can talk in the morning before I leave for work."

Scooting a little closer and slipping my arm under her head, but being careful not to jostle her too much, I kiss her hair and rest my arm over her hip. That seems to be the only area on her torso that isn't hurting. Then I listen as her breathing evens out. It doesn't take long before she's sound asleep.

Why am I drawn to her? She's beautiful, sweet and funny, but her unpredictability drives me crazy. She's right, I need to take a step back and decide what I really want and not be clouded by my need to protect or the draw of her beautiful body. I, of all people, know the kind of life she's had and I need to be careful with her.

At 4:30 in the morning, my phone buzzes on the nightstand and wakes me. Marina sleeps through it. I shift away from her as gently as I can.

"Hello?"

"Dex. It's Charlie Perkins. Listen we got a report of a homeless guy named Marvin Stanger taking a beating. Officer on the scene says he's in bad shape but won't go to the hospital. Stanger mentioned your name. Any chance you can help us out? Blaine is on the scene and doesn't want to force the guy, especially if he really is a friend of yours, but says he's bad enough he should go to the ER."

"Damn. Yeah, I know him. Where is he?"

"They said to tell you he's in his usual spot."

"Tell your guy I'll be there in 10 minutes."

I dress quickly and drive the truck over to where I know Marv stays. Sure enough, there are two squad cars, both with their lights on, blocking the alley. Both officers are hovering over someone against the wall on the ground. I jog over to the officers, one of whom I recognize as they turn toward me.

"Marv, what's going on?" The closer I get the more apparent his injuries become. One eye is swollen almost shut. There's blood all over his face, down his neck, and on the collar of his coat.

"I'm only talking to you. Tell these assholes to back off!"

"Hey guys, give me a few minutes, okay?" They nod and mumble as they wander back to stand by the closest squad car.

I put my back to the wall and slide down next to him like always. "What the hell happened?"

"Some guy was here asking questions about you. He was a weird dude. I wasn't too worried about him because he was a wimpy looking fucker, a video game or computer-type kid."

"Kid? He was young? I ask because I can't understand why someone would be looking for information on me, much less a kid."

"Young enough to be my son, but not yours. Twenties maybe? I told him to fuck off. I thought he got the picture that I wasn't talking, until he showed back up with a huge stick. Caught me totally off guard. He was gettin' the best of me until I snatched the stick from him and got in a few licks. He hauled ass then. Who'd you piss off, man?"

"Why was this guy asking you questions?"

"No fuckin' clue but you owe me a steak after this."

"I'm not buying you a damn steak unless you let someone look you over and stitch you up. You know you need a few of those, right?"

"Fuck you. Besides, I don't have insurance."

"Screw the insurance. I know a guy. Come on. Otherwise the cops will force you and I don't want them to put you on a psych hold for 72 hours. You might be an asshole but you're not totally crazy."

"Fuck off Dex. But you're right; I don't want to get locked up. You know someone?"

"Yeah, let me make a call."

By eight that morning he's been stitched up and looked over. I take him by my apartment so I can get my uniform. He has to fill out a report so I'm taking him to work with me. He's pissed as hell about it, but I figure this way I can guarantee he eats today and maybe we can figure out who the hell was asking questions about me.

When we get to the apartment, I stick my head in the door to warn Marina. She's sitting in the chair with one of my sweatshirts pulled over her giant T-shirt while eating a piece of toast.

"Mari, go put some pants on. We have company." Surprise flashes in her eyes for a split second before she hurries out of the room. Her ponytail swishes behind her as she retreats. With no makeup on her natural beauty startles me every time. When she strolls back in, her hair is down and brushed and she's wearing a pair of those tight-ass yoga pants designed to bring a man to his knees.

I move out of the way and finally let our guest in. "Marina, this is Marv."

Her smile is breathtaking as she steps forward to shake his hand. She doesn't even seem fazed that he's rough around the edges and smells like a garbage can. When she gets a look at his face she asks. "Oh my God! What happened to you?"

"Looks like the same thing that happened to you." He chuckles a little. She touches her face self-consciously before responding, "I doubt you became a stunt double and dove out of a car and rolled down a ridiculous hill in the dark." Her eyes twinkle.

How can either one of them make a joke about this stuff?

His laugh is hearty. "Nah, just a punching bag for some freaky kid."

She lifts an eyebrow. "Come in. I'll fix you some coffee. Dex, you want some?"

Why does it piss me off so bad when she calls me Dex? I lean down to whisper in her ear, "Jase, it's Jase to you." I pull back to stare at her to make a point.

"Fine. *Jase*, do you want some coffee?"

"Nah, I'll get it at the station. Put his in a travel mug. They're on the second shelf in that first set of cabinets. We need to go so he can give his statement and I have to get to work."

Marv grumbles as I close the door to my room and prepare for work.

Their laughter is loud considering they look like they had a cage match against each other. What in the hell do they find so funny? You'd think at a time like this they'd be more subdued.

"What are you two doing out here?" I mumble as I reach for a cup to get some water after joining them.

"Nothing really, sharing war stories about life on the street," Marv says. "Can't believe a pretty girl like her lived on the street." He smiles at her and winks, making her giggle.

"We need to get going, man." The thought of her living on the street pisses me off and I don't want either of them to sense the irritation in me in case they misconstrue it.

Marina doesn't say much to me but she's watching me cautiously and I'm not sure why. I thought we ironed some things out last night.

"Marina, can I see you in the bedroom for a second?"

She nods and follows me.

I close the door behind her, move in close and she cranes her neck back to look up at me. My arm slides around her tiny waist, turning her toward me as gently as I can. I kiss her forehead before I ask, "What's going on with you this morning? You're all fun and games with Marv and then tiptoeing around me like you're afraid I'll go off at any second."

Her green eyes assess me for a moment, seeming to take in everything about my face. *What's she thinking?*

"When I woke up to an empty apartment I thought you'd

hauled butt after our conversation last night." Shrugging, she glances away.

"Mari," I push the chunk of pink-streaked hair behind her ear so I can see her whole face. "The station called me in the middle of the night because Marv was hurt and gave them my name. You were sleeping soundly so I didn't want to wake you because I knew you wouldn't be able to go back to sleep if you knew you were alone. You need rest to heal. I knew I'd be back before work and figured I'd see you then."

"You realize being ditched is a serious fear I have? Right?"

"I knew you didn't like being alone, but I didn't get being left was part of that. I'm sorry; I didn't mean to upset you. I thought after our conversation last night you'd be okay."

"You mean the one where I told you to sleep on it and we'd talk today? Because when I woke up and you were gone, I figured it meant you changed your mind."

"Mari, we have a lot to talk about, but I have to go to work now. However, I didn't change my mind. I still want you." My lips brush against hers and her eyes stay closed like she's savoring the kiss as I pull away. "Tonight I want to take you to dinner so we can talk. I don't care where we go. Pick a place. I'll come home from work, shower and change, and then we'll eat and talk. Today, please rest, you need it. I have a house phone over in the corner on the end of the table, if you didn't notice it before; you can call whomever you want. I left my number on the counter, call if you need me. Don't open the door for anyone, please."

My day flies by. After Marv gives his statement and sits with a sketch artist for what was probably the longest hour of the poor artist's life, I take him back to his spot on the street. I agree to leave him there but only after an argument. I thought he should come to my place for a few days and take the time to recover. That didn't go over well.

When I arrive home, Mari is ready and lying on the couch. As she stands to greet me, I cringe involuntarily. *What in the hell is she wearing?* A short jean skirt sits snug around her hips and is short enough that her ass cheeks are practically hanging out. A tight T-shirt that says Led Zeppelin and leaves nothing to the imagination covers her chest, and to top it all off she's wearing her combat boots. My question must be obvious because she makes a face and says, "This was the best I could do. I'm rolling around in Goodwill clothes these days, remember?"

"Mari. Grown women don't dress like concert-going teenagers."

Her switch flips from sad to angry in half a heartbeat and she props her hands on her hips. "Dex, you're such an asshole sometimes. If you don't like me being me why are we even having this dinner together? Sure, if I had my clothes from before the break-in I could look a little better, but this is me, big guy. You'll never see me in some conservative sweater set from an uptown boutique. It's not my thing. I guess while you're in the shower you need to decide if you want me or the person you wish I was. I'll be here when you decide." She stomps back to the couch and lies back down.

I should be pissed at the attitude she threw at me for being honest, but instead I feel bad. I didn't mean it the way it came out. I don't really care what she wears as long as all of her important parts are covered. Although I love to look at the body beneath the clothes, I don't want to share that view with anyone else. If she bends over in that skirt, everyone will get a view they won't forget. She's also correct in her thought process. From what I've seen of her prior to this, even before her stuff was stolen, she walks on the wild side when it comes to how she looks. I either need to accept that or walk away now because there is no way she's going to change.

Even though I'm irritated at the whole confrontation, I like this side of her personality. I've always been attracted to strong women and this is the first glimpse I've gotten of that side of her. The rest of the time it seems she lets people push her around and drag her into things she may not want but doesn't back away from either.

The question I need to answer for myself is, can I be her man and take her as she is? Beautiful doesn't begin to cover the description of Marina. From her appearance, you'd think she's a wild child. She's not into drinking, drugs and partying, but she is into self-expression so I think artistic is the better term. Marina is exotic, beautiful and unique. Can I handle a woman like that? It's never been a certainty that I can handle a woman at all. My need for solitary moments has always suggested I'll do better with short-term situations and lack of attachment. I've never found a woman who would willingly give me the space I need to find peace. Evidence suggests that Mari wouldn't be capable of giving me the space and definitely not the quiet. The woman can talk.

Draping my towel over the rack, I turn and face the mirror. My eyes zero in on the first tat I ever got. Stu hounded me for weeks until I agreed. He had several by that time, but my first one was across the upper portion of my chest. It was original artwork Stu created while we were deployed the first time and it hurt like a bitch. There wasn't anything at that point in my life that held any meaning so I decided to use his design. Over the years I've added to it with more on my chest and all over my arms. However, it's all stuff that stays hidden from the public eye unless my shirt comes off, which it never does because of the burns. From this angle, I can't see them. They mar my back with twisted, ugly skin that appears rough but feels more like leather than anything. I don't look at them often but I know they are there, my constant reminder of how I lost Stu. God, I miss him.

It's funny that I stand here thinking of Stu since he's the one who used to ride me like a freaking bus about finding a woman and settling down. He wanted that for me. The other married guys in my company always had a million questions about what it was like getting strange pussy all the time. They were fascinated since they'd all been getting the same for years. But not Stu, he always told me that a good woman, a loyal woman, would be worth coming home to, worth sinking my dick into the same pussy every night, worth every fight and every tear, every smile and every penny.

I always thought he was crazy, until recently when I started to think about Mari every second of every day. It's totally messed up that I yearn at times to hear her loud-ass laugh or see that damn nose piercing sparkle when she smiles in the right light. And let's not even mention the overwhelming need I have to protect her. I've never felt anything stronger in my life. We're so different though. I hide my differences from the world while all of hers are on display. Some of it though is what turns me on to her. I guess it's time to clarify a few things with her.

When I slip into the driver's seat of my car, I turn to her and ask, "Where are we going?"

She glances back from looking out the window and says, "I'd just like a pizza. There's a place at the mall that serves it by the slice. Angling her head to look back out the window, she returns to her quiet state and I sit, confused.

"Why the hell would we eat pizza by the slice at the mall?"

"I'm obviously not dressed to go out anywhere else. I'm okay with that. If it's not what you want, I can order a pizza there and you can go grab something else."

My chest squeezes tight as I register the quiet, dead tone of her voice. It's so unlike her.

"Mari. We aren't going to the damn mall."

"Dex...never mind. I'll see you when you come home." Before I can respond, her door is open and she's out of the car, closing the door quicker than I can even yell her name. *What the hell!*

Jumping out of the car I follow her. It only takes me a few

steps to reach her since she still isn't moving comfortably yet and my legs are so much longer than hers. I grip her shoulder to get her attention, knowing I can't grab her and pin her against a wall like I want to.

"What?" she yells as she spins back around, and as soon as I see her eyes, I understand the hurt she's feeling and I'm gutted because I know it's my fault.

"Mari, why are you going back inside?" I'm finally thankful she can't keep quiet or keep a thought to herself.

"I feel like driving somewhere for dinner with you is like walking to the executioner willingly. The way you looked at me when you saw me tonight tells me all I need to know. I don't need to go to dinner to have you tell me you know it's not going to work. I knew that already, though I'm dumb enough to keep coming back for more. But damn it, Dex! Stop putting me in a position to make the wrong choice. It's not fair to me. I'll always fall for the sweet that comes in the dead of night when you don't have to see who you're screwing. I'll always be wild and unconventional and you'll always be straight-laced and controlled."

"Mari, that's not what's going on."

"Yeah, it is. You don't want to admit it because you know I need saving, which is your forte. You're also lonely for some female attention and I'm right under your nose, but it's not *me* you want. Not even close. I never want my man to look at me like I'm the dirt on his shoe when I spent time tricking myself out to spend an evening with him. If you don't look at me like I'm the most beautiful thing you've ever seen and feel it deep in your bones then I'm not the one for you."

"Mari—"

Holding up a hand to stop me, she continues, "Different choices. That's what everyone keeps saying to me. I'm listening but it's more than that for me. I want so much more for *you*. I want you to have everything you deserve. I *know* where you came from, what and whom you came from and I want a better life for you. I want you to have the whole package. You deserve to have the most beautiful woman in the room, the one you don't have to re-dress before you leave the house. Just leave it alone, Dex. Get something to eat without me and leave it alone."

She doesn't give me a chance to talk, she turns on her heel to walk away and anger explodes like fireworks in my head. "Mari!" I yell and the echo is so loud as it bounces off the apartment buildings that surround us, that she pauses and turns to me with wide eyes. Stomping up to her, I lean down and smash my mouth to hers as my right hand snakes behind her neck to hold her where I need her to be. I can't grab anything else for fear of hitting bruises. I want her attention but I don't want to hurt her.

"Mari," I gasp, pulling away. "Shut up for once. Stop the mother-fucking chatter and let me talk!" Her eyes flutter open and she studies me, wide-eyed and quiet. "Mari, you're the most beautiful woman I've ever seen. I knew it when we were teenagers and I knew it when I saw you in the parking lot on your knees. My point about the teenager clothes—about your look in general—is that you don't need to hide behind the layers of makeup, the piercings, the crazy-colored hair. You don't need to wear clothes that barely fit or look like they belong on a teenager because you are a gorgeous, grown woman. If you'd let yourself really be you, you're perfect. Do I love the tattoos and piercings? Some of them I do. Do I love the makeup? No, but not because it's ugly. Because it covers up *you*."

I stroke my finger along her jaw and continue, "Most of the women I've seen over the years needed to put on layers of makeup because what I woke up with in the morning wasn't as pretty. That's not true with you. I want the Mari that's buried, the one you hide with constant talk and layers of stuff. Can I live with you in a short skirt and combat boots? Yes, if it's the only way I get to have you. But the first man that looks at your ass practically hanging out the bottom of one of your skirts is likely to get a beatdown. I don't want date night with my woman to end in a fight. I want you to save some of those things for my eyes only."

"But you said—" she begins to protest and I kiss her again, this time threading my fingers into both sides of her hair and holding her to me as I slip my tongue inside her mouth and tease her with it. God, I love the way she kisses.

When I feel her relax I pull away. "I'm shit at relationships because I've never really had any. I've avoided them my whole adult life. Too messy, too many emotions and I'm terrible about anything being out of alignment, especially life. I'm an orderly guy and love never is. My communication skills suck and sometimes I say shit that comes out wrong. Marina, give me a chance. Please. Go to dinner with me, let's talk and try to figure out how to make this work. I want to be with you because you're you, not because you're right under my nose." I kiss her forehead and her nose and her lips softly one last time. "Please?"

Chapter Twelve
MARINA

Oh. My. God! Did he really say all of that? I'm probably being an idiot by going. In my gut I know this is a bad idea, but strong stoic Jase has laid it out for me in such a beautiful way that I can't ignore it. Nodding, I meet his penetrating gaze. "Yeah, Jase, I'll go." When I use the name Jase instead of Dex his eyes close and his lips meet mine again, so much softer and sweeter than before.

When he breaks contact, I step into him and wrap my arms around him, holding him as tight as my sore body will allow. He smells and feels so good, different than the boy from all those years ago, but somehow the same. "Take me to dinner, I'm hungry." The man rarely smiles but when he does—dear God help us all!

At a little mom-and-pop Italian restaurant not far from his place, we sit in a small booth towards the back. The murmur of conversation fills the quiet air around us and the scent of garlic and olive oil has my stomach rumbling. Candlelight from the votive on the table dances along the features of his face.

When his expression shifts from relaxed and content back to serious, I pick at the rolled silverware in front of me.

"Mari, I was serious when I said I want to be with you. You protest about being able to change but I know that if you said no to some things you wouldn't end up in half the predicaments you do. I'm not asking you to change who you are but I need you to think hard before you make decisions. What you do will reflect on me. If you ended up on your knees in a parking lot and we were dating, that wouldn't go well for either one of us."

"I get what you're saying, Jase, and I'll do my best. You just can't expect miracles because, seriously, there are some things I can't control, like the kidnapping and the stolen stuff."

"All I ask is that you try to limit the things that you know could lead to a poor outcome."

The rest of dinner we have lighter conversation and as he opens up and talks a little more, I can't help but watch his lips move and think about how nice they feel against my own. His touch is tender as he holds my hand across the table and strokes his thumb over my knuckles. Although I'm excited about the possibility of us, I'm equally terrified of this not working.

Jase pays the bill and I smile as he helps me to my feet by taking my hand. When we get back to his place, after we take off our shoes and socks, he guides us straight to his room. Pausing us beside the bed, he pushes my hair over my ear, his eyes never leaving mine. "There are a million things I want to do to you tonight, but I don't want to hurt you and I probably would without meaning to. However, I still want to feel you against me so my plan is to peel these clothes off and hold you skin to skin while we sleep."

Have I ever been with a man who just wanted to lie skin to skin with me? Not that I know of. I nod and grip the snap on my skirt, intending to remove it, when his hand covers mine. "Let me. Do you need to take off your makeup or take your medicine?"

My hands fall to my sides. "Both actually. I'm backing down on the painkillers, but I need one to sleep, otherwise everything aches and I can't relax."

"Okay, do what you need to do, but don't take off your clothes. I want to do that."

After removing my makeup and earrings, I step back into his bedroom and find him wearing only his jeans while seated on the edge of the bed. The lines and sections of muscle all over his body are sexy as hell. Add the ink and he's flat-out flammable. Most of the guys I've been with are thinner and more wiry-looking, so it's a visual treat to see him like this.

"Come here, baby," he says, holding out his hand. When I get close enough, he places both hands on my hips and pulls me in closer between his legs. "I'm going to take off your shirt." My fingers grip the hem of my shirt out of habit and he gently brushes them away. "I want to do this."

Carefully he pulls it up over my head and tosses it to a chair in the corner. He continues by running a finger around the waistband of my skirt before he unbuttons and shuffles the tight fabric over my hips, allowing it to pool on the floor at my feet. His fingers hook in the sides of my G-string and he tugs until it drops to the same place as my skirt. As he lifts his head he places soft kisses along my ribs where the worst of my bruises are.

My heart aches at his tenderness. I've never had someone be this gentle or delicate with me. My life is a series of abrasive moments and people, so this is more than special. I know my skin is hideous to look at with the black, blue and purple coloring, but he acts like it's nothing.

"Carefully crawl up on the bed and lie down." I do as I'm told, allowing my head to rest on the pillow and my eyes to locate his. He makes quick work of his jeans and shoves his boxers down with them. When he stands up, his cock juts proudly in front of him, hard and huge. "You're killing me, Marina; I want you so bad it hurts." When he prowls toward me, I wonder if he's going to go for it and I almost welcome it. Screw the pain I'll certainly feel, as long as I get the pleasure served along with it as he buries himself inside me again.

Moving in closer, his tongue sneaks out to swipe at my hardened nipple and I shudder slightly. The bed dips near my shoulder as he settles in next to me, the length of his body pressed to mine while his head is propped up in his hand so he can look at me. Those aquamarine eyes burn right through me, melting me into a sexual puddle of goo. I tickle my fingers up into his short hair, raking my nails along his scalp gently. As he relaxes into my touch, he begins tracing the patterns of my tattoos with his pointer finger and it's both sexy and soothing.

"What's this?" he asks quietly.

His finger moves along my hipbone so I answer without looking down, "It's the symbol of hope."

"Why hope?"

"Because at times, that's all I had. I've never had money. Sometimes I didn't have friends. Never had love. But I've always had hope that there would be a better day."

"God, Mari. You gut me with that shit."

"It's the truth."

His perusal of my tattoos continues. Swirl, stop, swirl, stop, long twist, swirl, stop. This time the motion is under my right breast.

I don't wait for him to ask. "The dragonfly, besides being beautiful, is symbolic of a couple of things. The Native Americans believed that when they showed up, your dreams would come true. The Japanese believe they're a symbol of happiness, strength and courage. Who wouldn't want all of that loveliness with them everywhere they go?"

"The poppies?" he asks as the pad of his finger swipes at the cluster of brilliant red poppies I know covers my left hip bone. Another twofold answer.

"Official flower of August, which is my birth month. Mostly it's in remembrance of my sister. If you look closely at the stem of the middle one, you'll see her name, Rosie. She hated the name

Rosanna, so I called her Rosie. She hated roses but loved poppies so it's kind of an inside joke between us."

My chest pulls tight when I think about Rosie. "I've always wondered what happened to her. Rumor has it my stepdad sold her to some Mexican drug lord. We were so close that it never made sense that she would leave of her own accord without telling me. I don't doubt that my stepdad was capable of doing such a thing after the way he used me. Of course, my mom always told me Rosie ran away because she was ungrateful, but I never believed it. You'll never convince me that she left me without a word to run away.

"For a long time after I aged out of the system, I looked for her around town, certain she would walk past me on the street one day. Then I swore I'd save a bunch of money to hire someone to find her for me but I can barely feed myself half the time. Whatever the case may be, I refuse to forget her, even if she did run away. She was the only bright spot in my childhood after Papa died."

"How old were you when she disappeared?" His voice is quiet as he moves on to the next tattoo.

"Twelve. She was 14. We shared a room, sometimes a bed, depending on how crazy things were at our house. Too many times my stepdad's friends would try to come into our room during parties, so we would block the door with our dresser and sleep in the same bed together. A twin bed is hard to share but when I didn't have her to share with me anymore, it seemed too big for me alone."

Matching the speed of a snail, he drags his finger over the curve of my breast, circles the nipple, tweaks it once sending a zing of pleasure straight to my clit, and continues his trail up near my shoulder to trace the cluster of little blue butterflies up there. My legs rub together restlessly and I squirm enough for him to notice.

"Mari, hold still." His voice is stern while his eyes are uncharacteristically playful. I melt into the mattress at his expression. Playful is not a word anyone would ever use to describe Jase, so the rare glimpse of it coming from him is swoon worthy.

"It's hard when you're touching me, especially so sweet. I haven't had much of that."

Instead of answering with words he slips his hand down over my unbruised hip and leans forward, placing his lips softly over mine. When his tongue slips inside, a happy sigh escapes. Jase doesn't just kiss me. No, he makes love to my mouth, never moving his hand from my hip, never going for more. I didn't know kisses could be like this. I never want it to end so when he finally pulls away my eyes flutter open and I'm sure I'm wearing a ridiculously dreamy grin.

"My darling Mari. Never been much for kissing but I could do that all night long with you. The only problem is my body has different ideas and it's getting painful."

"We can—" He stops my words with his fingers to my lips.

"Don't say it. I won't be like every man you've ever known. I won't take you for my own gratification when I know it'll hurt you."

"But—"

He shakes his head as he says, "Nothing you say is going to change my mind. We'll have to wait until you're healed up. I'm a grown-ass man and can take care of business if I need to."

"Maybe I should put on some clothes then."

"Don't even think about it. I've waited years to have Marina Rossi in my bed like this and I refuse to give up the full experience."

Two weeks have passed since I started staying with Jase again and we've formed a routine without me realizing it until this afternoon. I cook us dinner every night and have it ready when he comes home. Then we eat, he does the dishes, we watch a couple of hours of TV and then go to bed. Every night he strips me down, removing one article of clothing at a time like he's savoring the vision. One night when I tried to do it myself while he was in the shower, he gave me an earful, so now I let him do it. Once I'm naked he spends the rest of the time tracing my tattoos while I answer questions about my life. In the beginning, I tried to ask him questions about him but he always redirected the conversation back to me so I stopped trying.

By the beginning of the third week my rent is due so I use my new cell phone to message Amber, a friend from my old apartment complex, asking if she could take me to the bank and then to my landlord because he, of course, has not come into the 21st century and doesn't accept electronic payments. I would've gotten help from Dee or Reggie but both have to work overtime this week and are unavailable.

Amber and I met while doing laundry in the basement of our old apartment building. She came in one night while I was standing on a washing machine avoiding a huge rat that was running around. She laughed for several minutes before she finally scared the thing away with a broom. Wild, full throttle, funny and a little bit of trouble is the best way to describe her. I also know she only works weekends at Stilettos for Studs, the local strip joint, so I knew she'd at least be off of work and able to help.

Now that I'm mostly healed I'm placing a few things on my agenda. First, I'm getting in touch with Judson. Quinn came over last week and said that they want me back out there to work when I'm healed. Surprised isn't even a term that covers how I felt about that. I'm sure it's because Jase and I are together but whatever the reason, I don't care, I'm happy. I love that job and didn't want to give it up. Second, I'm going to seduce my man. I've had enough of sweet time. I need a little rough and a lot of naughty. But more than anything, I need that physical connection with Jase.

He may have the patience of a saint but I don't. I'm healed enough that I can get down to business so I hope he's ready for what's coming tonight. I'm pulling out all the stops. I love his hands all over me, love the way he looks at me when we're lying there talking, but I'm ready for his heat and his passion. Those things have been locked up too long.

Dinner is ready and waiting on the stove. I have a light layer of makeup on and have curled my hair to lie in soft waves over my shoulders. Dee freshened up the streaks in my hair last week when I was lonely and bored. Now mixed in with my natural brown are fresh, shiny streaks of violet, pink and turquoise, exactly the way I like them. I avoided the teasing comb and hairspray, praying it would hold up without that stuff. I'd love to have some sexy lingerie to wear as I greet him tonight but that stuff costs more than I can afford so I went with the next best thing...nothing. I borrowed a pair of sexy red stilettos from Amber and that's the extent of what I'm wearing. The belly button and nose rings don't count.

My plan is to be seated with my heels kicked up on the dining room table, ready for him when he walks through the door. He foils that plan when he shows up 10 minutes early. I'm bent over the bathroom sink wearing nothing but the heels as I swipe the scarlet lipstick on my lips. I'm rolling them together to even out the color when Jase leans against the doorjamb scaring the crap out of me. The lipstick falls from my hand, marks the bathroom counter and drops into the sink, but I'm too busy trying to steady my heart rate to worry about it.

"Mari." His voice is lower than usual as his eyes travel the length of me. His predatory perusal reminds me of the Big Bad Wolf and I shiver at the intention I see there.

"Going somewhere?" His eyes flick to my shoes and back as he asks.

"No. I wore them for you. I thought they looked sexier than bare feet." I hope I gauged this right and this is something he'll find sexy. He takes two large steps inside and the bulge in the front of his pants comes into view. A low moan slips from between my lips as he grazes the backs of his fingers from my chest down over the tips of my breasts until they rest on my hips. I'm finding it hard to breathe since he moved in close, the desire clear in his eyes. He pulls me against him, his lips press to mine. "You still have a few light bruises. I don't want to hurt you, but damn, you look amazing."

"Jase, you've been so gentle with me and I appreciate it, but I'm ready. I need it, need you. Please Jase. If it hurts, I'll stop you." He thinks it over for what seems like forever, building my need further with anticipation before he gives in and kisses me hard. Gripping my ass cheeks, he tugs me all the way flush against him. The kiss goes from a little heated to a full-blown inferno in seconds as I reach for his pants. I fumble with the belt so badly that he finally breaks the kiss to quickly strip to his boxer briefs, leaving his uniform in a pile by the door. The head of his cock is teasing me as it peeks out from the waistband and I lick my lips as I lower in front of him.

Just to tease him a little, I nuzzle him over his briefs and he groans bracing himself against the wall. When I finally free his cock and wrap one hand around the shaft, I place the other on his thigh for balance and find his thigh muscles bunched so tight they're rock-hard. I tease the underside of the head a little with a twist and twirl of my tongue before I swallow him down one inch at a time with each bob of my head, savoring him as I go. Jase gets impatient and punches his hips forward, gagging me. My eyes water a little as I pull back to look up at him.

"I'm sorry honey, it just feels so damn good."

I smile around him and go back to work, moving a little faster with my hand, pumping him as I go. My other hand slips between his legs to fondle the soft skin of his sac and I feel his muscles quiver a little when I give it a gentle squeeze. I let go with the other hand and slide it around to hold his ass as I take him all the way to the back of my throat and hold.

"Mari, fuck!" I thought the Spanish accent he uses with my name was heavy before. That was nothing. I've never heard it like this. I'm rewarded further when a string of Spanish words spill from his lips, none of which I understand. I glance up, my mouth full of his cock and find him biting his lower lip, eyes so heavily hooded they're almost closed and I'm so turned on I can probably come without him ever touching me. I slide down one last time before he loses patience and grips me under the arms, lifting me back to a standing position. His kiss is hard and fast before spinning me to face the mirror. He flattens his palm on my back and pushes me down so my chest almost touches the counter.

I can feel his length settle between my ass cheeks as he takes a deep breath. "Mari, do you trust me?"

"Yes, Jase, why?" I answer, breathless and ready.

"Because I don't have a condom and I'm ready to fuck you without one." I swear my clit swells further knowing there's going to be nothing between us and I slip my hand down between my legs to provide some relief as I tell him, "Yes, yes, yes, just fuck me."

Moving back a little, he guides himself to my entrance while I work my clit with eager fingers. I'm so close. The slightest thing is likely to send me over the edge and I need it so bad. Weeks of waiting, smelling his warm skin next to mine, feeling his gentle fingers trace my tattoos. The slow build-up has finally reached a crescendo and I'm so ready. Thank goodness he doesn't waste a second. He powers forward and after three amazing, breath-stealing strokes, I'm pushed into that beautiful oblivion where everything is happiness and sunshine. My arms turn to jelly and instead of bracing me, they give out as Jase continues to power in and out of me at a punishing pace. Of course, to make it as unsexy as possible, I clunk my head on the mirror and the sound causes him to stop.

"I'm sorry," he says, out of breath.

I lock my elbows and push back against him. "Don't be. Keep going!"

He begins again, but it's a little slower this time and I know he's trying to calm it down so I rock back into him, making the impact harder. Our eyes meet in the mirror and my sex clenches tight as I take in the erotic sight in front of me. Pausing, he lifts my leg behind the knee and props it on the counter which opens me up and gives him a better angle. I whimper as he enters me, this time not holding back in the slightest. Each smack of our flesh, each groan from his lips drives me closer to a second orgasm. I'm so close, hovering in that intense pleasure that comes right before you climax. He readjusts my hips a little and between the firm grip he maintains on my hips, the new angle, and increased force, I come again, yelling his name, trigging him to follow me. His cock swells and explodes inside me, filling me like I've never been filled before and after a few strokes, he collapses against me as I rest my cheek on the cool countertop. Totally worth the wait and effort. God that was amazing.

Now that the excitement is fading, the position is becoming uncomfortable so I'm glad when he pulls out and reaches around me to grab a cloth to help me clean up. After that, he lifts me in his arms and takes me to his bed to continue what we started. A few hours later we eat dinner in bed and sleep tangled up like every other night, except now we're both sated.

Chapter Thirteen
MARINA

On Saturday morning, as we're getting ourselves ready to go out to the ranch, Jase's phone rings and instead of answering it when he glances at the caller ID, he steps out of the room. He hasn't done that at all since I've been staying here this time and something about it makes me nervous. I pull on my jeans and thread my belt through the loops. The depth of Jase's voice vibrates through the wall, but it's still impossible to hear what he's saying.

After a couple of minutes it gets quiet in the living room. I step in front of the mirror and use bobby pins to hold the hair back that I've carefully twisted into place. Once I'm satisfied with my reflection, I step out into the living room holding my boots in hand. Jase is seated but has his boots on already with an ankle crossed over his knee. The expression he wears is contemplative, but the vibe he's giving off is uncomfortable.

"Hey, you okay?" I ask.

Glancing at me like he forgot I was here, he says, "Yeah, yeah. I'm fine. You ready?"

The tiny grin that he's been wearing for the last couple weeks is gone and the Jase I first encountered is back. I'm not quite sure what to do or say but I know I'm not returning to grumpy, closed-off Jase. Not without a fight. I maneuver to stand in front of him, between the coffee table and where he's seated on the couch. "If something happened, you know you can talk—"

"Mari, I'm fine. Let it go," he snaps and stands abruptly to cut me off. Then he slips around me with minimal contact and strides to the door. I have no idea what to think of this crazy one-eighty he's done in the last 15 minutes. One thing I know for sure though is that he's stubborn and won't easily be moved in any direction except the one he wants to go so I clamp my lips shut and follow him out the door.

The flatter areas of town quickly turn into the foothills as we climb up near Daisy Rivers Ranch. Although Jase's mood has laid a huge stone on my chest, I can't help but smile as we climb up the long gravel driveway to their house. I love it out here. If I could name one place as my happy place—that had nothing to do with Jase's naked body or his bed—this would be it.

We pull up and Carlo bounds out of the house toward the truck. He adores Jase and I love to see the kid so happy. He surprises me as he bypasses Jase with a "Hey, Dex!" and runs right for me. He reaches me but then stops abruptly and his brows knit together. "Are you still hurt?"

"I'm much better." As soon as I flash him a reassuring smile, he throws his arms around my waist and holds tight. Tears spring to my eyes at the sweet gesture but I swallow hard and force them back. To have someone so excited to see me that they can't contain it is a salve for my soul. When you've gone through life like I have, not feeling loved, little things like that mean the world.

"I missed you," I tell him as I hold him close. He and I are kindred souls, I'm glad that he found a forever home and people who really love him. It's what I always wanted. As I glance up, I see Judson appear in the doorway with baby Lila. Quinn nudges him out of the way and approaches with a smile, and I greet them with a half wave. "Hey guys."

WE SPEND A FEW HOURS WITH THE HORSES AND KIDS, AND after I help Judson clean up the dinner mess, I go in search of Jase and Quinn. They're nowhere inside so I venture out to the porch. As I open the door I can hear their voices carry on the slight breeze. With a funny feeling in my gut, I approach more quietly than I normally would.

"So, Leslie's set a date for the wedding. I knew it had to be something big with how quiet you've been today. How did you respond when she told you?"

"I was quiet at first. I knew it was coming. Joe, her fiancé, said something to me while I was there, but I guess I didn't expect it this soon. I'm not ready for this."

"Are you sorry it's not you?"

My tummy does a somersault and I know without a doubt I don't want to hear the answer to the question. If he's already upset about her getting married, I don't want to hear what he has to say about the speedy nuptials. If I hear the answer I'll never be able to act like I didn't know what was said, so I call out to them. "Hey guys! You out here?"

Conversation between them halts instantly as Quinn answers, "Over here." I'm so glad I made my presence known. I can't even stomach the thought of hearing him say he wishes he were marrying her.

"Lila is going in for her bath and Carlo is watching *Star Wars* so I thought I'd see what you two are doing. Am I interrupting?"

With a quick glance at Jase, she says, "No, you're not interrupting. Come sit down."

The fake smile I've perfected over the years tips my lips. He scoots forward, preparing to get out of his chair, and asks, "You ready to go back to my place?"

I nod, not sure what to say. Leslie has been a niggling concern in the back of my mind since the first time he got a call from her. His sudden change in behavior at the revelation that she's getting married forces a physical ache in my chest I almost can't ignore. I don't want to be a place holder until another beautiful, traditional beauty comes along. Or a stand-in for the woman he really wishes he could have.

I promised myself that I'd make changes after this last fiasco. I wanted to make better choices so that my outcomes would be different but I totally ignored the warning bells with this one. I so badly want him to be "the one" that I looked past the obvious.

The truck radio plays a country song while we sit in silence on the way back to his apartment. I can't hear the words to the song over the screaming doubts in my mind though. I'm not sure what to do about any of this. The desire to have a boyfriend and a life that's no longer lonely is overwhelming, but the desire to have *him* be my man is practically all-consuming. When we enter the apartment, I walk toward the bedroom to change into my pajamas so we can watch TV like we've done every other night. After I've tugged the T-shirt over my head, Jase enters the room, sits on the edge of the bed and removes his boots. His silence is strangling me so I ask, "What do you want to watch tonight? I can go get it ready while you change." Without even looking up at me, he says, "I'm pretty tired; I think I'm going to turn in."

My heart sinks, weighing my chest down, but I've got to try. I'm not willing to accept defeat after only a few hours. Maybe being close to me in bed will help. Maybe when I'm naked next to him he'll have to remember that he wants me, that he's been happy with me the last few weeks. Damn, I hate how desperate I sound.

"Okay, well, I'm pretty tired too. I'll go turn the lights off in the living room, wash my face and then I'll join you." A grunt that sounds suspiciously like "whatever" comes from him while he continues undressing. I hurry out of the room to shut off the lights and do a quick face wash. I'm back to the bedroom to join him within minutes. Unlike every other night, he's curled on his side facing away from me. I yank my clothes off, slip in between the sheets and scoot in close with my best attempt to spoon his much larger body.

For the first time in forever he's wearing basketball shorts. That's a bad sign. I slip my arm around his waist and slide my hand down his abs, hoping to get his attention. As I reach the band of his shorts, his hand clamps down on my wrist.

"No, Marina. I'm tired. Maybe tomorrow."

Embarrassed, chastised, and now angry too, I roll away, climb out of bed and shuffle my T-shirt and sweatpants back on. I can't lie there in his bed feeling that level of rejection only a foot away. It's bad enough being stuck in the same apartment, but the same bed? I can't do it. I won't do it.

Huddled in the corner of the couch with my knees pulled up close, the TV flickers something I'm not even watching into the darkness and I think about where I'm at and how I got here. I think about when Jase gets over this and accepts that Leslie is getting married and becomes interested in me again. Sure, it's been less than 24 hours since all this happened, but in my quest for a different life I can't settle for second best. If that's who he really wanted, so much so that he can shut me out and shut me down then I would never really get what I wanted with him. Yes, I want a husband and children. But more importantly, I want a boyfriend first who loves me so much he can't see straight. So, when that same man who loves me like crazy asks to make me his forever, I'll know for sure I'm making the right decision. I won't have to worry if Leslie gets divorced or widowed again, or if someone more suited to his tastes rolls up, that I'll lose him. I want the security that comes with true love and forever.

As the night drones on and I can't sleep because I'm upset and out here alone, I decide that if he's still like this in the morning, then it's time for me to go back to the mattress on the floor of the crappy apartment I walked out of three weeks ago.

At five in the morning, he comes out in his running gear. I suspect it's to go talk to Marv but with the guise of running. His eyes narrow on me when he realizes I'm sitting there.

"You been awake all night?"

I nod, afraid that if I open my mouth either a sob or a list of cuss words will slip out, neither of which is appropriate this early in the morning.

"Marina, you know you'll never fully heal if you don't get rest."

The burning is back in my chest and the heat from my temper is bubbling to the surface. "I'm fine."

After studying me for a few seconds too long, he shrugs and proceeds out the door.

Screw this. He's obviously ready for me to go or is too closed off to deal with me being here. While he's gone I shower and pack the little bit of stuff I have into the bag I brought it in and place it beside the bed, out of view. I eat breakfast and go back to the couch. He has the swing shift this week so I know he'll be back soon to get ready for work.

After he showers, changes and leaves for work with little more than five words for me, I message Amber, asking her to take me back to my place. Dee works today and I don't want to wait for her to get off. I write Jase a note thanking him for his hospitality and leave it on the table. In it I promise to give his apartment key to Judson the following day when I start work again.

It shouldn't be so painful to walk away from someone who clearly loves someone else, but I'll be damned if it isn't. I think because things had been wonderful for weeks I should've realized, with my track record, it wouldn't last. I was so caught up in my own happiness that I let my worries and normal concerns slip under a rock somewhere. I enjoyed his routine and his closeness, his strength and his beauty, and had no interest in facing the fact that I may not be what he really wants.

When midnight rolls around and I have every light in the apartment on because a weird sound outside the door made me nervous, I'm starting to second guess my decision. Maybe I should have stayed with him and used him for his safe space, his TV and his full refrigerator a little bit longer. I'm hungry because the last quarter jar of peanut butter didn't quite cut it for a lunch/dinner combo without bread or jelly. Since the only other thing I have left in here is crackers, tomorrow should be interesting.

Despite my fear, I have to take a taxi to the ranch tomorrow and that has my anxiety level up too. I'm almost unable to breathe, thinking about the kidnapper from the last ride alone from the ranch. I still don't have a car though, so I have to suck it up and I need to get to my job so that come payday I can buy some groceries. Tomorrow night I may just have to drag my butt down to the local soup kitchen. It's only about five blocks north of here and although it's not great food, it's at least edible and usually warm.

At one o'clock in the morning, there's a knock on the door. Paralyzed with fear I sit on the mattress, afraid if I get up to check the peephole, the squeak in the floorboards will be too loud and alert someone to my presence. Another set of knocks echoes through the apartment.

When I still don't answer, I hear, "Mari, open up the door. I know you're here. I can see every light in the place on from street level. You're the only broke person I know who keeps all your lights on all night long. Open the damn door or I'll kick it in."

Damn it! Why is he even here? It makes no sense. I'm not in the mood to deal with him but I can't afford a new door so I stand

and make my way over there. When I open it I'm practically blown away by the waves of anger he's throwing off. Why the heck is he mad?

"What the hell, Mari?" he barks at me as he grips my shoulders and pushes his way inside. Shocked, I say nothing while he slams my door and locks it. I shake my head because I can't find the words to say anything quite yet. He's upset that his distraction is gone? I don't get it.

"Seriously, Mari! What the hell?"

"What do you want, Dex?"

I thought he couldn't get madder but when I use the name Dex, his nostrils flare and the muscles in his shoulders and neck flex. A pissed off bull in a pasture doesn't look crazier than he does right now.

"What do I want?" He steps closer so I have to bend my head back a little to see him. If this would have been a couple of months ago I'd be afraid of him. Now that I've been around him again I know he'd never physically hurt me.

"Yes. I can't figure out why you're here. I left you a note. I said I'd give your key to Judson. If you want it now I can go grab it. Just give me a second." I turn to walk away and he snatches me by the arm, pulling me back against him.

"You know what I mean. What are you thinking? You're not safe here."

Really? He's pissed because I came back to an apartment he doesn't think is safe? Please. Sometimes emotional health trumps physical safety. Right now is one of those times.

"I'm thinking I don't need to get my heart broken. I'd rather face a crazy man than another broken heart. Besides, no one is after me. Whatever that was before, it's over. There's been no sign of anyone all night. I'm fine. Go home, Dex. I don't need you in my face for no reason. I appreciate you taking care of me, but I'm back to normal and I go back to work tomorrow. It's all going to be fine."

"Damn it Mari! What the hell happened between Friday, when we talked about you driving my car to and from the ranch while staying at my place, and today?"

"Nothing. It was just time for me to go."

"Bullshit!"

"It's not bullshit Dex, it's the truth."

"Stop calling me Dex!"

"It's your name!" I yell at him. My chest is heaving I'm so damn mad at him. Why won't he go away?

His eyes search my face as he straightens himself up to his full height. He steps around me and heads for my room. "I'm done with the games. If you won't grab your stuff I will and then I'll drag your ass back to my place. Unless you want to fight me the whole way, you'd better lose the attitude and get moving."

Wow. He's freaking clueless. All he did with that little speech is piss me off more.

"Dex," I emphasize the name to piss him off. "I'm not going with you. You and Quinn and Judson and Dee want me to make better choices, so guess what? I *am*! I don't need or want you to take care of me. I've said it a million times, I'm not your charity case and I don't need you. So turn your ass around and march it back out my front door and don't come back!"

He steps even closer so that our torsos touch to piss me off more I'm certain. Anticipating my retreating step he grips my arms and holds me still. I'm so spitting mad I could claw his eyes out.

"What the hell is your problem? You were fine yesterday."

I'm so angry I can't control the words coming out of my mouth or my train of thought or my actions. I can only feel the red-hot anger pushing its way up from my gut.

"You're right. I was fine. I had no problems. It's *you* that had the problem and as soon as I figured out what it was, I knew I wasn't going to stick around anymore. You saved me. Your job is done. You helped heal my body, your job is done. I need nothing else from you so go the fuck away!"

"I'm not going anywhere until you explain yourself. None of what you said makes sense."

"Are you kidding me?" I screech. "Friday night we had sex and you wrapped yourself around me like a boa constrictor to go to sleep. Saturday morning you were all smiles and fun until your goddamn phone rang! Then you hid while you took the call and closed me out the rest of the day. No talking, no hand holding, no smiles, no nothing. When I was coming out to the porch to find you, I heard you tell Quinn you were upset that Leslie set the date for her wedding."

"If—"

My hand goes up to stop him. "Let me finish. You wanted to hear this, so listen good. I heard what you said to Quinn. As soon as I came around the corner you clammed back up again. Then you were silent all the way back to your place. At bedtime, for the first time in almost three weeks, you went to bed without me, completely clothed. When I tried to instigate things with you, I got shut down so fast my head spun. It didn't even faze you that I went to the couch. You slept like a baby while I sat out there all night coming to terms with the fact that I'm a placeholder, a time-passer while you wait for the one you really wanted to come after you. I'm not that woman anymore. I refuse to be, so let me go. Find someone else, I'm sure it won't be a problem!"

My whole body is shaking with anger and I can feel the tears building, but I refuse to shed them. He will not see my pain. Not again.

"God, you're maddening! Why didn't you say all that to me at my place?"

"I never intended to say it anywhere. I assumed we were done and I wouldn't have to say it at all."

His mouth crashes to mine before I can utter another word and I fight it at first but he forces his tongue inside my mouth and wraps his arms tight around me. I do my best to push him away but he keeps at me until he backs off just enough to nip my bottom lip with his teeth as he growls, "Stop it. Don't fight me," and seals his lips back over mine. This time the buzzing that starts in my core is so strong I can't ignore it and I open for him, meeting his tongue stroke for stroke. I've never had an angry kiss before. I've had angry sex, but never an angry kiss. My hands shove up inside his shirt and push until he breaks the kiss to rip it off over his head. Mouth back to mine, he shoves at my sweatpants until they're at mid-thigh. "Fuck, no panties!" he grunts as he grips the flesh of my ass.

I'm unable to comment back while his mouth continues to feed on mine. He breaks the kiss as he backs me into the wall and works his way down my neck. When he reaches my T-shirt, he yanks if off and tosses it aside.

"Mari," he whispers, his voice hoarse with desire.

I pinch my own nipples and pull, needing relief.

Quickly he spins and turns me to face the wall so my back is to his front, almost knocking me off balance. My hands move up level with my shoulders so I can brace myself against the drywall.

"Jase," I breathe. One of his hands runs over my ass cheek and he slaps it hard.

"Ow!" I squeak, half irritated and half turned on.

I can hear his belt buckle jingle as he loosens it and the jeans he's wearing slide down his thighs. Grabbing my hips, he yanks back so our bare flesh meets and his cock is hard against my ass crack. Less than a second later his hand disappears back behind me, lining us up and he shoves in hard and fast. The unexpected power behind the thrust has me flush against the wall. It's pleasure and pain all mixed up to create the sexy combination of passion and anger. He bends at the knees and hooks his hand behind my left thigh, lifting my leg. When he has me where he wants me, he begins a hard and fast rhythm and it's all I can do not to fall over.

My skin is hypersensitive and it's possible he's bruising me with his grip on my thigh as he works that angle, but I can't seem to care. My orgasm builds, starting at the tip of my toes and roaring through me at the speed of light, practically blowing me apart with the sheer force of it. Nothing I do at this point will stop it. I come, screaming his name at the top of my lungs as the leg holding me up buckles. He grips me tighter and pounds into me at an alarming rate until I feel him thrust hard one last time as he fills me. His body weight traps me against the wall and we stay like this for a couple of minutes, gathering our breath and our sanity.

Chapter Fourteen
MARINA

Slowly, all my senses return and the humiliation of being used floods my system. I realize I've just allowed myself to be fucked against a wall in the middle of an argument with a man who loves someone else. Not only allowed it, but begged for it, totally participated in it. Enjoyed it even. Shit!

I push against the wall and work to squirm free but he pushes harder, pinning me in place. His voice is softer now, "Mari."

"Please don't," I whisper.

"Mari, listen to me. If you don't like what I'm saying to you then I'll let you go, walk out the door and you won't see me again."

I don't reply because the ache in my chest is so strong after he says he won't see me again that I'm afraid to speak. No matter how mad or hurt I am I can't imagine not seeing him again.

"Leslie and Joe set a date to get married, you heard that part correctly. Yes, I'm upset but not for the reason you think. God, I hate talking about all this shit."

"Then don't. Just let me go and you can keep quiet the way you like it," I snottily reply.

He pulls back just enough to smack my bare ass and I yelp.

"Quiet and let me finish, woman." A tingle runs to my sex and I chastise myself for getting turned on again in the middle of a fight.

He continues, "Leslie is getting married. She'll no longer be Stuart's wife. His wife and kids will belong to another man. Stu spent so many hours talking about them I felt like they were my own. No one loves their wife and kids the way he did. I ache for him and all that he lost. He was the best friend I've ever had. When I'm in Colorado I can pretend that he's still alive in Florida with his family, enjoying the life he should've had. I don't have to think about reality unless I talk to them or see them. Now it's real, every day. Leslie's no longer going to be Mrs. Stuart Larkin."

"You don't have to face it until you see them again. Why are you freaking out now?" I ask sounding like a total bitch. I wiggle enough to turn around and face him.

"They're coming here. The kids are staying with me while they honeymoon. Les thinks it will help if they're distracted by a vacation. We talked as long as we did so we could set it up. My vacation time renews in a few weeks and I can take off to be with them. She needed to coordinate it with my schedule. I get to spend a week with my best friend's kids while he spends the week in the ground and his wife takes a new husband. Can you see how that fucks with my head?"

He leans back and runs his fingers through his inky black hair, giving an exasperated tug. "We were in the same explosion and he died while I walked away. Do you know how shitty that feels? He had so much more to live for than I did, but I'm here. I breathe while he can't, and the thought of watching his kids so his wife can spend a week with another man is more than I can deal with. My head is a fucking mess, Mari. You have no idea how much he loved them."

I step into him in an attempt to comfort him and I'm stunned silent when his first tear hits my shoulder. Jase has never cried in front of me and I doubt many others have seen it either. I hate when anyone cries, I can't stand for anyone to be sad, much less a man as strong as he is. The pain he must be feeling to allow a breakdown like this makes my heart hurt for him. I squeeze him tight around the middle while he cries quietly.

"I'm sorry. I was jealous of her. I've thought since the first time I saw your reaction to her call, you had a thing for her. When you went from really hot with me to freezer-cold, I thought you were sad you missed your chance. But to be fair, you locked me out and shut down. For a girl like me who has never gotten a single thing she wanted in life, it was easier to believe the worst in the absence of information."

He wipes his face with one hand while he's still wrapped around me, like he doesn't want me to see the tears I could feel falling. "Grab your stuff. You're coming back home."

"This is my home."

He leans back as his brows knit together. Then he makes a big production of looking all around the room and says, "This is no one's home. Come on. You belong in my bed, at my place." He tilts my jaw up in his large hand, never breaking eye contact and softly says, "I care about you, Mari, so much. Please, it's been a really long day and I don't want to sleep on a mattress on the floor but I won't leave you here."

The weight of all the emotion I've been carrying around for two days sits heavy on my shoulders. We've been through enough for one day so I quietly gather my stuff again and ride with him to his apartment. This time when we have sex he enters me slowly and takes his sweet time, showing me that I'm the one he wants.

LATER THAT WEEK WE'RE LYING IN BED WITH ME ON MY BELLY while he traces my tats again. For someone who doesn't like them very much, he seems fascinated, but this is the first time he's explored the few I have on my back. As he works his way up my shoulder, his nail drags slowly across my skin on his way to my neck. Softly his lips follow the trail until he brushes my hair all the way over my shoulder.

"More ink?" he asks, surprised.

"What?" I twist my head to find his eyes as he answers my question.

"I didn't see the ink on the back of your neck before. I take that back, I did see a little of it sticking out of your collar awhile back, but I haven't noticed it since then."

"How is that possible? You've seen me naked a hundred times it seems."

"I guess your hair was covering it."

As he begins tracing the newly discovered tat, his finger pauses and his voice comes out on a whisper, the accent strong, "Mari."

I wait for his reaction. This is the one tattoo that could potentially mean something to him. All mine mean something to me, but this, this is all him. I wasn't sure if he would recognize it or if it would matter when he did.

"My grandmother's locket. I didn't even think you remembered that old thing."

"Are you kidding? You gave me your grandmother's locket and I was afraid that something would happen to it with the way I live and it would be gone forever. This way at least I always have it with me. Turns out I made a good choice by doing that. I had it until all my stuff was stolen at the apartment. Other than the few pictures I have of my family, it's the one thing I've always protected. I was a little less devastated when I remembered I still had it on me, even if I didn't have it with me. I'm sure it sounds stupid, but I've never had anything that beautiful before and I was desperate to keep it a part of me."

He doesn't say a thing and I wonder if he thinks I'm an idiot for everything I just told him. Before I can open my mouth to ask, his lips find the ink. The heat of his breath on my sensitive skin makes me shiver. "Hold still," he commands so I do my best to follow his instructions. Warm strokes with his tongue test me as he traces the image. Damn, that's sexy as hell.

"I can't believe I didn't see it all this time. I'll never miss it again," he murmurs. He spends a long time with the tattoo before sliding his lips down to the base of my spine. His mouth brushes the dimples above my hipbones and I moan softly. He spreads my legs and lifts my hips so he can crawl between them. I do my best to angle so I can see what he's doing back there, but this isn't a good position to watch anything. The whole slow, sweet seduction of the last half hour has me dripping for him, so ready I'll probably come as soon as he touches me. It would be embarrassing if it wasn't so amazing.

He holds me captivated as he runs his fingertips from my ankles over my calves, up the backs of my thighs, over the cheeks of my ass, across the plane of my back until both hands meet at the locket tattoo. It's all I can do not to beg him to make love to me now. But I know he's taking his time to worship my body and his new discovery is all part of it. He's been slow and sweet before but this is something very different. As fantastic as it is, it's something I've never had before and I'm a little nervous. One of his hands grabs hold of my hip while the other situates his cock so it slides in smoothly when he presses forward with his hips. I almost can't breathe, he's so deep when he's in this position. The motion of his hips is slow and controlled to start and only pauses when he pulls my torso upright against his. His fingers find my beaded nipples. "Jase," I hiss, pressing back harder against him.

Plucking, pinching, tugging, he's working them hard as I get off on it. When one of his hands stops and slips down between my legs, I grip my breast and work it while he attacks my clit with perfect precision. He's taken his time to build this orgasm for me and it's so big by the time it consumes me, I almost pass out from the sheer bliss of it.

When my muscles relax, he pushes my chest back to the

mattress and hammers into me relentlessly. My sensitive pussy clenches tight as he draws out another orgasm until he finally comes and collapses on me. The last thing I feel before I pass out from exhaustion is his lips meeting that tattoo again.

THE NEXT MORNING WE'RE COMFORTABLE LYING IN BED, NOT talking, only holding each other. I realize yesterday may have been more words than he's used to using in a day so I don't push for more, but he surprises me by speaking first. "Mari, I think you need to give your landlord notice and get out. Dee is ready to move on and you have nothing there."

"She hasn't come right out and said it but I know it's time. I have nowhere to go, Jase. I can't get rid of it even if it's mostly empty."

"You can stay here."

I stop breathing. *Did he say stay here?*

"That's not a good choice, Jase. We're brand new and we've done an awful lot of arguing. I don't even know if you can put up with me past a couple of weeks. That would be another bad decision in a line of bad decisions."

"Okay, so you stay here until you can find something else. You're here every night anyway and I won't ever be okay with you going back to that place. It's not secure and you have nothing there anyway. I had someone look into the leasing policy. You can give notice today and stay here for a bit. You'll be saving money to get something nicer or at least more secure so when you're there I won't worry. You're welcome to stay with me as long as you want, though."

"If you want me to live with you I need a better reason than it's convenient, so I won't move in, but you're right that I need somewhere new so I'll take you up on the offer temporarily. Dee wants to stay with Reggie and I hate being alone, especially there.

I'll do it if you can take me by there today to grab what little I have and give my notice."

"Yeah, let's do that."

After we execute our plan for the day I call Dee to let her know what I've done. Her sigh lets me know she's relieved without her having to say it. Tomorrow I start looking for somewhere to go in a month or so. I'm back to working at the ranch and I'm making good money so it shouldn't take me long.

Three weeks pass and there has been no sign of my stalker, thank goodness, and finding a place to live has been more difficult than I could imagine. To afford living somewhere safer, I'll need a roommate, which means bringing a stranger into my house. After everything that's happened, I'm nervous about that idea. Although things with Jase have been great overall, I don't want to wear out my welcome and I don't want him to feel obligated to keep me here because I have nowhere else to go. Ray will be out of Reggie's in a couple of weeks and I can go there if I'm desperate to give Jase a break, but not until then.

Chapter Fifteen
MARINA

Tonight Leslie, her new husband, and the kids come to town. We'll have Rushton and Skylar for five days while she and her new husband go skiing in Vail. They had a courthouse wedding yesterday afternoon in Florida with a few people in attendance and that was it. Jase is excited to have them here, I think. I'm a little nervous they'll take one look at me and think I'm a freak like he did when he first saw me again. I've always liked my particular style and was never self-conscious until Jase said all of those things to me a while ago. With the kids though, I have no idea what they've been exposed to over the years so I'm nervous. I could be the strangest person they've ever seen. When they arrive in town we're meeting them for dinner and then bringing the kids back with us while those two drive to Vail.

As I come out of the bathroom ready to go, Jase's head tilts as he studies me. He takes two steps toward me and stops while eyeing me from head to toe, followed by four more steps to be right in front of me. He knows how nervous I am so him scrutinizing me is making it worse. I fidget under the weight of his inspection.

I tried to tone my look down a little by replacing the small hoop that goes through my left nostril with a tiny diamond stud and removing the Monroe piercings above my lip. I'm wearing makeup, but it's more subtle than usual. I'm in a decent pair of jeans and boots and a top I borrowed from Dee, which means it's way more conservative than what I'd normally wear.

"Mari, you don't have to be someone you're not. You look beautiful, but you don't have to change for them. The kids won't care at all. They may ask a hundred questions about your hair and the piercings though. Skylar will be the worst. She's curious as hell about everything, but that shouldn't matter."

I worry my lip with my teeth before I answer. "It's not the kids. I didn't want to feel out of place with you, Leslie, and Joe. I didn't want to look like a teenage runaway while the rest of you are dressed like normal adults."

His fingers slide up into the hair at the nape of my neck and hold me so I can't look anywhere but at him. "You're beautiful. Just relax. I know your sudden insecurity comes from the shit I said. I'm sorry for that. I want you to be happy with who you are. I am. Do you want to change into *your* clothes?" I shake my head and glance away, but he pulls me closer and kisses me hard. "Trust me, Mari. You can be yourself. They'll like you just the way you are. I do."

He spins me a little, sweeps the hair off my neck and tugs the collar of my shirt down a bit so he can see the locket tattoo. A sweet, tender kiss is placed over it before he moves my hair back into place. If I were chocolate, I'd melt.

When we walk into the restaurant a half hour later they're already there, seated and waiting. Leslie is the first to stand and large, jagged stones settle in my gut when I realize how beautiful she is. Short but sexy, with smooth blonde hair and her general appearance is that of a Dallas Cowboys Cheerleader. The light in her eyes when she recognizes Jase makes me wonder why she married Joe. It's obvious there's something there. *How am I going to survive this dinner?* I can make sure I'm busy when they pick up the kids after the honeymoon, but I have to get through this meal. Doing my best to hide my discomfort, I paste my fake smile on and reach out to shake Joe's hand first. He greets me warmly and I like him right away. Some souls are easy to read and his is one. I'd bet money that he's gentle and sweet and easy going but fiercely in love with her.

I shake with Leslie next as the kids jump all over Jase, yelling, "Uncle Dex! Uncle Dex! Uncle Dex!" Before I can say anything, Leslie leans toward them and shushes them. "Kids, settle down. You've got all week to get crazy with Uncle Dex. We're in a restaurant so quiet down." To their credit, they hush immediately as Dex pulls them both close and ruffles their hair.

Once we're seated the little girl is the first of the two kids to speak to me when she says, "You have a diamond in your nose! Are you a princess?" The wonder in her voice makes me smile as she continues to inform me, "Only princesses have diamonds in their noses." All of us laugh except Leslie, who looks horrified as she tries to stop the words coming out of her daughter's mouth. "Skylar Larkin, hush. That's rude!"

Jase turns wide eyes to Leslie and reaches across the table to place his hand on hers. When they make contact, I swallow hard, fighting the jealousy that's threatening to overtake me. "Les, it's okay. Marina knows she has a diamond in her nose." Then he gives the little girl a wicked smile and says, "She's definitely a princess, don't let her tell you any different." He pulls his hand back as the little girl squeals with delight. I can't help but laugh. She's adorable and broke the ice for me without meaning to.

"Skylar and Rushton, this is Marina."

"She's your princess girlfriend?" Skylar asks her eyes alight with excitement.

"Yes, she's my princess girlfriend." I warm from the inside out as I watch his interaction with Skylar. It's so rare to get such a wide, relaxed smile from Jase.

When I glance over to smile at Rushton he stays quiet but smiles at me.

Jase's hand slips up under my hair to graze the tattoo he loves so much before he grips the back of my neck for moral support. He must sense the little bit of lingering discomfort I have because it's a sweet gesture and settles me quickly. Through dinner, things become more relaxed and Leslie and I talk a little. She seems to be excited about the honeymoon and Jase's time with the kids. Although I find her studying me out of the corner of my eye, it doesn't feel weird. It's almost like she's trying to figure me out. I'm sure Jase has never had a woman like me around. I'm guessing they've always been more like her.

I'm buried in my thoughts when Joe asks, "So Dex, how did you meet Marina?"

"Foster care. When we were teenagers." He doesn't elaborate further and surprise fills Joe's eyes, but I find it curious that Leslie doesn't seem surprised. Is it possible she's heard about me before now?

"What's a foster care?" Skylar pipes up, looking directly at me.

"Well...it's a place kids go to for people to take care of them." How do you answer a little kid who has a family that loves her, in a way she might understand?

"So we might go there too?"

"Um..." I look to Jase for help.

"Bunny, not everyone is as lucky as you are to have your mommy and daddy and Joe who love them. Marina and I didn't have a nice family like yours so they sent us to live with another family and other kids like us."

"No one loved you?" Her eyes are huge as she asks, like she can't even fathom it.

"My grandma did but she died and there was nowhere for me to go. It's okay though because that's how I met Marina."

The rest of the table sits uncomfortably quiet for a second until Skylar decides to speak again. "Uncle Dex—"

Leslie interrupts her, "Sky."

Jase says, "It's okay, Les. Do you have a question, Bunny?"

"No. I just want to say that you don't have to live at foster care anymore because I love you. So now you can live at your own home."

Jase's eyes soften, and I'm telling you, there is nothing hotter than a man who looks at a little girl with that kind of tenderness.

"Foster care is only for kids and I'm an adult so I already live in my own apartment. That's where you're staying this week. But let me tell you that as soon as I met your dad and your mom and your brother and you, you became my family so I didn't have to be alone anymore. Just because you live far away doesn't mean you aren't my family. I'm so glad you love me back though. I'm a lucky guy."

Dear lord, my lip starts to tremble at the triumphant look on her little face, like she's so proud of this whole scenario. Just as I get it under control, she takes it a step further.

"Marina, I can love you too. If you were a little kid, you wouldn't need foster care either."

That does it. A few tears spill out and drip down my cheeks. I try to wipe them away but it's futile. This little girl completely unraveled me.

Jase places his fingers on my cheek and turns my face to him. He wipes the remaining wetness away and kisses me softly. "Don't cry Mari, you've got me." I smile a little, trying to push down the big fat tears that are building at the back of my eyes. I know I've got him for now. I don't think I've got him forever though, but I try not to think about that. I want to savor everything in the moment with him.

The server shows up with our meals right in time to break the serious moment and Joe does his best to keep the rest of dinner light and easy. When it's time to leave, we transfer the kids' suitcases to Jase's car and everyone says their goodbyes.

THE DAY BEFORE LESLIE AND JOE COME TO PICK UP THE KIDS, we take them to the ranch. I'm going there to work, but Judson and Jase will take them on a trail ride around the property. The kids are giddy with excitement and I can't help but be too. Jase has spent the week taking them all over Colorado Springs and even into Denver to keep them busy. When I get home from work every night they're all exhausted.

"You get to play with the horses every day? You're so lucky!" Skylar says as she bounces in her booster seat in the back like she has jumping beans in her pants. "I love horses. They're the best."

"What do you think of horses?" I ask Rushton.

"They're cool, I guess. But they're really big and a little scary. Do you think I'll be okay?"

"Of course! They like people and are really good with kids. Trooper sometimes kisses my neck when I get too close while I'm working in the barn. He's my favorite."

"A horse kiss!" Sky's whole face lights up.

"Yes, it's super ticklish and will make you squirm. His breath is kind of stinky so you may get a whiff of that if he tries to kiss you."

"Eww! Gross!" The kids squeal in unison, making Jase and me laugh.

AT THE END OF MY WORKDAY I TRUDGE INSIDE TO MEET everyone. Judson made dinner so Quinn could see the kids. When I come out of the bathroom from washing up, I pause to take in the scene in front of me. Carlo, Skylar and Rushton are talking animatedly with each other and Lila's in her highchair happily banging her spoon on the tray. Quinn, Judson and Jase are trying to hold a conversation above the noise and everyone looks comfortable and content. It makes my heart both happy and sad all at once. I've wanted this scene my whole life. I've wanted this kind of family normalcy and love so bad I can't stand it. This is what I've been missing for most of my life.

I'm not sure how long I stand there before Jase calls to me, "Mari, you okay?" I shake my head a little to bring myself back into the moment and plaster on the smile.

"I'm good. Sorry, I was thinking about something. What's for dinner? It smells wonderful!" As I sit in the empty chair on Jase's right side, he squeezes my knee and I lean in to peck his cheek.

"Did Judson work you too hard today?" he asks.

"Of course, but it was good. I love being in there even if it's cold as hell."

Everyone laughs at my answer. When dinner is over, we pack up the kids and head back to his apartment for our last night with them. Joe and Leslie will be here tomorrow and want to take us to dinner before they leave the following day.

THE NEXT NIGHT WE HAVE A FABULOUS DINNER AT AN ITALIAN restaurant with Leslie, Joe and the kids. Everyone is relaxed and talkative and I'm much more comfortable than I was when the kids were dropped off. Joe and Leslie hold hands until our meal arrives and the conversation between her and me flows more smoothly for me this time since my nerves are gone. It's obvious the kids had a great time with us this week, but I know I'll miss them so much more than they'll miss us. Being surrounded by voices, conversation, questions and smiles this week has been a dream come true. I'm so envious of Leslie and Joe and the life they're about to start together.

After dinner, we meet Leslie in the hotel bar for a drink while Joe gets the kids to bed. We're laughing and carrying on about some of the things Sky says until Dex goes to the bathroom and Leslie and I are left alone.

"I'm so glad Dex got his head out of his ass. I knew when he mentioned your name that you were more than just some chick he slept with," she says as she smiles.

My brow furrows. "How did you know that? If he mentioned it when he was with you guys the last time, we weren't even speaking."

"I've known him a long time and I've never seen him get upset about a woman. Every muscle he has tensed up during that phone call when he heard something happened to you."

"Oh. I still don't think he's all that crazy about me, but he's worth sticking around to find out."

"I knew if you could get past us sleeping together and understand it was nothing, like Joe did, that you were worth keeping. I don't think you have anything to worry about. I've never seen him like this. I'm happy for you both."

As soon as I register what she said to me, a vise closes around my chest and I can't breathe. *Get past them sleeping together?* He lied to me. Not a lie of omission, but a flat-out lie. I don't want her to see the meltdown that I can feel coming on. With that one sentence from her, it's total heartbreak so powerful that I'm in physical pain. I do my best to continue with conversation, changing the subject and asking about her future plans with Joe, but I'm so preoccupied with my own heartbreak that I don't process her responses. I'm so overwhelmed that when Jase comes back from the bathroom, I say, "My stomach is a little upset. I hate to ask, but do you think you can take me back to your apartment?"

He senses something is up because he pauses and searches my face, probably looking for clues about what changed while he was gone. "Sure. Let's go."

We say goodbye, give Leslie hugs, and return to his apartment. The only noise in the car on the way back is the growl of his engine and I'm having a hard time breathing. How do I deal with this? Do I say something? They obviously have nothing going on now, but can I stay with him knowing he lied to me? I don't think it's something Quinn, Dee or even Leslie would put up with. Lying feels like a deal-breaker for me. Does this bother me enough that I should even say something? The more I ponder this, the more I realize, it doesn't just bother me, it tears me up. I'm not going to shove something under the rug as big as lying so I can keep a boyfriend. If he lied about this what else has he lied about? He wouldn't tolerate this from me so I need to have enough respect for myself not to tolerate it either.

The question now is what am I going to do about it? I could scream and yell like some kind of teenage drama queen or I could tell him what's bothering me like an adult. Although my stomach burns bad enough that I'd like to throw a hissy fit, I won't.

"We need to talk," I tell him as we enter the apartment.

"All right," he replies as he pulls off his boots and sets them neatly by the end of the couch.

"Why did you lie to me about sleeping with Leslie?" He stands up straight and stares at me for a second. His Adam's apple bobs as he swallows hard before answering.

"Marina."

"Jase, I don't want a bullshit story. I want to know why. I know you did. She mentioned it tonight while you were in the bathroom, in the middle of conversation like she figured I already knew."

"I didn't lie specifically." When I'm about to protest he holds up a finger so he can continue. "You asked if I slept with her when I was there that time. I didn't. I slept with her a long time ago. I should have told you the exact truth, but things were volatile between us and I felt like if you knew you'd think something was still going on. I was trying to keep from messing with your head."

"So, let me get this straight, you're telling me you lied for my benefit?"

"Mari—"

"Um, no. Your time to talk already passed. See, I'm thinking the only person that benefitted from the lie was you."

"You're not looking at this the right way."

My head jerks back, surprised that he's trying to spin this on me. Nope, I'm not going to listen to that nonsense. Snatching my coat back off the hanger behind me, I shrug it on and say, "I think I need a little bit of time to cool off. I may be a lot of things Jase, but I'm not stupid and I'm not so needy that I'll stay with someone who could so easily lie to me. Especially someone who wouldn't tolerate the same in return. I know you well enough to know if I lied to you I'd be sitting on the curb with my shit in hand, looking for somewhere to live. I'm taking a walk. We can finish this when I get back."

"I don't think it's safe outside, Marina."

"Too bad. I've lived in worse places than the streets of this neighborhood." With those parting words, I open the door and slip through before he can say anything else. When I'm several blocks away from his apartment I hear my named called, but it's not Jase. *What the hell?* I turn around and search the area the voice came from and walk back to where the alley opens up between two concrete buildings. There's a large green dumpster about halfway back on the left side that's surrounded by a bunch of trash that should be in it not around it. It's dark further back and I'm unable to see anything in that section. On the right, there are a bunch of broken down cardboard boxes and huddled up next to them, wrapped in an old coat and a blanket, is Marv. I breathe a sigh of relief as I walk toward him.

"Where are you going this late at night alone? Where's Dex?"

I roll my eyes. "Well hello to you too, old man."

His scruffy cheeks lift in a half smile and a dark hole where a few of his teeth are supposed to be becomes visible.

"Don't get smart with me, Marina. It's not safe for you to be out here without Dex."

"We had a fight and I needed some air."

"This is not the place to be getting air." He waves his hand out in front of him to indicate the neighborhood.

"Please. This is a vacation spot compared to where I lived when I was on the streets at one point." Tilting his head, his eyes narrow on me like he's trying to understand me.

"I know we talked about it a little at Dex's apartment but you never told me when or why you lived on the street."

"From the age of 18 until I was 20. I aged out of the system and had nowhere to go and no money to get a place. I lived like that until a friend from school passed me on the street one day and took me in."

"Fair enough. Now sit and tell me about this fight."

"I don't want to talk about it."

"Girly, you don't have a choice. You're in my house and I want you to go home so I don't worry. You won't do that until you decide not to be mad anymore. Now get over here and spill the beans."

I probably shouldn't, but I have no one else to talk to, so why not? I spend the next few minutes explaining what happened and how it all went down. He's quiet for the most part until I say, "That's it. That's the story."

Certain he's going to tell me I'm being stupid, I hold my breath as he speaks. "That was an asshole thing for him to do. I get why he lied, but I also understand why you don't like it. It probably makes you wonder what else he's lied about and I'm sure he'd lose his mind if you did the same.

"Here's what I can tell you: Dex keeps mostly to himself and I assume it's because of all he's been through in his life. I've picked up bits and pieces over the years. But he's wired inside and out to protect the people he cares about and will do anything to make that happen. You two are a good match like that. It's unlikely he'll get taken advantage of by you since you're the same way. However, I think you're going to have to consider letting this one go in an effort to keep a good thing. I mean, make sure you blister his ass so he won't be quick to do it again, but I think you need to forgive him.

"Never seen that boy care about a woman before. In fact, most of his women come and go in one night. He's broken, but I believe you can fix him. Take it from a lonely old man like me, sometimes you need to overlook an issue if it was done with the right intentions. I threw away something really good a long time ago and it's the only thing in this life I regret. Don't be like me. I know Dexter is a good man, an honorable man. Give him the chance to make it right."

"What if I can't?"

"You can. Now turn around. I believe you'll find him half a block back, waiting for you to come out of the alley. He backed off a minute ago when he realized you were down here talking with me."

"He's here?"

"Did you think he'd let you walk this neighborhood alone at night? I can tell by the look on your face you really thought that. If you did, you need to spend some time getting to know him because he would never leave you unprotected. Now go on. Put him out of his misery."

I pause as I think about everything he's said to me. He's probably right but I need to talk to Jase before I make any decisions. I can't believe he followed me even though we were in a fight.

"Marv, are you hungry? You eat anything lately?"

"I haven't been too hungry. I'm fine."

"Marv—"

"Don't worry about me, Marina. Go take care of yourself. I'm fine."

"Okay," I say as I bend over and kiss his cheek, noting his garbage-ripened scent. I need to get Jase to bring him to the apartment for dinner and a shower. "Thanks, Marv."

When I turn the corner, Jase is standing half a building back, leaning on the wall with his hands in his pockets. We both stand still, taking the other in without a word. This goes on until he stands up straight and walks toward me. When he's close enough, he pulls me to him and wraps his arms around me. I'm stiff to start but soften as he speaks. "Mari, I'm sorry. I didn't want to hurt you or make you wonder if something was going on between Leslie and me. It's not. I didn't want you to worry, but you're right, I'd be pissed if the roles were reversed."

"Jase."

"Shush. I get it. I know I did wrong. Please let me apologize and go back to my place. We can talk about it where I know you're safe."

I allow him to lead me back to his apartment. When we get there, I hang my coat back up and remove my shoes. I sit at the end of the couch and wait for him to sit too. He sits at the opposite end and waits for me to speak.

"Do you get what the issue is here?" I ask him, unsure if he knows why he's apologizing.

"I said I was sorry and I meant it."

"Yeah, I heard you, but I feel like it's an apology designed to shut me up, not one of real remorse. If I would've lied to you, I'd be kicked to the curb. Now I wonder what else you've lied to me about. I also wonder how long you two were sleeping together."

Leaning forward to rest his elbows on his knees, he clears his throat and stares at the floor in front of him as he explains. "Stu was the first person since I was eight years old to love me. He was more than my best friend; he was my brother. He trusted me to take care of his family so when I moved to Tampa with the intentions of taking care of them, I just sort of slipped into his role. It was like I didn't know how to separate caretaker from man of the house. Neither Les nor I were working, so we spent every day, all day together. She's beautiful and we were both lonely so now that I look back, I realize it was building long before anything happened. One night we got drunk out by the pool after the kids went to bed, and one minute we were talking and the next..."

"Keep going."

"It was sloppy, it was weird and it was fast. Probably the worst sexual experience of my life other than my first time. When it was done, we both cried. God, it was awful and I was so embarrassed.

"I felt like I betrayed him. He trusted me with his wife and kids, and instead of looking out for them, I took over being him in every way possible but didn't realize it until I had sex with his wife."

"He was dead, Jase. It's not like he was just out of town. It happens. You were both vulnerable and attractive and attracted to each other. I'm surprised it didn't happen sooner."

He shakes his head sadly. "The next day I woke up and called a headhunter and asked him to find me a job somewhere other than Tampa. It didn't take long and the next thing I knew, I'd moved back here."

"What did Leslie say after the sex?"

"What was there to say? I apologized, probably a million times, and she cried. There was nothing to say; it was a mistake and we both knew it. When it was time for me to go, she asked me to stay and I explained that if I didn't leave I'd simply be a replacement for Stu, not someone who really belonged there. She seemed to understand after that."

"Are you in love with her? If there was no Joe, would you still be with her?"

When he turns to me, my heart aches. *Please don't say you love her.*

"No, Mari. Not like you mean. I love her like my sister, which I think is why the sex was so bad. I'm not *in* love with her."

By the look in his eyes, I can tell he's not lying this time. I breathe a sigh of relief and he moves over to kneel in front of me. His fingers slide into my hair and he holds me so I can't look anywhere else but his amazing aquamarine eyes. "I'm sorry. I'll never lie to you again. Let me tell you this too, Mari, when we were at dinner with them, there was only one woman in the room who got my blood pumping, one woman I was thinking about taking home and stripping down, and one woman I wanted to wake up next to tomorrow morning, and it was not Leslie. Only you, baby. Please believe me."

I must be a sucker because I believe every word of it. His mouth meets mine in a tender, tentative kiss but it doesn't take long to become more. His lips shift to my cheek and slowly work down along the sensitive expanse of my throat. With a swipe of his tongue in the hollow at the base, I'm squirming. "Jase," I hiss.

"Clothes off, baby," he demands in a gravelly voice laced with need. Leaning back on his heels, he gives me space to strip down and as soon as my bra drops to the floor, he pushes me onto my back. The kisses resume down along the swell of both breasts. He stops momentarily to tease my nipples to tight buds before moving further south. Each kiss feels softer than the last and I whimper with desire. *Please put your mouth on me.* I don't say it out loud, but my hips lift, begging of their own accord.

"Patience sweet Mari," he mumbles against my skin while he buries his nose in my sex. With his skilled lips and tongue, he works my clit slowly at first as the damp heat between my legs grows. When I cry out in frustration he slips two fingers inside me and curves them to find the secret spot buried within. Now that his fingers and mouth are working me at an escalating pace, it's not long before I dig my fingernails into his scalp and call his name.

With my body still shuddering, he strips his clothes off and settles between my legs, pushing my knees up high. As he slides in, my body twitches with the aftershocks of my climax and the promise of another on its heels. Jase leans in close and takes my mouth as his hips roll against mine, pushing his thickness in deeper each time. He breaks our kiss and stares at me as he works me, his eyes shining like the water in the Caribbean and I'm mesmerized by the passion held inside. My hips lift to meet each thrust and we're working feverishly to cross the finish line together. "Touch yourself, baby, I need you to come one more time." I'm close so it won't be difficult. Slipping my hand between my legs, I work my clit until I pull another sweet orgasm out of both of us.

Jase collapses on top of me and kisses the skin at my neck while he comes down from the sex high we just experienced.

"I'm sorry, Mari."

"I forgive you, but no more lies. I don't care how painful the answer will be."

"I promise."

Chapter Sixteen
DEX

Life has been good with Mari since she found out about Leslie. The things that once drove me crazy like the constant chatter and the need to be touching me at all times, have gotten better. Partially because she's relaxed and doesn't seem to need that continuous sound to fill the dead air and also because I've grown used to it. As for the touching, that's been the change on my part. I've never felt the need for physical contact and now I can't get enough of it. For me, it's both arousing and soothing with her.

Today I noticed a change in her appearance and if you would've asked me when I first found her again if I'd be happy with those changes, I would've answered yes. Now, not so much. I love that she's not hiding her gorgeous face behind a bunch of unnecessary makeup, but I think the piercings fit her character and if she wants them, I don't want her to remove them because of some asshole things I said a while ago.

Thank God she can't remove the tattoos. I could spend hours tracing those just to touch her smooth skin. Never have I found tattoos on a woman attractive until I saw her without clothes the first time, but It's the locket behind her neck that gets me every time though. Seeing it there, knowing it means so much to her, digs deep inside me, pulling up things I never thought I'd feel. I only wish that the actual necklace would turn up somewhere. I've been in touch with all the pawn shops from here to Denver with a special request if it shows up. It was my grandmother's and that in itself makes it special, but for her to love something that much and have it taken away makes me want to move heaven and earth to get it back for her.

I could buy her a new locket, in fact I'm going to, but it's the sentimentality behind that one that matters most to me. She protected it during the remainder of her time in foster care, and continued to do so when she was living on the street. She deserves to have it back.

QUINN AND I ARE LEAVING A RUN-DOWN APARTMENT COMPLEX with a repeat offender, wife beater when my cell phone rings. I miss the call because I'm busy wrestling the loser into the car. As I slide into the front seat, I hit play on the message, not recognizing the number.

What the hell? The call was from Mari and she's been arrested. She starts crying too hard for me to understand her so I end the message and start the car. Quinn must sense my change in mood because she asks, "You okay? What's wrong?"

"I don't know. Can you call the station and find out why Marina was arrested?"

She gasps. "Marina?"

I grind my teeth together and take a deep breath in through my nose. I thought all the cops on this shift knew I was dating her, so why I didn't get a courtesy call, I don't know. I also don't know what would've gotten her in trouble. She was supposed to go straight home to my place after eating dinner with Judson and the kids. I knew she wouldn't sleep well but at least I knew she'd be safe at my place.

Quinn calls, listens, tells them we'll be there shortly and hangs up the phone. "It's not good, Dex. She was with a girl at a known cocaine distributor's house when a raid went down. Detective Downie says she was standing in the middle of the living room holding a suitcase full of it. She swears she didn't know what was in the suitcase, but Downie doesn't believe her considering how well-known this drug dealer is. This is bad for her and it won't look good for you either."

"Fuck!" I roar and hit the gas with new fervor. I don't know why I'm in a hurry to get there, but I am. *What the hell was she doing? Was she trying to earn extra cash?* I know she was talking about getting her own place again, but it was going to be a little longer until she had enough money. I guess it doesn't matter why she did it, only that she did and effectively ended us and maybe my career with her dumb-ass decision.

When we finally get the idiot from the backseat into the station, Quinn takes over so I can figure out what the hell is going on with Marina. I'm so fucking furious I could explode, but I can't decide who I'm most mad at, the cop that didn't call me or Marina.

When I enter the room Detective Downie stands abruptly, drawing attention from several cops nearby at their desks. When they follow his line of sight, a few more stand and move in closer to him. If I'm pissed, there isn't one of those boys who could contain me, but I'm don't plan to do anything more than have a few words with him.

"What the fuck, Downie? You couldn't give me a heads-up about this shit? I had to hear it from Marina in a crying phone call? You know that's not how things roll around here."

"You couldn't have gotten her out of it, Dexter. She had several pounds of blow in that suitcase she was holding."

"I don't know what the hell happened tonight but I do know I deserved a goddamn phone call. I wouldn't have tried to get her out of it. But I'd at least like to hear the circumstances before she calls me to bail her ass out. I didn't have a clue about any of it. Was she selling the shit?"

"She says no. This house has been under surveillance for weeks and no one has seen her before. The girl she was with has been seen frequently."

"Who is the girl?"

"Amber Johnson."

"Doesn't ring any bells. What was Mari doing there? You've been told she's not usually there so there has to be a story."

"Marina says she went to the residence to help Amber move her stuff out. Marina waited in the living room for her. When Amber was done packing, she brought Marina the suitcase and asked her to take it to the car."

"Why was Amber leaving?"

"The owner of the house, Jeremiah "Jay-Freak" Boone, her boyfriend, decided it was time to put a beating on her and let me tell you, it was a nasty one."

"You didn't believe Marina was there to help her move?"

"Would you? Looks like she was helping her friend steal a ton of blow from a man that beat her. Shit happens all the time. When you see Amber, you'll understand. I'm surprised she didn't set the place on fire. But she probably figured she could at least sell the blow and get the money to get out of town. Only problem was Jay-Freak showed up and the raid carried forth like we planned. Marina was caught up in it all. I can't just let the girl holding pounds of the stuff walk away without checking the story. She needs a lawyer, Dexter, even if she didn't do anything wrong. It still looks bad. You need to see the captain when you're done. She's in interrogation now if you want to see her."

"Fuck!" I storm out and march toward the interview room knowing I'm close to losing my shit. To make this day worse, Gino strolls past me in the hall and decides to mouth off.

"Heard your girl's in lock-up. I think she might need a little visit later. Think she's lonely?"

Without thinking it through I turn and throw a punch so hard he flies off his feet and into the wall with a huge thud. A woman from an office right by where Gino sits, rushes out as I say to him, "You go anywhere near my girl or any other woman who isn't interested and I hear about it, you won't make it to your next promotion. I've heard enough whispers over the years, and I know what you did to Marina the night we found her, to know what kind of douchebag you are. Keep your fucking hands to yourself, you son of a bitch!" I turn and continue on like nothing happened and I can hear the female cop behind me say, "It's about time," and laugh as she returns to her office leaving Gino in a heap on the floor.

When I enter the interrogation room, the cop that's with her stands and looks at me. "I need a minute with her, man." I gesture toward Marina. Her tear-streaked face and doe eyes tell me she's in the middle of hell but I can't seem to calm down enough to approach her softly.

The cop walks over to me and says, "You've got about 10 minutes, man." Then he pats my arm as he passes.

"What the hell happened Mari? I've heard the arresting officer's story but I want yours."

"Amber called when I was leaving the ranch. She said her man beat her up and she needed help getting her stuff. Dex, I've been in her situation before, I couldn't leave her to go back in there alone. I knew he was a dealer, but I didn't know he kept it at his house or that she was taking his stuff. We were only there for about 10 minutes. I sat in the living room while she packed. When she came out, she handed me one of two suitcases and we were turning to leave when Jay came home. He said about five words to her and then the cops busted in the front and back doors. I was scared, but I figured once they saw how beat up she was and that all we had was her clothes, they'd let us go. I had no idea she was taking off with Jay's cocaine or that I was standing there holding it."

"Why didn't you call me when she called you in the first place? What if he would've been there, ready to pass out more beatings?"

"Number one, you were working. Number two, I knew you'd hate Amber on sight. I've known her a long time and she's been there for me too many times to count. There was no way I wasn't going to help her when she called. I had no idea she was stealing his product, though. This isn't my fault. If you see Amber, you'll understand, you'll know why I had to help her. I could never walk away from someone in need."

I pace the room as I run what she's said through my head. This is a typical Marina mess. "What happened to making better decisions? You promised me. What made you think going into the house of a known drug dealer was safe or logical?" This time her eyes lower to the table and she rubs her lower lip with her teeth, but gives me no answer.

"Come on Mari, you've got to give me something."

"I'm sorry if this embarrassed you. I only meant to help a friend and I'd probably do it all over again if given the chance—minus the drugs in the suitcase. Being who I am means never letting a friend walk through hell alone. When you see her you'll know she walked through hell."

"Anyone who puts you in the position she did, knowing you could get in serious trouble, isn't a friend, Mari. Why can't you see that?"

"I can now, but when I made the decision to help her, it was based on previous friendship status. I didn't realize what kind of friend she was until they opened that suitcase. I can't go back and fix it now, Jase."

"I don't think I can help you with this, Mari. You need a lawyer. I'll get you one, but there's nothing else I can do. I'll be lucky if I don't lose my job."

"Why? You weren't there, you didn't even know about it."

"If the woman who shares my bed and my home gets busted for having a shit-ton of blow at a known dealer's house, it comes back on me. It's part of my contract. Even if they don't fire me, this may have tanked my career. I've got to go see my captain and get you a lawyer."

"Jase." Her eyes plead with me to understand, but I can't. I'll never understand how she can get herself into this stuff. She doesn't consider consequences before she does anything.

I call a lawyer and explain the situation the best I can. Then I call Dee and tell her what happened. My boss sent me home and explained that internal affairs will have to investigate before I can come back to work. I'm not the kind of person who does well with idle time when I'm under a bunch of stress. Even after running, about a million sit-ups, push-ups and pull-ups, I'm still not able to settle enough to sit down, much less lie down.

I figure it's time to go see Marv. Quinn isn't allowed to talk to me until they interview her later today. When I reach him, he's gnawing on a granola bar of some sort. I have no idea where he got it but I'm glad to see he's eating. After some basic pleasantries he squints his eyes and studies me.

"What's wrong, boy?"

"Marina."

"Damn, that girl's an angel. You'd better get your shit straight so you can keep her."

"You have no idea what you're talking about. She might cost me my job."

He doesn't even flinch or ask why. "You can get another job. You won't find another girl like her."

"She was busted with several pounds of cocaine."

He shrugs. "She's not a druggie. We both know what those look like and she's not one. Where did she get it? Did she say why she had it?"

"Wrong place, wrong time, or at least that's what she says. The girl she was with got beat up by her man and said she needed help getting her stuff out. She didn't tell Mari that 'stuff' meant a ridiculous amount of coke or that Mari would be the one to carry it out the door. By the time it was all said and done she got caught up in a raid, literally holding the bag."

"Then you'd better be there when she gets out because that girl is tough as nails, but spending a night in jail and you being mad at her on top of it... I'm sure she's in hell. She has a tender heart."

"I don't know what to do."

"You hire her the best lawyer you can afford because I'm guessing she can't afford much, and you get her cleared, but you stand by her the whole way."

"Why are you so big on me staying with her?"

"Because I've known you for several years and you've always been closed off. I'm a man, I get it, but you take that closed off shit to a whole new level. It's been obvious since the day you found her again, that she helped you find your heart. You keep everything so close, never letting anyone in, never reaching out. It's a lonely life. If you find a woman like her, no matter what kind of trouble follows her, you hold tight."

"What do you mean I don't let anyone in? I've got Judson, Quinn and the kids, and Stu's family. And I think you and I passed being acquaintances a long time ago."

"It's not enough, Dex. Women like her don't come along often. She's true to the core, sweet and she's got a great ass too. Just listen to this old man, okay?"

After ending the conversation, I run another couple miles so I can contemplate what Marv's said. I know he's right. I know I'm in love with Mari and I know that I'll struggle without her. Luckily, I already called the lawyer for her before I left the office, so she should get out first thing in the morning. I need to make sure I'm there to pick her up so we can talk about all of this.

As I'm approaching my apartment building, a strange sound like I've never heard before draws my attention to the narrow alley that runs between buildings three and four. I turn to see what it is and something hard catches me across the side of the head. My vision goes black and I feel myself falling.

WHEN I WAKE UP MY HEAD IS POUNDING AND MY MUSCLES ARE cramping. My wrists and ankles are bound too tight and I've lost feeling in both. I try to stretch as I open my eyes and find that I'm tied to a radiator in what appears to be a small apartment that I swear I've been in before. I wonder if I've responded to a call here. I blink a few times to clear the blur of my vision. The place is familiar, but at the same time it's not. Where am I? Am I alone in here? Tugging and wiggling my hands, I look for a weakness in this cord I'm wrapped in. So far there isn't one.

The sound of someone whistling a cheerful tune halts my movement. Footsteps approaching alert me to a presence entering the room, out of my line of sight. I crane my neck back enough so I can see who it is. The skinny guy that appears is not what I expected with his shoulder-length, black, stringy hair and powder-white skin. He's wearing a black, Nirvana T-shirt and faded black skinny jeans. Worn-out black Converse shoes are on his feet and the guy actually has black eyeliner around his eyes. This is almost the exact description Marv gave the sketch artist after his beating. Mari said the guy who tried to abduct her had long black hair too. Shit! It all makes sense. Without a doubt this is the guy who tried to take Mari and I'm suddenly so thankful for her arrest. At least I know she's safe from this crazy freak while she's locked up.

With the realization that this is Mari's stalker, the familiarity of the room makes sense. Everything in here is hers and by the looks of it, we're in the same building she used to live in. I never saw her stuff, but I read every line of the report and know the description of what she had. It looks as if he recreated her apartment for her in this specific unit. If my assumption is correct, there should be a collage of pictures of Mari with Dee on the wall near the kitchen and a red, white, and blue plaid blanket folded up on the floral couch.

"I see you finally decided to wake up. You might be a little sore. Can't guarantee I didn't break anything getting you in here. You're a heavy bastard."

This guy has to be stark raving mad and working on pure adrenaline, or with someone else, to have gotten me in here as dead weight. I'm at least twice his size, if not more. The freaky blend of contentment and insanity that I'm seeing in his eyes is scary as hell. Under the thumb of a deranged son of a bitch is not somewhere a control freak like me wants to be. I have to focus on how I'll get out of here. I need to start by throwing him off his game.

"You know Marina's in jail, right? You can't get to her."

"She'll find her way here once she realizes you're here. It doesn't seem like she can stay away from you for very long, no matter what kind of prick you are. She should find my appreciation of her more to her liking after being with a big, heartless ape like you." He wanders out of the room again and I can feel the panic attempting to rise in me. It's not in my nature or my training to give in to panic so I need to keep a lid on it.

My brain is moving a little slowly as the throb from the hit continues to hurt, and my blood runs cold as it dawns on me that he plans to lure her here using me as bait. I wish I could get out of these bindings, but there is almost no stretch to them at all.

Several hours go by and the light that was peeking through the blinds gets brighter, suggesting that it's late morning or early afternoon. The crazy guy's continued whistling can be heard clearly where I'm tied up and it's obvious he's in the kitchen. I'm dying to take a piss, but I'll be damned if I'm going in my pants. I refuse to let him humiliate me.

I try to dissect the situation in my head and as I do, it becomes clear that this guy, who stole her stuff, lives in the building. Which also explains how he knew her schedule so well when she claims to never have seen anyone following her. I must be deep in thought because I don't hear him approach this time.

"I've already sent her a text from your phone, asking her to come here."

"She won't come. I told you she's in jail, and we broke up because she can't keep herself out of trouble. She's as done with me as I am with her."

"Well that will work in my favor once she gets here, I think. I was afraid it would take more convincing, but if you've already dumped her, then this will be easy."

The whistling starts again, sending chills down my spine. This dude is totally ass over ankles crazy. With new-found fear coursing through my veins, I search for anything that might work to fray this cord enough to tear it off. When I finally locate a sharp notch on the underside of the radiator, I rub the cord between my hands as hard as I can across it, over and over. After what seems like forever, the cord starts to tear a little so I work more feverishly.

Chapter Seventeen
DEX

The doorbell rings and I freeze. God, please don't let that be Marina. After he opens the door and greets her I can hear her saying, "Um, hi. Dexter said to meet him here?"

"Sure, come on in." He closes the door behind her, locks it, and I know the moment she's sees me tied to the radiator she realizes this isn't the meeting she thought it would be. Her face loses all color and at the same time her eyes grow wide. I shake my head as subtly as possible and I'm praying she gets my message. Please let her be as strong and as smart as I think she is. Mari needs to go with the flow until I can get loose.

She swallows big before she turns to the obviously excited crazed man behind her. He's practically hopping on one foot over this. With his hands clasped and pulled up under his chin, he's waiting for her to say something.

"Wow! You found all my stuff! This is so amazing! But, um, what is Dexter doing here?"

"I thought you'd need him to get you here."

"I couldn't figure out why he wanted me to meet him here. We broke up. Apparently, I'm not high class enough for him. My recent arrest didn't help that. Why didn't you just tell me you found my stuff and invite me over? I would've come, I've been dying to get my stuff back and I love to meet new people."

This guy is no idiot and she's piling it on kind of thick. His head tilts as he studies her. The smile has slipped from his face.

"Are you fucking with me, Marina?"

"Why would I do that?" The innocent act works well for her.

"You never noticed me before."

"Where would I have seen you?"

"At that bar, The Angry Lager, last summer."

She seems to study him for a minute before she asks, "Was your hair shorter?" She motions to her neck. "If you lift your hair I should see a tattoo of scales running up the back of your neck in like blue or green. It's hard to remember exactly. The lighting in that place was terrible."

Nodding excitedly, he lifts his stringy locks and turns to show her his neck. She gulps and flashes a look at me that says she's about to lose it.

"You do remember." His voice is awed.

"One of the coolest tats I've ever seen. I can't believe you cover it with your hair." Her voice only shakes a little.

He pulls his hair around so she can see some of it but it's not quite long enough to stay like that when he moves. I go back to work on my hands while he's preoccupied.

"So, I'm thinking you and I can go by Dexter's house and get my clothes and come back here. It's like I'm coming home again! I'm so excited to have my stuff back! How can I thank you?"

"We aren't going anywhere anytime soon. I have a nice dinner ready for us and we need to decide what to do with the big guy now that I know you don't want him. I don't need him and I can't let him go or he'll arrest me."

"Okay, we can come back to him. I'll need to get clothes and a shower soon, though. I'm gross after sitting in that cell all night."

"You've got nothing to worry about because I have all your clothes too."

"You have all my clothes too?" The little squeak at the end of her words gives away her fear and I hope he didn't hear it. I'm almost free of these restraints. The burn is getting to me but nothing beyond what I can handle. I'd rather have nasty rope burns than be stuck at his mercy. As Mari follows him to the bedroom, I tug and tug and tug until it finally breaks.

Glancing around I try to find anything that can help me knock him out. It's the only chance I've got with my ankles tied and he'll catch me before I get those undone. My best bet is the dining room chair halfway across the room. I roll and push myself to my knees and do the best I can to scoot over to where the chair is. If I hop he'll hear me. Mari catches a glimpse of me and I hear her beg, "Wait! Show me the scales again. I've always wanted to touch them. I'm surprised I didn't get up the courage to ask at the bar. You never noticed me staring?"

"No. You were always talking to that douchebag bartender."

"Well I probably didn't want to come across as a little creepy. I've been told guys don't like that."

When he's turned fully away from me, I maneuver to my feet and slip a little further to the side so the dividing wall to the kitchen is my cover. Once the chair is above my head, I wait. Thank God I'm a patient man because it takes forever. My arms are beginning to shake from fatigue when he calls to her from only a few feet away from me, "Can you wear the little blue dress with the white flowers?"

"Sure," she replies and steps a little past me so I can reach him. He must catch a glimpse of me because as I'm swinging the chair down he punches out at me. I connect with some part of him, which part I'm not sure though, and he screams like a girl. But I'm off balance from his punch so I hit the floor with a thud. Crazy guy stumbles backward holding his shoulder and arm. I may not have hit him square on but I did some damage. I swipe at his leg, trying to pull him to the ground, but he kicks me in the cheekbone, stunning me. My hands fly to my face and I instinctively protect it. *Fuck!*

I hear a lot of rustling and grunting, and by the time I can see again, Mari has the guy pinned face down with the arm I hit pulled tight behind his back as he shrieks. If the whole thing wasn't so insane, I'd be laughing at the little wisp of a woman who has the crazy man completely under her control. She's breathing hard and practically snarling at him she's so angry. I'm a little afraid of what kind of adrenaline crash she's going to have.

I reach down and fight with the knots on my legs as she lets off just enough to stop his screaming. Curse words are flying left and right between the two of them and she's telling him off. I can't understand what he's saying but she's loud and clear.

Once I'm free I dart for the phone on the counter and dial 911. As soon as I have someone on the way, I relieve Mari. She's still spitting mad as she moves away from him.

"You stole all of our stuff! You tried to kidnap me! Did you think I'd fall in love with you after that? Why didn't you try asking me out instead of watching me from a dark corner of the bar every night for over a month? I don't think I was hard to approach. I know I was never rude to you. You left me with nothing! I had to wear clothes from Goodwill!" She's screaming now and I understand she's upset but I need her to calm down or the cops will have her in cuffs too.

"Mari," I say, but not loud enough since she continues yelling at him.

Louder this time, I snap, "Marina! Knock it off. I can't think so I need you to settle down for me, please."

The rise and fall of her chest reminds me of an angry gorilla and I'd like to get up and help soothe her, but I won't give this guy a chance to run.

"Mari. Trust me, okay? Just trust me."

Huffing, she stomps over to the couch and plops down but stays quiet.

"You're hurting me!" the idiot below me whines.

"Yeah, I'm not really caring too much about that right this second."

Within five minutes everyone arrives—cops, paramedics, my boss, and Quinn. Quinn called Dee and she's on her way too. Once they've taken custody of the freak, I usher Mari out of the apartment to the parking lot. I need a quiet place to talk to her. There are so many things I need to say because so many things are clear after an event like this.

When we're outside, I realize she's not making eye contact, instead, she's looking at the people milling around the parking lot. Some are watching us with curiosity and some are huddled in groups talking.

When I reach out to place my hand on her shoulder, she flinches, but I grab her anyway, as softly as I can so I don't hurt her. She's had a long 24 hours and I don't want to make it worse than I already have.

"Mari, look at me, baby." Her eyes are still focused on the group off to our right. "Mari, please."

When she finally looks at me, I say, "I'm so proud of you. You saved us both. If you didn't think so quick on your feet, I'd probably be dead and you'd be handcuffed to the headboard for that guy. I've never seen someone untrained assess a situation and react like you did."

Her eyes fill with tears and I'm waiting for them to spill so I can be the one to wipe them away. I'm a little disappointed when they never fall. Instead she blinks several times and wiggles out of my grip.

"Dex, I'd love to curl up in your arms and forget about the last 24 hours, but I can't do that. You didn't stand by me when I needed you. You didn't hold me and help me through yesterday when I was scared and sad. You left me alone. Do I need someone now? Yes, but not as much as yesterday. The fact that you're praising me on how I handled that situation in there feels good, I know you mean it, but you haven't trusted me with anything else I've done since we met. I'm always going to be this well-meaning, nightmare of a girl because my heart is in the right place, no matter where my rationale is. I'm finally okay with that, but I know you never will be.

"I'm in love with you Dex, all of you. The quiet you, the closed-off you, the soft-hearted you, the open you, the sweet you, and all the you's that I'm not naming. The funny part is everyone takes me for stupid. They think because I end up in bad situations that I must be dumb. I'm not, I just live in the moment and do my best to help the people around me. But here's the thing: I'm finally at a point in my life that I want someone to love me and respect me for who I am, the way I deserve, no matter what stupid shit I pull. I want someone who knows that no matter how bad a situation looks, my heart was in the right place. You've proven more than once you don't feel that way. I can't live with the fear that every decision and move I make could send you back out my door as quickly as you arrived."

As she lays the last of the words between us that are effectively crushing my chest like an enormous combat boot, Dee's car pulls up and parks behind her. She turns to knock on the window and holds up a finger, telling Dee to wait where she is. When Mari turns back to me, the tears have returned and one slides slowly down her face. She reaches up and cups my jaw with her little hand. "I'm sure I'll see you around. Thank you for trying to protect me. It means the world to me. Tell the detective he can reach me at Reggie's." Her soft lips touch mine and she turns to go without another word.

I'm left standing there, stunned, as she climbs in Dee's car and pulls away. Every word she said is correct. A direct hit with the arrow of truth and I've never been more in love than I am now. I always thought I wouldn't get married because I was afraid of love and preferred being alone. The truth is now clear to me. I never wanted to get married because I didn't think anyone had a heart big enough for me. There's never been a woman that I loved so much it hurt somewhere inside, in a place that you can't find with a physical touch, and I sure as shit never respected a woman other than Quinn and Leslie enough to settle down with her. Until now.

The problem I have now is, how do I convince her that it's every part of her that I need, that I want, that I love? I have to find a way because I love her and I refuse to live without her. I don't care how many times I have to bail her out of jail or explain to my boss I have no idea how she got into trouble. I just need her. How could I have been so dense? How did I not see this before now?

WITHIN 48 HOURS, MALACHI ROBINSON, AKA MARI'S FREAKY stalker, was charged with breaking and entering, theft, stalking, kidnapping, two counts of assault, and a couple of other things they added for good measure. He should go rot in jail but the guy is so batshit crazy that the state is pushing for him to be placed in a mental facility long term instead of a regular prison. I'm all right with that as long as the guy is off the street.

It turns out that he's been stalking Mari since the first night he saw her at The Angry Lager the summer before. He even moved into her apartment building to be closer to her. He followed her everywhere and had a detailed description of what she did every day for months written in journals. He knew her schedule and patterns better than she probably did. He stole all of their stuff so that when she moved in with him—which he really thought would happen voluntarily—she'd be more comfortable. It never occurred to him that she would stay with me when she had nothing left and that's what sent him over the edge. His obsession grew to epic proportions, causing him to quit his job and confront people we both knew. When he was staked out at my apartment, he learned my patterns too and thought Marv would be an easy target to get information from.

The scariest part of it all is that he had a ton of information pulled up from the Internet on how to dispose of a body without leaving a trace, which is what he had planned for me. Malachi really thought if he got rid of me, she'd fall madly in love with him and they'd live happily ever after. The guy is nuts, but we no longer have to worry about him.

While I was preoccupied with Malachi during my 18 hours of captivity, internal affairs cleared me. I was surprised that it didn't take weeks, because it usually does. Amber came clean as soon as they put a little pressure on her and told them that Mari didn't know the drugs were in the suitcase and was only there to help her move her personal belongings out. Because the information matched the evidence, they dropped the charges against her and in turn dropped any issues they had with me. I got lucky. Other guys have lost their jobs over less.

Almost a week after Mari walked away, a week of hell for me, I'm ready to face her once I collect this one last thing. I've called in every favor and pulled every string I could think of, and I'm standing by the evidence office waiting for my boss to release what I came for. This little piece is the only thing that may help me win her back.

Judson says she's been at work every day busting her ass but has been very quiet. That's not like her at all. He and Quinn were worried when they came to me about it, until I told them my plan. Nervous little butterflies make my stomach their home as my boss turns the little ziplock bag over to me.

"Dexter, they processed it and took all the pictures they need. Try not to lose it in case something comes up. I hope this helps."

I smile as I dump the locket out into my hand, turning it

over. I haven't seen it in person in 12 years. In fact, I never thought I'd see it again. My grandmother was a beautiful woman with a heart of gold and when she passed away my heart broke. This is the only remembrance of her I have and I'm glad I gave it to Mari all those years ago. She's the only one my grandmother would have found lovely and genuine enough to own it after her.

I open it to see whose face she put in there. If there is a man's picture in there, I may have to remove it and pretend it wasn't there when I got it. My fat fingers fumble to get it open and a tiny piece of yellowed, folded up paper pops out and falls to the floor. There are no pictures inside so I bend down to pick up the paper. When I finally unfold it, I find the name *Jase* written in feminine cursive handwriting. I'm absolutely dumbfounded as I realize how many years she carried my name in her heart. The scrawny young man who saved her once and held her twice is who she chose to place in her most prized possession. My phone buzzes in my pocket so I shove the paper back in the locket along with another little surprise and close it before I place it in my pocket. The phone number belongs to Judson.

"Hey man!"

"Dex, you need to meet me at Colorado Springs Regional. Marina passed out and it took a little bit to get her to come around, so I threw her in the truck and rushed her to the hospital. I'm not sure what's going on but I think you need to be here."

"On my way." I hang up and hustle to my car. If something happens to her before I can tell her how I feel, I'll never forgive myself. I should have sped this process up or showed up sooner to beg for her forgiveness.

I bust through the doors of the E.R. to find Judson waiting for me. "Is she okay?"

"Yeah, she's awake and seems okay. They're running some tests but I think she's just tired. She told the doctor she hasn't been sleeping well. She wanted to leave and was a little pissed that I brought her since she doesn't have health insurance, but I wasn't taking a chance. Come on, man, I'll take you back."

When Judson pulls the curtain back, Mari's tired eyes glance up and meet mine. God, she's beautiful even with the dark rings around her eyes and the wild hair that still has pieces of hay sticking out of it, I'm guessing from where she landed in the barn.

"What are you doing here, Dex?" She looks confused. "Aren't you supposed to be working? You're not in uniform."

"I was coming to you. I took the day off. I was finishing my last task when Judson called to tell me you were here."

"He didn't need to, I'm fine. I don't want anyone making a big deal out of this. We all know I don't sleep well."

"Judson." I look over at him. "Can you give us a few minutes, please?"

He glances between us and finally says, "Sure. I'll be in the waiting room."

Once he's gone I move over to the side of the bed and lower the rail. Her eyebrows are drawn together in confusion, but I make room and sit on the edge of the bed by her hip. Before I begin, I tug a piece of hay out of the top of her hair and smooth the remaining strands down.

"Mari, you were right the other night with what you said. You deserve someone who knows your heart, understands your mind, and respects your loyalty. You need someone who finds you beautiful full of tattoos and piercings and crazy hair colors. You deserve someone who will always love you and protect you and support you.

"I was just too damn stubborn and stuck on 'normal' to know that guy was me all along. I get you. I understand why you do the things you do and I love that about you. I never had loyalty like yours from any woman, so I didn't know what it looked like. I love you, Mari, like I never thought I could love someone. I need you to make me a better person. I need you to love me and hold me and soften me up. I've been so used to handling things on my own that I didn't see how badly I needed all of that until you came along and showed me. I shouldn't have let you walk away the other night, but I needed to make sure I was doing this for the right reasons."

"Dex—"

"No more Dex. I hate when you call me that. You're the only person who knew me as Jase. The only person who knows where I came from and what makes me who I am. Jase is the man you held in your heart, not the man you hold at arm's length."

I readjust and pull the locket out of my pocket and dangle it in front of her.

Startled, she jerks a little and flicks her eyes back to me. "Is that...?"

I nod. "Open the locket Mari."

"I know what's in there, unless that crazy guy dumped it."

"So you knew it was still in there?"

"Your name?"

I nod.

"Yes, I kept it there on purpose."

"Open it, Mari."

A gasp invades the quiet of our little area as she pops the locket open. I'm studying the expression on her face as she discovers what's inside.

"Jase, is this...?" When her eyes meet mine again they have tears in them.

"Marry me, Mari. Let me love you, respect you, and bail you out of jail when you end up there. Let me show you what it's like to have a family that loves you and you can show me the same in return. We haven't really had that apart but together we can build something strong. We can make our own family and give them everything we never had. I never wanted that before you."

As her hand shakes, the paper and the ring fall from the locket on to her shirt. I rescue them from the covers and take her left hand in mine. "Will you marry me, Marina Elena Rossi?"

She rubs her bottom lip with her teeth for a split second before she nods and smiles. I can't help my sigh of relief. She grabs my face with both hands and pulls me in for a kiss that's more appropriate for being at home than in an emergency room bed. I pull away but rest my forehead against hers.

"Mari, I love you."

Before she can reply, a short, roundish Asian man with silver-rimmed glasses and dark hair steps into the area, pulling the curtain closed behind him. He's flipping through some paperwork in his hand when he says, "Ms. Rossi, I'd like to review a few things." He looks to me and asks, "Can you step out for a few minutes, sir?"

"No, I'm not going anywhere. Especially when it concerns her health."

"That's her call, sir." He glances to Mari.

"He can stay."

"How are you feeling?" he asks as he flips another page of printed data.

"Better. I haven't been sleeping so I think I just overexerted myself. I'll be okay."

"Well, it's going to be very important that you get your rest, Ms. Rossi, because you are resting for two. Your blood work indicates that you're pregnant. According to the nurse's notes, you don't recall when your last period was so you'll need an ultrasound and a pelvic exam to determine how far along you are, but getting the right amount of sleep and good nutrition is very important now."

This time when all the breath leaves my body, it's for a whole different reason. He wouldn't have shocked me more if he had said she had some horrible disease.

"Mari..." The timing couldn't be more perfect. "You're gonna have our baby." This time it's me who loses it. I couldn't have stopped the tears if I tried. Leaning down, I kiss her stomach through her clothes, not caring who's around for this, not caring how out of control I feel. The only thing that matters to me is in this bed and I'm going to make sure they both know it.

"Doctor, can you give us a few minutes, please? Just five." I hear her ask him right before the curtain moves and she says to me, "Jase. Are you sure you're okay with this? It's what you want?" Her fingers run over my short hair and I lift my head. I hate that I've made her doubt me.

"It's the only thing I want. I just finished telling you that I want to build a family with you. I almost can't breathe. I've never gotten what I wanted before. Not one thing and this time I get it all. How did I get so lucky?" I lower my head back to her belly again but I pull her hospital gown out of the way to place a kiss below her belly button. Her fingers run through my hair and when I lift my head, I see she joined me in the festival of tears. Damn, I love this woman.

"Mari, I have to take back what I said, though."

"What?" her voice breaks a little.

"You can't get arrested. At least not while you're pregnant. I'll kill a man if they put cuffs on you while you're pregnant."

Loud, hysterical laughter spills from her and I can't help but smile.

"I promise not to take any chances while I'm pregnant."

I laugh this time and lean in to consume her with a kiss. In the middle of the make out session, the doctor comes back in and clears his throat. We separate and grin at each other.

"Alright Ms. Rossi, I've written you a prescription for prenatal vitamins and I am referring you to an OB-GYN. You need to be under the care of a doctor and they can do the necessary exams to find out how far along you are. I'll send the nurse in to remove your IV and give you discharge paperwork. You need to take it easy—at least until you see an OB and they clear you to return to work, and," he looks to me, "make sure she gets some sleep, please."

"Yes, Doc. I can do that. Thank you." He nods and slips back through the opening in the curtain.

After the nurse gets us situated with the discharge paperwork and removes the IV, I help Mari out of bed and attach the necklace around her neck. She fingers it with a little grin playing on her lips and then I lead her out of there. I thank Judson and take her back to my place.

After dinner and some together time in the shower, I take her to bed with nothing but her new engagement ring on her body. Taking my time to trace every line and curve of her tattoos, I tell her all the things I never thought I'd tell anyone. All the things that roam around in my head but I never give voice to because I never thought there would be a person who'd really want to know. No one ever did when I was growing up, not after my grandma passed away.

"When we name our baby, I want to name it something with a strong, important meaning. Not just some trendy name that every kid in the same first grade class will have."

Mari's fingers glide across my hair and down to my cheek where she urges me to look at her. "You're already thinking of what we will name it?"

"Well...yeah. Aren't you?"

"Not yet. I'm still trying to get used to the idea that I'm going to be as big as a house soon. You're not going to like me when I'm big and fat, waddling along like a freaking penguin." The wrinkles in her forehead prompt me to crawl up closer so our lips touch when I tell her this.

"You are the mother of our baby and the beginning link in our family. Don't you know how precious that is to me? You could gain 400 pounds and I'd still think you were beautiful. You might have to give up a few piercings for a little while but nothing you do, short of leaving our family, will ever stop me from loving you and this baby."

"It's so weird how excited you are. I've never seen you excited before about anything and it's kind of freaking me out. I'm used to the too-cool-for-the-rest-of-us Jasen Dexter. The guy whose feathers never get ruffled. I'm surprised you haven't called Leslie and Quinn yet."

"I want to wait until we see the doctor and get a due date. I know those women are going to have a hundred questions and I want to be able to answer some."

"I love you, Jase."

"I love you, too. Now give me a kiss so we can get some sleep. I'm getting you in to a doctor tomorrow so it might be a long day." Her giggle is music to my ears.

THE NEXT MORNING I'M UP EARLY FIXING HER BREAKFAST AND getting ready for the day. I didn't tell Mari but Quinn is good friends with her obstetrician, Dr. O'Doyle, and I helped the doctor out of a speeding ticket while Quinn was on maternity leave. I texted her this morning and was able to get Mari an appointment at 8:30, before regular office hours. She said she was booked all day but could squeeze us in early, so I jumped on it.

Chapter Eighteen

DEX

I'm giving Dr. O'Doyle the stink eye as she holds the ultrasound wand in her hand. She just explained that she'll be inserting that into the vagina for this procedure.

"What happened to the ones that go on the belly? I see those on TV all the time."

Both women laugh at me before the doctor continues. "Dex, we don't know how far along she is and if it's really early, this will allow us to see things in there more clearly."

The doctor takes her time clicking and moving the mouse for the computer screen and the inserted wand. Trying to see anything on the screen is weird so I keep tilting my head and squinting.

"Dex, why don't you pull up a chair near the bed and sit down."

At the same time Mari and I both blurt, "Why?"

Dr. O'Doyle's smile is genuine when she says, "Just trust me, guys."

I grumble as I follow her instructions. What if there is no pregnancy? What if the doctor at the hospital was wrong?

"Settle down, Jase," Mari says, squeezing my hand. Who knew that she'd be the calm one of the two of us?

"Okay, you two," the doctor says as she turns the screen so we can see. Then she hits a switch and a bizarre whooshing sound fills the silence of the little room.

"What the hell is that sound?" I ask, a little freaked out.

"That is the sound of your babies' heartbeats." Before I can register all of what she said, she points at the screen with her finger and draws imaginary circles around two little spots that are fluttering like crazy. It's clear that the fluttering matches the sound we're hearing and I'm mesmerized. That's my kid in there, with a heartbeat, and I have no idea what else because I can't tell what any of that is. I squint to see it better and Mari asks, "Did you say *babies*? Like with an s, plural?"

Wait, what? My eyes jump to the doctor. Oh, my God. She did say babies and drew *two* circles. Holy shit! Two babies. The doctor removes the wand and clicks a few more buttons on the computer.

"Jase?" Mari's voice calls to me, soft and hesitantly. When I look back at her, it's apparent that she's scared.

I can't help the big, fucking, pussy tears that fill my eyes. Her eyebrows hit her hairline as she swallows hard. I hate the fear I see in her eyes. Standing abruptly, the chair flips backward, making a loud clanging sound and both women jump. I take her face in my hands gently and move in close so she can feel my lips. "You know how happy I was last night?" She nods a little. "Double that." The tears roll down my cheeks, all kinds of unmanly, but I don't care. I think I've cried more in the months since she's been back in my life than all the years before this combined. "Don't be scared, honey. We've got this. Together. You and me." The trembling of her lips can be felt against mine so I press mine against hers and hold. When I pull away and smile at her, she smiles too through the tears on her face. When I glance over at the doctor, I find her smiling bigger than both of us. "I love my job!" she tells us.

"By the way, you're measuring at almost nine weeks. Let me print the images I took so you can take them with you and then I can give you a due date." Fifteen minutes later, Mari is dressed and we're on our way to the ranch. We're both dying to tell someone so we decided on the Rivers. She's already called Dee and asked her and Reggie to come to our place for dinner.

Two months later, the night before Mari and I are getting married, she's staying with Quinn, Dee, Leslie and Sky at the ranch. Carlo, Judson, Joe and Rushton are staying with me at the apartment for the bachelor party, which basically consists of us going to the local wing joint, eating until we all feel sick, and watching the baseball game until we have to go to the airport. Mari's wedding gift is coming in on the 7:15 flight from Dallas. We're all standing by baggage claim when a woman, the spitting image of Mari, minus the hair color, tattoos and piercings, comes strolling into the area glancing around, likely looking for us. I step aside, away from the little crowd gathered in front of us and wait for her to spot me. It's weird looking at the clean-cut version of Mari. From the moment I saw Mari again, until a couple of months ago, I thought I would like this version better. Rosanna's beautiful, I'll give her that, but she doesn't have the flare and spice that my Mari does. Once she sees me, she must know right away because she dumps her stuff on the floor and runs for me. When she throws herself in my arms she's blubbering and the only thing I can make out is "my baby sister" and "you found". Carlo and Rushton gather her belongings and we usher her to the car. I want to get her to the ranch before Mari falls asleep. She falls asleep early these days, not long after dinner, but the doctor says it's normal so I try to go with the flow.

We pull up the long gravel driveway lined with piles of snow and my heart is hammering in my chest. I hated keeping this secret from Marina, but she's impatient and I knew she'd never be able to wait two weeks to see Rosanna if she knew I'd found her.

I started looking for her a couple of months ago when Mari first told me about her. I tried using all the resources at work and when that didn't pan out I hired a private detective whom I met through one of the veterans' charities I help with. Javier Suarez is a former Marine and one hell of a tracker. It wasn't long until he'd traced her to a small town in Montana. Her story is one I don't wish on anyone.

We get out of the car and Carlo leads the way while Judson carries her bags. I bring Rosanna in right behind me, doing my best to block her from view while the other guys follow her. The girls all look up from where they're sitting on the floor and it looks like they're painting toenails.

Mari says, "You can't crash our bachelorette party. It's bad luck!" She tries to sound mad but she's so busy grinning at me, I know she's not, and she steps into my arms.

"Well, I had to bring you your wedding present."

Her face falls. "We were supposed to do that? Oh, no! I didn't know."

"No, honey, we weren't, but there was something I knew you needed tomorrow."

"I already have my locket, it's in the guest room. I checked."

"No, Mari." I continue to block her view and hold her face in my hands so I can kiss her lips quickly. "I love you more than anything and I want to give you everything you've been missing." She's confused until I lower my hands and turn to the side to reveal Rosanna.

"Rosie?" It's not quite a whisper and not quite her normal voice. Then a screech like I've never heard before comes from both of them and they scramble to get to each other, knocking me to the side a little. There are so many tears and so much snot,

I know they're both going to need a shower, and the rest of us have joined them. I've never seen anything like this reunion and it's killing all the testosterone in the room.

When they finally pull apart to look at each other, Mari turns to me. "How?"

"I started looking a while ago. When I couldn't find her on my own I hired a private investigator who found her. I called her and asked her to come for this."

"You found my big sister." Mari turns and addresses Rosie this time as she runs both hands over her hair and shoulders like she's trying to physically comprehend her presence. "I thought I'd never see you again! Oh, my God!" Mari pulls her in for another quick hug.

"Well I'm here for a week so we can catch up. We have plenty of time."

Mari's smile drops and her lip quivers a little. "I'm going on my honeymoon. I won't be here."

I step in now to share the rest of the surprise. "No, honey. I moved the dates of the honeymoon. I'll work this week while your sister is here and then we'll fly out the same day she does. I wouldn't let you miss this time with her."

The crying starts again and I'd love to be upset by it, but I know they're tears of happiness. I kiss her one last time and hug her sister before we leave again. As we pull away I vow to do as many of those types of things as I can to make her happy. She deserves to wear that smile all the time.

THE NEXT DAY, I'M AT THE MOUNTAIN ESCAPE RESTAURANT and lodge we rented for the afternoon, standing in front of the floor-to-ceiling windows that look out on the snow-covered mountains, waiting for my bride-to-be. On one side of me is the justice of the peace and on the other is Rushton, Quinn and

Carlo. I felt it was only right to have Stu's son at my side for this moment. He'd be so damn happy about me marrying Marina. Judson is sitting in the first of two small rows of chairs facing us, holding a squirming Lila, and next to him is Marv. I couldn't have been more shocked than I was when he arrived today in an ill-fitting suit and outdated tie. I didn't expect to see him here because he blew me off when I asked shortly after we got engaged. He told me a few minutes before I took my place up here that Marina approached him after I did and worked her magic. He even had a shower, brushed his overgrown hair and shaved. I was blown away. Some people would probably be embarrassed to have a toothless, homeless old guy at their wedding, but I couldn't be prouder. Marv has been a great friend. I'm a walking testament to the idea that love and friendship can be found in the least likely places with the least likely people, and I'll never again find shame in that.

The second row has a few of the guys from work and their wives. On the other side of the aisle, Reggie is seated next to Joe, Skylar and Leslie. Behind them are a few of Marina's friends from over the years. I don't know any of them well but they're an eclectic group.

A selection of songs that we chose is playing softly as we wait. When the song changes to *A Thousand Years* by Christina Perri, Dee comes into view wearing a long, simple red dress that she and Marina picked out. Once she's made her way all the way down the aisle and is standing opposite Carlo, Marina appears in the doorway as a tattooed angel in a formfitting white lace wedding dress that goes all the way to the floor. She told me that some women try to hide the baby bump if they're in a wedding dress, but I thought that was dumb so I encouraged her to get a dress that showed every inch of it, and this one certainly fits the bill. We're both excited about our growing family and see no reason to hide it.

Rosie is next to her in a basic black floor-length dress, ready to escort her down the aisle to me. Quinn told me that as soon as it sank in that Rosie was there she asked her to walk her down the aisle.

A small, pretty bouquet of red and white flowers is in her hand but it's her smile that holds me captive. Mari's hair is down and full of volume. The colored streaks are gone and it's all dark brown except the blond tips. It's a subdued version of the Mari I love, but I couldn't be prouder of her than I am right now. In the next couple of minutes, I'm about to get everything I ever needed but didn't realize was possible.

EPILOGUE

Epilogue: Dex

10 Years Later...

"Did I really say I wanted this many kids or did we end up this way because you can't keep your hands or your lips to yourself?" Mari asks me. I can't help my bark of laughter because I know the answer is a combo of those two things. As I survey our living room, which currently looks like a small tornado carried the entire toy store to our house and dumped it off haphazardly, I understand why she's asking. She's exhausted and doesn't want to tackle cleaning up.

"Don't laugh at me, you big jerk. It's not funny, I'm so tired."

"Yeah, baby, I know. But I've told you a hundred times the kids can clean this up. They're old enough now and don't need you following them around doing everything for them. If we don't teach them how to follow directions and rules, they'll be hellions. If we don't teach them to do things for themselves, they'll live with us forever. Don't get me wrong, I love them, but I'm counting on them evacuating the nest when they're 18."

She sighs. "I know, but I want to be a good mom."

"No one questions that. I don't know a better mother than

you and I know some good moms. It's okay for the kids to do a little work. Let me handle this, you go relax in the tub for a little while. When you come back down, this will look like a new room." I kiss her head and help her up. When she's hesitant to go, I smack her on the ass. She yelps, giggles and hurries upstairs.

I tiptoe down to the game room in the basement, certain I'll find the four oldest offspring down here. Damaris, is the youngest at two years old and still taking naps, which is where she is now. She sleeps at the weirdest times and we quit trying to fight it early on.

The twins, Andrew and Amanda, are playing each other in air hockey. By the numbers on the scoreboard and the triumphant smile on her face, I'd venture a guess that Amanda's winning. I stay quietly off to the side, observing them. Belinda, who is second after the twins, is curled up in a chair in the corner with a book, while Carlin, who is turning six years old tomorrow, is parked in front of the television with some show about cartoon fairies on.

"Yes!" Amanda yells and fist pumps twice, bringing my attention back to her. "I'm the champion again!"

I glance over at Andrew to see how he's taking it and by the angry scowl I'm going to say it's not well.

"Mom says you shouldn't gloat so much. Someone will knock you off your high horse and the fall is going to be ugly, Mandy." He crosses his arms and turns toward the stairs, stopping when he sees me.

God, I love my son. He's such a good-hearted kid; even when he's upset he still won't throw out nasty insults. Physically, he's the spitting image of me at 10 years old, but the boy has the same soft heart as his mother. Injured animals stop him in his tracks and if there's a baby anywhere nearby, he gravitates right to it.

His frown flips upside down into a smile before he yells, "Dad!" and runs at me, crashing into my middle almost hard enough to knock me off my feet. I wrap him up tight and squeeze.

"Hey, big guy! You getting your butt kicked again?" He pulls back just enough to give me a dirty look. "I'm kidding, relax." I ruffle his hair and step back, making room for Amanda to hug me. I swear, this is the best part of every day, getting to come home to my family.

"Dad, she always cheats. She blocks the hole with her fingers and then shoots when I'm not looking."

"Daddy, I'm just not wasting any time. I can't help it if he's so busy yelling at me that he can't keep defending his goal." I bend down and kiss her forehead. "Be fair when you kick his butt, Amanda."

About that time, Carlin has unglued herself from the television and is climbing over the furniture backwards to get to me. Her wispy little frame flies at me and I lift her high in the air and nuzzle her belly before I lower her enough so she can wrap her arms around my neck.

"Daddy, did you know I'll be six in one day?" Holding her tight, I take a second before I respond. I want to savor every minute that she's five because time seems to be flying by too fast. "Yeah, kiddo, I know tomorrow is your birthday. Are you excited?"

"Yes! I'm so excited to have a pony party at Aunt Quinn and Uncle Judson's house!"

"I know. It's going to be a lot of fun."

I kiss her hair and set her down so I can cross the room to where Belinda has her nose buried in her book. Who knew eight-year-old girls could read for days and not realize the world is still turning around them? She still hasn't seen me.

Belinda's an exact physical replica of Mari, whereas the other girls are a good mixture of both of us. She's serious and focused like I am, though, making her somewhat of a challenge for Mari. When I reach her, I lean down and pull the book from her hand.

"Hey!" she protests. "I was at the good part!"

"Bee, the only thing I want when I get home is a hug from my babies." I smile as I say it because that term sets them all off every time I use it.

"Daddy! We're not babies!" They all scream in unison. My laughter comes out hard and long and they all stop protesting to stare at me.

"What?" I ask as I sit down on the couch across from where Belinda is curled up. Patting my lap, I invite her over since I still haven't gotten my hug. She accepts the invite and leans her head against my chest. Her soft brown hair hangs halfway down her back and I run my fingers through it a few times before I finally pull her in tight and wrap my arm around her.

"Come here guys, we have to talk," I call out to the rest of the group. Groans and grunts can be heard the whole way. Carlin climbs on my other leg and mirrors her sister's head on my chest, Andrew sits next to us on the couch and Amanda sits on the floor in front of me with her long legs stretched out in front of her, crossed at the ankles.

"Listen, I came home and found Mommy upstairs cleaning while you guys are down here partying. It looks like a toy-store tornado hit the living room."

"You say that every time you come home, Dad," Amanda whines.

"That's because it's summer and you're here all day long to make a bigger mess than normal. Here's the deal: Mommy is taking a bath and relaxing. I'm going to order some pizza for dinner while you guys clean up that mess upstairs. I don't want her to touch another toy. This is your job. You make the mess; you clean it up. That's how the world works. No one gets a free ride."

"Damaris does," Carlin tells me in that sing-song voice of irritation. "She never has to clean up."

"We'll start teaching her to help, but I'll remind you that when you guys were that age you didn't have to do much either, so suck it up." They all groan.

I ask them to tell me about their day and listen patiently as they all give me their own version. Once they're done, I usher them upstairs to clean while I call for pizza. After that's taken care of, I let myself into the bathroom to find my sexy-ass wife floating in the tub with her head back and her eyes closed. Her now full breasts break the waterline and a thousand thoughts come to mind about what I'd like to do to her beautiful rosy nipples.

"I know you're staring at me. It's making me self-conscious," she surprises me by saying.

"I'm always staring at you. Why would you be self-conscious now?"

"Probably because I'm fat."

My head jerks back. *What the hell is she talking about?* "What? You've never been fat a day in your life."

"Well..." She squeezes her eyes tight like she's fighting tears as she trails off and I know it's time to put her out of her misery.

"Babe, I know you're pregnant. You're not fat. You never have been, even when you were round with the twins."

Sitting up abruptly, she knocks water out of the tub and the shock on her face is priceless.

"You thought I didn't know? Come on baby, I'm an observer and I know your body better than I know my own. I figured it out about a week ago."

"Why didn't you tell me? I've been terrified to tell you."

"I wanted you to come to terms with it first, but you shouldn't be scared because I'm as responsible as you."

"I know you didn't want any more. I didn't really either but..."

Before she can say another word, I lock the bathroom door, strip off my uniform and slide in behind her. Now there's water flooding the floor of the bathroom but I don't care. We only have about 15 or 20 minutes before the kids finish and the pizza guy arrives.

"Turn around and face me." When she turns around and straddles my hips I harden in an instant. Damn, that's how we ended up with another mouth to feed. I wrap my arms around her and pull her against me so we're chest to chest and the feel of her full breasts has my cock ridged and ready.

"We said we wanted a big family. We wanted to fill our house with love and laughter, and we have. So there's one more mouth to feed. Who cares? It's another baby we made out of love and there's nothing wrong with that. I can't promise that I haven't been praying for a boy, though. Lord knows we're drowning in estrogen in this house, but I'm not upset about another baby."

Her lips respond for her as she takes mine in a happy kiss. I didn't mention that my wife is insatiable when she's pregnant, but she is, and I have no complaints there. Without breaking lip-lock, she shifts and slides down over me. I'm thanking God that I locked the door on the way in because I swear the kids can smell the flow of hormones and they always need something when we're at this stage of naked fun times.

I grip the soft globes of her ass and squeeze as I lift and guide her in the rhythm that I need. Even after having the kids she's still so tight, such a perfect fit for me and she feels so damn good. Now that she has the rhythm, I lift one hand to palm her breast, lifting the weight of it and squeezing it gently, flicking my thumb across the hardened nipple.

"Ahhhh," she drops her head back and cries out softly.

"Shhh. The kids will come knocking if they hear us. Faster, babe." The faster she moves the more water splashes out. It's all I can do to be quiet. She's past the point of quiet though so I clamp my hand down over her mouth as her pussy flutters all around me, squeezing and tugging with her orgasm. Watching her come apart forces my own release so I drop my hand from her mouth. She leans in to kiss me, keeping my groan quieter.

"I love you so much Jase. You always surprise me. I thought for sure you were going to be mad."

"Not a chance."

Marina

When I hang up the phone with Rosie, I realize I forgot to ask about her son and husband, who have both been down with the flu for the last week. I was hoping they'd be well enough to come to the party, but I forgot to ask. I'll include them in my head count and hope they can make it. If I call her back I won't get anything done. It doesn't matter that she lives down the street from us, if we get on the phone we can talk for hours. I don't have time for that. Tomorrow my middle baby turns six and a week later, Rushton graduates from the Air Force Academy. He chose the Academy to be closer to Dex, I think, although he's never said. We've enjoyed having him close these last few years and will miss him when he leaves for pilot training after graduation, but we're happy that we had the time that we did.

Leslie, Joe and their nine-year-old daughter, Frannie, arrive later this evening for both Carlin's birthday and Rushton's graduation and are staying with us. We're all excited to see them. So much has changed since I first met them and I laugh sometimes at the fear I felt at that first encounter.

Now that the dishes are put away and all the kids are in bed, I can do my second favorite thing with my husband: nothing. After the kids go to bed every night, we're on the couch together binge-watching the latest Netflix series. I like watching TV, but this is more about the quiet time with Jase. He always sits so I can lay my head in his lap and he can run his fingers through my hair as we watch the shows. This is so relaxing for me, a time where I can just enjoy some time with my husband with no obligations.

Over the years, Jase has done everything he said he would. He's given me the family I always wanted, he's brought me peace I never knew existed, and he's made sure that every day I know I'm loved and cherished for who I am.

Rushton

Two years later...

I call Uncle Dex to give him my pilot training graduation date and he gets really quiet. Misunderstanding what he's thinking, I say "Uncle Dex, I know you have your hands full so if you can't make it, I understand." I would totally understand; I mean, he has six kids, and all of them except little Eden, are into sports and activities. I get that he doesn't have enough time to even breathe, much less travel to Arizona for my graduation, but I had to at least ask.

Since my mom married Joe, he and I have grown pretty close. He ended up being a great friend, full of guidance and wisdom during some difficult teenage years and I appreciate that more than he could understand, but he still isn't my dad. The closest I've got to my dad is Uncle Dex and I really want him there to pin my wings on for me. It's an important day, and his support would mean so much.

He clears his throat several times and I hear his voice break a little before he says, "Rush, I wouldn't miss that day if I were on my death bed. I'm so proud of you and I know Stu would be too. I'll be there. I'll probably have the whole herd too because the kids always want to see you, but even if we don't all come, I'll be there. I promise."

Closing my eyes tight to battle the tears that fill them, I breathe deep for a couple of seconds to get control. "Thanks, Uncle Dex. It means a lot."

"Yeah, for me too, kid. Text me the details and I'll be there."

ONE MONTH LATER...

Thank God the Air Force encourages a big family celebration at the completion of pilot training, because I'm not sure I could've kept any of them away. I swear I have the biggest group here for this ceremony. There are 18 if I include my two best friends from high school that showed up at the last minute. Uncle Dex, Marina and their six kids, Mom, Joe, Skylar, Frannie, and my grandparents from both sides, all flew out here for this and are taking up a huge chunk of seats in the back, left-hand corner.

When it's my turn, they announce my name and I walk up to stand in front of the flag, facing the audience filled with family and friends of our graduating class. A bunch of obnoxious cheering from the back corner drowns out the speakers so I miss the first few words of what the announcer says, but I hear, "Pinning his wings on today is his uncle, Purple Heart recipient, former Army Sergeant Jasen Dexter."

The announcer goes on to say a few more things about my upcoming duty station in Georgia, but I tune him out. I can't concentrate on anything but the pride in Uncle Dex's eyes as he accepts the wings and works to put them on. The whole time his mouth is tight, an attempt at hiding his emotional reaction. I've seen that expression a lot from him over the years.

When he's done, he lightly pats the wings and looks me dead in the eyes, his filling with tears and says quietly, "I know he's here with us and he's even more proud of you than I am." His lip trembles a little and I'm left stunned as he turns and faces the audience so a bunch of pictures can be snapped of us.

In all the years I've known him, Uncle Dex has never cried in front of me. Not at any of the memorial services for my dad, not when he moved to Colorado, not ever in my presence. Seeing this unhindered show of emotion leaves me hanging on by a thread myself, and I'll be glad when I'm not standing in front of all these people.

As the weekend comes to a close and everyone is in the parking lot saying their goodbyes, I stand observing the chaos around us. All the people I love who have supported me all these years are preparing to go back to their everyday lives. For me, this whole weekend has been about my past and my future coming together in a collision of understanding and accomplishment. My dreams up to this point have come true and now I realize it's time to dream new dreams and have new wishes, and one of those is to find what my parents had with one another and what Dex has with Marina.

I have my education and my career, but now I want to find the kind of happiness that can only come from having a family of my own. Uncle Dex found that not only in Marina but also in Andrew, Amanda, Belinda, Carlin, Damaris and Eden, and according to him, in a man-to-man conversation we had in private, he also found those things in my sisters and me and the Rivers family too. I want to wake up every morning like him and know without a doubt I found my heart.

Before they load up to leave in their SUV, Uncle Dex calls me to the side. When we're far enough away from nosey eavesdropping ears, he steps in a little closer than normal, places his palm on my shoulder and looks me in the eyes. I take a deep breath because I know something big is coming. Dex talks more than he used to, but he's still a man of few words.

"You've been a man for several years now, but you're finally out of school, ready to start your life and your career. There are women out there who'll be interested in you only because you're a hot shot fighter pilot. Choose carefully. Look for someone genuine, look for a pretty face if you want, but make sure she has a beautiful soul to match that. Your instincts are good, follow them and don't stop until you find the right one.

"I'm proud of you, kid, and even though you're a grown man, I'm always only a phone call away. It doesn't matter what branch you're in, military life can be hard. I may not understand specific circumstances that you find yourself in, but I understand you and I'll always be here for you."

He hugs me and strides away before I can say another word. Jasen Dexter is the greatest gift my dad could've ever given me and I'll never forget to be thankful for what he's brought to my life.

The End

Coming in August 2017

Finding Passion - Colorado Veterans Book 3

ALSO BY TIFFANI LYNN

Colorado Veterans Series
1. Finding Purpose
2. Finding Heart
3. Finding Passion

Betrayal to Bliss Series
1. Strangers at Sunset
2. From Strangers to Lovers

Eden's Odyssey Series
1. Finn's Shot (Free ebook)
2. Tangled with Tyler

Stand Alone Novels
1. Love, Lust & Life

Made in the USA
Columbia, SC
21 October 2017